Love

(and other uses for duct tape)

To Joyce
Thank you for making people love to write and read

For Aunt Patty
Because she, too, is missed

And for Em and Doug
Without you two there's no point in duct tape

Carrie
Jones

Love

(and other uses for duct tape)

flux ™

Woodbury, Minnesota

First Edition
First Printing, 2008

Book design by Steffani Sawyer
Cover design by Ellen Dahl

Flux, an imprint of Llewellyn Publications

The Cataloging-in-Publication Data for *Love (and other uses for duct tape)* is on file at the Library of Congress.
    ISBN-13: 978-0-7387-1257-4

Flux
Llewellyn Publications
A Division of Llewellyn Worldwide, Ltd.
2143 Wooddale Drive, Dept. 978-0-7387-1257-4
Woodbury, MN 55125-2989, U.S.A.
www.fluxnow.com

Printed in the United States of America

You THINK YOU KNOW PEOPLE and then it turns out you don't.

You think you learn this and then it turns out you didn't.

People keep changing who they are and defining themselves by their own choices, and that's cool most of the time, but not all the time. No, it's not cool all the time at all.

Before I know

George Burns said, *Don't stay in bed unless you can make money in bed,* which sounds like a good song:

Don't stay
In bed
Unless you can make
Don't stay
Make bed
make it in bed

"So." Em FLIPS BACK HER hair, slams herself into the seat next to me at the cafeteria. "How's the problem?"

I stir my Postum. The wheat grains dissolve into the water, turning it murky. "The Problem?"

"I thought maybe you…you know? Something happened last night," Em leans forward, waiting, waiting, waiting, just like me.

Tom's almost through the line. He's dimple-grinning at the lunch lady. She blushes and hands him back his card. His strong fingers smash it into the pocket of his jeans. Then he turns, makes eye contact with me, even though we're all the way across the cafeteria.

I swallow. My hand clutches my mug of Postum like that will make me steady. "The Problem is still a problem."

----o----

Tom's duct tape saying of the day, plastered across the back of his hand, is from George Burns, who is dead but used to be an actor who played God in a movie, I think. I know he always had a cigar in his mouth, which is so phallic I just can't believe it. But, truth is, I'm thinking that everything is phallic lately. That's because I'm sexually frustrated.

The quote stuck on Tom's hand?

"Don't stay in bed unless you can make money in bed."

I'm trying just to tap the shiny tape with my finger in a totally nonchalant way, but instead I draw my fingertip all the way across it. "Interesting."

"You think?"

"Yeah."

We're in German class. Somehow the air suddenly changes.

It stops smelling like Crash's sweat-wet socks and starts smelling like Tom, like Old Spice deodorant and pine trees.

"You're too sexy for me," I whisper. "I can't handle it."

He wiggles his eyebrows. I tip up the edge of the duct tape. There are tiny man hairs under there.

"That's going to hurt when you take it off."

"I know." He gives me this look, this meaningful boyfriend look. "But it's worth it."

I'm not sure if he's talking about the duct tape or me. His cheek twitches and he looks away.

"You're blushing…"

"I know."

"You have practice today?" I fiddle with my mechanical pencil, pushing the lead out. It's a tiny dark line. Too many clicks and it'll topple onto Tom's desk.

"Yeah."

"Baseball…Baseball…Baseball…" I tease.

The lead falls out. I pinch it up with my fingernails and Herr Reitz, our German teacher, clears his throat as he makes his entrance from the door in the back of the room. Today, he's wearing lederhosen, these German pant things. Every day it's something, lederhosen or a Valkyrie outfit like opera Viking ladies. Once, he dressed up as Shakespeare, another time he was Big Bird from Sesame Street, all huge and yellow. Today, he looks like he belongs on the side of a box of cookies.

He throws his arms up in the air and yells, "Tah-dah!"

White tights do not look good on skinny man calves, especially skinny man, German teacher calves.

We all fake clap as he makes his way to the front of the room. He bows. He twirls.

"Hey, why do you dress up every day?" Crash shifts his weight in his seat, folds his legs up beneath him so he's taller.

He looks for support from us. We nod, because, let's face it, we're all wondering.

Herr Reitz shrugs, smiles. "I used to do opera in Germany."

"That explains it all." Crash slumps back in his seat. "But now you're stuck here."

For a second Herr Reitz loses his smile, but he gets it back and says, "I'd hardly say I'm stuck."

"We're all stuck, dude," Crash moans.

Which is far too true. We're all stuck, stuck in a million ways, stuck with each other, stuck in Eastbrook, Maine, tiniest city in the universe, stuck with waiting for senior year to end, stuck like the duct tape on Tom's wrist. What could be worse? So, even though I'm stuck at this stupid desk, I make my move and get it over with.

"I think we should do it." I cringe the moment I've whispered it. Why did I say it in German class? There is something so wrong with me.

Tom cocks his head to the side. "What?"

Even his whisper is sexy.

I regroup.

"Today's the day my mom and I go to my dad's grave," I tell Tom and turn around quickly before I see the pity in his eyes.

"Belle!" Herr Reitz says. "Today we are going to learn how to say who we are."

Bob, my ex-boyfriend's new boyfriend, snorts.

"We did that in German 1," Crash moans. "Can't we learn how to say, 'Will you come back to my hotel with me?' or something useful?"

Herr Reitz pulls his hand to his chest in an overdramatic I-once-did-opera pose and pretends to be shocked. "Crash? Are you telling me that knowing who you are isn't useful?"

Tom crosses his arms over his chest and smiles.

Crash just looks horrified.

"Dude, I know who I am."

For a second I hate Crash, who has a father, who has never had a significant other turn out to be gay, who has an identity. Then I stop, because, well, it's not nice to hate. That's what they always teach you in Sunday School when you're little, or else in an old John Lennon song: Love your neighbor. No jealousy. Do not hate. Blah. Blah. Blah.

----o----

After German, Tom takes off for baseball practice. When I get to my locker, I spot Em, my best friend. She's dancing through the hallway. Her little butt moves in some sort of swishing pattern that reminds me of Spanish dancers. She swings her hips around right by the lockers, smiling, grabbing her notebook for law class, our first class of the day on Mondays.

Em's a happy person, even with the whole dead dad thing. She's the kind of person who smiles and jumps up and down at the thought of really good ice cream. She'll open her happy-duck mouth with the thin, long lips and quack, pretty much, but she doesn't usually dance in the halls at school.

I just stand there for a second and smile at her. Even though Tom's smell, tree bark, man musk, still lingers in my nose. It's Friday. It's almost the weekend. It's May. Tom's not mad at me. I will not be a born-again virgin much longer. All is good.

Em swirls around and shuts her locker, then does this shimmy step towards me.

I laugh. "What are you doing?"

She grabs one of my hands, swirls me around.

Andrew walks by and says, "Yummy. Girl show."

I glare at him. He chuckles. It's not quite a laugh and then he walks away.

Some little freshman boy, whose name I can't remember, but whose mom works at the bank gives us a thumbs-up sign. Em just keeps dancing through it all, pulling me into it, whirling to some imaginary beat. My gig bag bangs against my back as she swirls me around again. For a second, I almost think I should reach in, haul out Gabriel, my guitar, and start in with a flamenco beat, give Em some real music to dance to, other than the stuff that's just in her head, but I don't because we have to leave.

"What are you doing?" I ask again, laughing.

"Celebrating." Em's hands go to her waist. She starts into some weird pseudo-funky Russian dance, all high knees and craziness.

"Celebrating what?" I ask, taking a step back.

"May. Senior year. Spring?" she says and twirls around again.

I stare at her, adjust my gig bag higher on my shoulder. "Spring."

Just that second Mr. Duffy, an English teacher, pokes his head out of his classroom and says, "You girls have senioritis."

Em rushes over to him, reaches out her hands. "Celebrate with us, Mr. Duffy. It's Spring. Come dance."

He shakes his head, but there's a glint in his eye. "You seniors get crazier every year. You're just aching to ditch this place and go start life. I know. I know how it is. "

He shuts the door, slowly. It clicks.

Em grabs my hand. "He really wants to dance with us. Really. You know he does. He just pretends to be Mean

Teacher Man but underneath those khakis is a ballet leotard and the overdeveloped thighs of a dancer."

I laugh. "I do not want to imagine that."

She pulls me down the hall, no longer dancing and orders me, "Come on. Let's get out of here."

Em and I have been friends since the beginning of high school. She's nuts and smart and I love her.

When my ex-boyfriend, Dylan, told me he was gay, Em was right there.

She started dating Shawn right around the time I started dating Tom, last fall, right after the Dylan announcement.

She puts up with me carrying Gabriel everywhere. I put up with her always taking pictures of everything and smelling like ice cream. She works at Dairy Joy. It's like the Joy of Dairy, or milk products and high cholesterol. It's the Unjoy of the lactose intolerant. It's ridiculous.

I think that's the funniest name for an ice cream place.

She puts up with that too.

After the random hall dancing, we head out to her little red car.

"So, how's The Problem?" she asks again. The wind twists her supermodel hair all around her face and she grabs it, bunching it in one hand as she unlocks the car. I stash my backpack and Gabriel in the back.

"Do we have to talk about The Problem? We're always talking about The Problem."

"That's why it's THE Problem."

"It's proper noun important, huh?"

"Yep."

We slam into the car, smash the doors closed against the wind and try to get the hair out of Em's face.

"Did you see Tom's duct tape message today?" I rub my eyes with my hands.

"Nope."

"It was, 'Don't stay in bed unless you can make money in bed.'"

"What's that supposed to mean?"

"I have no idea."

Em pulls out of the parking spot. The baseball team starts straggling out of the school and jogging towards the field for practice.

"There he is," she points and lets go of the steering wheel.

He's jogging. He's in shorts. He has the best legs, soccer legs, thick with muscle. He plays soccer, too. He does everything, except the one thing that I want him to do, which figures.

"You're panting," Em says.

"Shut up."

"You're having an eye orgasm."

"Shut up!" I cover them, then peek out.

"Don't hit me. I'm driving. You'll make us crash." She smiles at me and honks the horn. "There's Shawn."

Shawn waves his giant arm at us. Em and Shawn do not have the problem Tom and I have. The sex problem.

"It'll happen. You know he loves you," she tells me, all sweet and mothering. "Someday, you'll bonk each other into oblivion."

"Bonk?"

"You want me to say the f-word? I'll say it. I just thought it was crude."

"Bonk's not crude?"

She opens her mouth.

"Do not say the f-word!" I yell before she can. "It is not appropriate here. There is no right word here."

"Okay. Fine. Someday you'll copulate each other into oblivion."

I punch her in her tiny arm, again. She shrieks and the car swerves towards the gutter thing on the side. She pulls it back into place. The wind kicks up dust that seems to swirl towards us, around us, embracing us. Dust.

"Today's my dad's death day," I tell her, back-kicking an old Dunkin' Donuts bag under the seat.

She nods. Her face quiets. Her eyes don't go pity-pity the way Tom's would, but they go pity–I know. She lost her dad too, but to cancer, not to war. "You want me to drop you off at the cemetery?"

"That's not how I do it."

"It's going to pour."

I check out the sky. Dark cloud after dark cloud presses down towards us like it's setting the scene for some ancient tragedy, some overdone play. "I know."

For the next minute I riff on how my stress levels are ultra high because of The Problem, plus the talent show Monday, and Em says, "You always worry about nothing."

I rub my tingling palm. "No, I don't."

She laughs and hauls a left onto the Surry Road at a good forty over the speed limit of twenty-five and says, "Yes, you do. And you are easily the most talented person in our high school. You are a shoo-in to win."

"What about Dylan?"

"Dylan is gay and has lost most of his fan base."

"That's horrible!" I roll my window down all the way so I can smell spring in Maine, ground warming, cars moving, wood chips. From two miles away, a wind blows the salt smell of the ocean.

"It's true," she sighs. "People won't vote for him as much this year. You might beat him this year."

I've never beaten Dylan, ever.

It's a demographics issue, basically. Underclassmen who are girls always vote for him after they're all done squealing his name, and there are way more underclass girls than guys in the talent show audience. Back before he came out, everyone voted for him because he was so good. Sure, I always had the crunchies, the morbids, and the girl jocks because girl jocks band together and support each other. Now, none of the guys will cheer for him. Except for the theater guys and some of the music guys, but only the ones who aren't afraid that people will call them gay.

Most guys don't go to talent shows anyway, except as favors to their girlfriends or to throw things at the stage and chant stuff like "homo" or "see your tits" or something.

Dylan also lost a lot of his female fan base because they are now all sympathetic to me, because, let's face it, it sucks when your gorgeous, perfect boyfriend is gay. So, I've got a lot of the pity vote. My head spins just thinking about it.

Thick dust covers Em's dashboard. I scrape my index finger through it and write the word HELP.

"I don't know why I do these things," I say. "I don't like the whole competition aspect, like by winning you're making other people lose, or that we place some hierarchical value on art and music."

"Shut up. You do it because you're good and you need an audience." Em presses down on the accelerator and we speed by Friend and Friend, where people are cruising around the parking lot checking out the ATVs. "Do you know dust is mostly sloughed-off human skin?"

"That's disgusting."

"Yep."

I jab my dust-encased index finger at her. "Whose skin is it?"

She shrieks and yanks the wheel. The car swerves and steadies itself. I wipe my finger on the door. There's a little rip in the paneling.

"I'm going to vote for Dylan," I say. When Dylan announced he was gay it was a big deal. The town was pretty much shocked because handsome, blonde, handy Dylan did not fit their stereotypes of what a gay guy should be like. You'd think by now that people would learn about stereotypes. We talk about this in Students for Social Justice all the time.

For a couple months people called him fag and harassed him, which, according to our civil rights' team bulletin board, is normal high school behavior. Sometimes things get so bad that kids have to leave school. Dylan didn't do that. I think sometimes he wanted to, but he toughed it out.

Anyway, at first I was pretty much shocked by the whole Dylan thing because I thought he loved me. He told me that all the time, whispered it in my ear after we had sex, wrote it to me in poems or when he instant-messaged me before going to bed at night. It was hard dealing with that, the fact that it was all some fairy-tale lie, but he still loves me, just not the way I thought he did.

He does.

I love him too.

Just not that way any more.

That new, bold, crazy, stomach-pit-aching, world-spinning, lust-pumping-through-every-neuron way is reserved for Tom.

"You are zoned out," Em says.

"Dylan is an amazing singer," I announce as we come up to the Y. "Do you think that I'm messed up because Dylan's gay?"

"Duh," Em nods.

She honks her horn at the Eastbrook squad car that's parked in the Y lot, facing out and ready to catch speeders. Chief Tanner, Tom's dad, Eastbrook's head cop, waves his radar gun at her, but smiles. She slows down.

"It's a good thing he likes you," I say and cross my legs, rub my hands hard against my thighs trying to get rid of the tingling feeling.

"I know."

We stop at the red light, one of Eastbrook's few, and she puts her blinker on, clears her throat and says, "You need to let the Mimi thing go."

I groan and don't answer. The red light flickers. Something is wrong with it. Does it want us to stop or not? It's like it can't decide.

"Tom does not like Mimi," she says.

The light flickers. Cars drive in front of us.

"Belle?"

"Whatever." I'm a tiny bit obsessed about Mimi Cote liking Tom. They went out in eighth grade. She's pretty open about her desires. She hates me. Enough said. "But maybe that's why there's a Problem. Maybe it's because he doesn't want to compare."

"Maybe he's just scared."

"Right."

"Guys can get awkward about the sex thing. Even Tom guys."

"Right."

Em taps her fingernails on the steering wheel. "Fine.

Don't listen. Anyway, I need you to come make a pharmacy run with me tomorrow."

I raise my eyebrows. "Is it that time?"

"I think so, and I only have two left," she whines and turns onto Main Street.

Emily is terrified of buying tampons from Dolly at Rite Aid. She's all uptight about it. I always have to do it for her. She won't even let her mom do it; it's like she's all upset about being an adult or something.

"Having your thingy is not something to be ashamed of," I announce. I announce this every twenty-eight days. We stop at a crosswalk because Jessica Osheroff, the *Eastbrook American* reporter is hustling across the street, slinging her pocketbook over her shoulder, pulling out her notepad.

"Yeah. Right. You just called it a thingy."

"Fine. Your men-stru-al cy-cle." I make the words long and slow, which cracks Em up. Jessica Osheroff glares at Em as if Em is laughing at her.

Since Jessica has crossed the street, we're moving forward again. Em finally stops laughing and says, "It's not just that. We have to buy condoms, too."

I stop laughing. "Condoms? You want me to buy condoms for you!"

"Shut up! The windows are open."

"Can't Shawn buy condoms?"

"He did last time. It's my turn and we're all out."

"Oh my God, you take turns? How often are you guys doing it?"

Em turns her head to give me an eyebrow wiggle. "You're just jealous."

"Yeah." I hang my hand out the window and feel the air

hit it, giving it a high five. "I can't buy condoms from Dolly. I'm not even doing it with Tom."

"I know. Believe me, I know."

"What's that supposed to mean?"

She sucks in some air and says, "It means we all wish you guys would just get it over with."

I try to glare at her. Her lip wiggles because she wants to laugh but isn't. Her lip always does that.

"I can't believe people talk about my sex life."

"Or lack thereof," she says like a teacher. She thrusts her hand in the air to make the point. I grab it and put it back on the wheel.

"Shut up," I taunt her.

"Make me," she says right back, matching my annoyed kid tone.

I crack up. So does she.

Then I say it again, because I can't believe it. "You want me to buy condoms for you and Shawn."

"Uh-huh."

I shake my head. "Fine. But you're coming with me and we aren't going to Rite Aid. We're going to Wal-Mart. They have those self-checkout lines there."

Em's face lights up. "That's beautiful! That is such a good idea."

"I am the best friend you'll ever have," I say.

She turns into my driveway and flashes a smile. "I know."

We weren't always best friends. We always knew each other and were friends but not in the ultimate friend way. Everyone in Eastbrook knows each other, pretty much because there's only about six thousand people who live here. I used to be best friends with Mimi Cote, but that ended in eighth grade. It wasn't just the Tom thing, I swear. It was a bunch of things, like the way she'd lie and pretend to get better scores on her projects than me, or the way she'd get annoyed that I was the flyer on our middle school cheerleading team (see, more small-town multitasking) and she wasn't and she'd always tell me I was getting too fat to be a flyer, which of course I wasn't, because I was tiny, tiny, tiny and it was only because I was getting breasts that Mimi even tried to pull the whole "you're too fat to be a flyer" crapola routine on me.

Pathetic.

There are lots of things that can make you not be a friend with someone, and fewer things that can make you a friend with someone, but I lucked out when Em got seated next to me freshman year in period-A study hall. She is easily the best friend I could ever have.

"I can't believe your mother's going on another date with Jim Shrembersky," she says in my driveway. "Where are they going?"

"Cleonice." It's our town's one fancy restaurant. They serve tapas.

Em laughs. "Hhm. Maybe we should buy some condoms for your mom, too."

I fling open the door and get out of the car. "I hate you."

She just laughs harder.

I wave to her as she starts backing out the driveway.

"You sure you don't want a ride to the cemetery?" she yells, her rear bumper missing our mailbox by five-tenths of a centimeter.

I smile. "I'm good."

She toots and zooms off down the road, my crazy, uptight best friend who has supermodel hair, a brain that doesn't give her seizures, a non-dating widow mother, a boyfriend who sleeps with her, who tells her he loves her, a perfect life.

My MOM AND I VISIT my dad every year. I bike there. I can't drive because I have caffeine-induced seizures, but I wouldn't drive anyway because that's not how I do this. Since I was six I've always ridden my bike up the steep hills of the Bayside Road. My mom always drives. It's part of our ritual, but neither of us talk about it. This year, of course, she blows it and brings Jim, her new boyfriend. It's not like I hate Jim, but he's not supposed to be here. It's supposed to be about my mom and my dad and me. She says that he'll wait in the car when we go visit the grave, but it's not the same. I'll still know he's there.

It rains today, too, but that doesn't change anything. Rain has come before. Jim, though, Jim hasn't come before.

People have traditions in their lives, you know. They have ways things happen, and then, all of a sudden, someone decides to change it. I hate that.

I hard-pump the pedals to get up the last big hill, steer around the crumbled asphalt that juts into the breakdown lane. The tires slick to the pavement and I don't fall despite the slippery surface, despite the rain slashing into my eyes, pouring off my helmet, obliterating the smells of the flowers, the spring-fresh grass, so that all I can smell and taste is iron and rain, metal and loss.

We don't dress up for the occasion. My mom says he wouldn't want that. He wasn't a dress-up kind of guy. I wouldn't know. I never met him. I was a baby when he died, a massive hole blown in his chest a half a world away.

The rain drenches my jeans and windbreaker/rain coat.

I get off my bike, see Jim sitting in the car. He's pretending to read a book, but he looks up the moment I walk by and he waves and gives a little half smile. His hair is thin and it's all wet. I can tell that even through the car windows. He got soaked somehow today, just like me.

I wave back. He's not a bad guy, Jim. It's just he doesn't belong here, not right now. My mom should know that. There's a way this is suppose to be, every year, and this isn't it.

My mom's already at the grave, holding a blue and green umbrella that's older than me. Maybe my dad once held that umbrella over her head, protecting her from the rain, the way he never had a chance to protect me. My mom's raincoat touches the ground as she bends down at the knees, strokes his name, the dates; a grave, her face. She clings to air.

So do I.

Leaning my bike against the big granite pillars that guard the cemetery, I head in. My feet squish in the wet grass. Water invades my running shoes. My toes adjust to the damp.

Normally, I bring Gabriel and play my dad a song. Gabriel was his guitar, and she's a wild, deep blue. I don't ever sing because that would be too cheesy, sort of crossing the line into schmaltz. Instead, I just play something soft and quiet for him. I think it calms my mother down, too. It gives us something to focus on in the awkwardness of a cemetery. My fingers always relax when they play the chords. You have to keep your left hand loose to play chords well. Anything jerky and it just sounds like crap. And when your fingers relax, your heart relaxes and you don't think so much about how you've never had a dad.

According to my mom, my dad used to love folk music, Bob Dylan, Richard Thompson, Tom Paxton, Ewan Mac-Coll, all that old-guy stuff. But it is too wet today, this death day, and I can't risk bringing Gabriel out in this and singing some Dylan. The rain would pound too heavy on her body. It would ruin her.

So, it's just me clomping through the wet grass towards my mom, just me alone without my guitar, but with my mom's new man friend witnessing it all from his spectator seat in the car.

Reaching out, my hand touches my mom's shoulder. She jumps up so fast the umbrella almost bashes into my face. I stumble backwards to get out of the way and fall on my butt. She laughs.

The sky above her lightens to charcoal gray. The water drops come down at me like slow-motion silver bullets. I can plot their course. The only color is from the flowers she's brought, bright zinnias, pink and yellow. The rain bends their petals but they somehow stay whole.

"You okay?" she says, reaching out her hand. It's wet. I take it.

"Yeah," I say as she hauls me back to standing position. "You?"

She nods, keeps my hand in hers, and tucks me under the umbrella with her. "Your father would be so proud of you."

She says this every year, even years when I fall on my butt in the wet grass. It's a cliché. It's what everyone in Eastbrook says to me. Your father would be proud.

"Why?" I ask my mom. It's the question I've wanted to ask her every year, and now, I guess, without Gabriel here to distract me, I ask it. Plus, I mean, really, would my father be proud knowing about The Problem? I doubt it. "Why would he be proud?"

A truck bellows by on the Bayside Road, past Jim in my mom's parked car, past the cemetery. Its wheels displace the water for a brief second, pulling puddles from the road, from the earth, before smacking them back down again.

"Why not?" my mom answers.

Lightning brightens the sky. Magic seems to whisk through the trees. The zinnias shake.

"That's getting closer," she shudders. "We should go."

----o----

We start walking through the grass. The wetness of it seeps into my shoes, sloshes around my feet and I just ask her, before we get too close to Jim and her car, "Do you think he'd love me?"

"Oh, honey, how could anyone not love you?"

This is a completely good-mother thing to say. My mother is that type of mother, the kind that doesn't think there could be anything wrong, ever, with her darling little girl.

But that's not true, especially when it comes to love.

Tom has never told me he loves me even though we've been dating for months.

My ex-boyfriend, Dylan, I always thought loved me, but he didn't, not "that way." He was gay. I was totally dependent on him for most of high school and then—poof—it turned out to be a big pretend.

"I'm not that lovable, Mom."

She shakes her head beneath the umbrella. "Yes, you are. I love you. You're a very popular girl."

If she wasn't so cute I would glare at her, but she looks like a wet puppy so I just say, "I'm not popular, Mom."

"Were you Harvest Queen?"

I shrug.

"Are you in charge of clubs at school?"

"Students for Social Justice and Amnesty International don't count. Those aren't the cool clubs."

She charges on. "Do you have friends? Lots of friends?"

Now, I glare at her.

"Then you're popular."

"I'm not 'popular,'" I say, making the little finger quotes that people make. "Not in the rah-rah pep-rally way."

I hate labels. I'm not sure why people get labels. But I do not want to be labeled, not popular, not folkie, not good girl, not slut, not anything. People aren't just one thing; my mom should know that. Like, her boyfriend has a horror movie collection but that does not make him a serial killer freak weirdo, although looking at his choice in media, you would label him that. He's also a really good 3-D photographer and newspaper guy. Everybody's like that. Including me. I hate when people pretend life is simple and straight, one label, one plot moving us from point A to point B, pretending our entire makeup fits into a one-word description.

"I'm not popular," I tell her again.

"Sweetheart," she says, itching at her ear. "Your boyfriend is a jock, a cute jock."

"He's not just a 'jock,'" I say, a little angry. "Jocks are not into duct tape, and they don't make little sculptures out of it or write sayings on it and they aren't as smart as Tom is."

"No one is 'just' anything, Belle. Didn't I teach you that?" Now she's finger-quoting at me.

"Yeah." I shiver in the rain, staring at her warm car and Jim sitting in it. "You taught me."

"Your dad would've been so proud of you," she says, reaching out and squeezing a lock of super wet hair. She smiles, sweetly and slowly. She looks pretty. I forget that my mom is kind of pretty despite the whole thinning hair thing. My dad must have really loved her.

The thunder ripples through the air. Sound waves of grief or anger or something, I think it's too symbolic, too heavy. All I need is a skull to lift up in my hand and a soliloquy. *Dear dead father... Would you have loved me? Your first-born daughter? Blah. Blah. Blah. To be or not to be...*

I would rather have a sunny day and a happy frolic with Tom on a beach somewhere. Okay, fine...a bed somewhere. I would rather have a father who was alive and loved me instead of a war hero. I would rather have dry socks and fingers that relax above guitar strings, ready to play chords.

My mom kisses me on the top of the head as she gets in the car. "You sure you don't want a ride back? It's pouring."

"It's dismal!" Jim says, leaning forward so he can see me. He rubs his hands together and he's got this massive smile smacked across his face. I guess horror-movie buffs like dismal weather.

"Yep," I say. "I'm sure."

Our ritual is already too different. The least I can do is bike home like normal and obsess about Tom.

My mom's hunched inside the car, trying to shelter away from the rain and it's obvious she wants to slam the door shut to keep the rain out, but if she did, it would keep me out too, and she's too nice a mom for that.

"I'm just going to pick up a few things for my trip next week, drop Jim off at the car place, and then I'll be right home."

I close the door for her and as my hands push the cold, wet metal I say, "Take your time."

Then I add, so I'm not rude, "Good luck with your car, Jim."

He gives me a dorky thumbs-up sign. "You just must adore this rain! It's torrential."

Torrential?

My mom honks. She drives off, taking with her the smell of car air-freshener in pine tree form and tic-tacs.

As soon as she leaves, I slosh back to the cemetery and my father's grave. The sky opens up for one second and a spot of blue edges out of the gray, like a promise, but as quickly as it appears it's gone again, swallowed up by the gloom. My fingers touch the zinnias.

I sit on the wet earth, my head resting against the marble. If I close my eyes, maybe I could see him somehow, but that's not what I want. I want to be able to smell what he used to smell like, feel if the skin on his arms was rough or smooth, super hairy, or just kissed with follicles.

"I wish I knew you," I say. The rain pellets my bike helmet. Thwonk. Thwonk. It makes a patter beat like Morse code, but I can't decipher the message. What does my mom do when she comes here? What does she think? Does she see old visions of him, dancing her across the floor at their high school prom? Does she feel the soft cloth of his flannel shirt against her cheek as he hugs her hello? Does she remember the day he left for the war? The sorrow-crinkles in his eyes when he refused to say goodbye?

"No good-byes," he told her, patting her belly, where I was swimming around, waiting. "Those are for movies and men who don't come home."

But he didn't. He didn't come home.

When your dad dies before you know him he becomes a fairy tale, like someone familiar that you've always wanted to meet but you keep missing each other somehow, almost as if you walk straight and they turn; you ride your bike down a road while they whiz by in an ambulance; you know they exist, that they existed, but it's something that you can never touch.

And the thing is, I think the people you know can be like that too. You think you're so connected. You think you know someone's soul and then it just rain-smears away and you're just left with words about them, words that explain about them, but you don't have them.

My fingers press against his headstone, but it's just wet stone, wet and hard and there's nothing there at all, just a name, letter-symbols of someone who once was.

That's it.

That's it when your dad dies before you knew him or when your husband dies before he kisses your baby. You just journey through it. You just keep going and going like some sort of crazy battery-powered pink bunny in a commercial. You bang your drum and you go on.

"Would you love me?" I whisper ask. "Do you think Tom loves me?"

My father, he doesn't answer. Of course he doesn't answer.

So, I get up and walk away.

Everything is different, just because of Jim in the car, just because you can't keep everything the same forever, I guess.

It rains harder but I can handle it. On my bike I can handle almost anything. It's like you're a superhero pushing through the rotation of the tires. It's all you and muscle and gravity, going forward, moving, all power.

I race my bike through the sheets of water. Massive puddles slosh up and spray my legs. The bike is like the storm, out of control, but I'm doing my best to stay upright and stable on the old, hilly Bayside Road. I would focus on the faded white line that shows the shoulder, but puddles obscure it.

This is hell.

Splash.

Only wet.

Can hell be wet?

Isn't hell supposed to be hot fire and searing pain? Isn't it supposed to be constant torture by your most hated enemies? For me, that would be Mimi Cote, the high school bully queen.

Why would her mother name her that? Mimi like me-me, like shallow materialism and greed at its best.

"Because life is full of cruelties perpetuated by our parents," is what Em would say.

Splash.

My cell phone waits in my pocket, tempting me to call Em, or Tom, for a ride, but I won't do it. I don't need help getting home. I'm no damsel in distress. It's just rain.

Splash.

This time the puddle wiggles my tire a bit. My jeans are heavy against my leg.

"I am so stupid," I say out loud, between gritted teeth. "I am a total idiot."

Clouds thicken the sky. Thunder rolls around the air like a curse. The zinnias in the cemetery must be struggling.

I pedal and then a black truck pulls up alongside me. The growling engine noise lets me know it's my neighbor, Eddie Caron. Eddie used to be one of my little-kid best friends and then he freaked out last fall, pushed me against a locker, put his hand on my...

Don't think about this.

Pedal.

Just pedal.

"Hey Belle!" He's rolled down the window. "Want a ride?"

"No, thanks," I manage to make my lips move. The bike's tires rip through another puddle, dark and foul. A used paper cup floats in it. Ahead of me, near Billy Ray's house, is a flat lake spreading out across both lanes of the road. On sunny days, there's a pothole there that I always have to veer around. The rain hits this massive puddle, striking it over and over again.

"You can't ride your bike in the rain," says Eddie. "You look like a freaking lunatic and you're soaked."

He leans his bulky body out of his truck window. I keep riding, pumping the pedals, smooth and hard so I can go faster even on the slick roads. He keeps the truck going the same speed as my bike.

"I'm fine!" I yell and push harder, like I'm somehow going to magically be able to outrun a truck with an engine, a motor and Eddie's big foot on the gas, like I'm suddenly Superman. Sorry. Too gender specific. Superperson.

Eddie shakes his head at me, squints his big dark eyes and doesn't give up. "You're being stupid."

The rain splatters down. Lightning shrieks across the sky.

"You're just being stubborn," he yells at me. I glance over at him. Rain has soaked his shirt. "You're going to fall."

"Will not."

"Will too."

Thunder booms. Rain splatters against my ears. Eddie keeps trailing me. "If I was Tom you'd take the ride."

"Yeah."

That's a no-brainer right there. Tom is my boyfriend. Eddie is the freak who grabbed my breast in the hallway and got suspended for it. I'm not supposed to think about that. I think about it and shudder in the cold rain.

"Belle, just let me bring you home. Okay?"

I start to shout something back, but at that moment something happens. My hand starts jerking the way it does right before I have a seizure, only I don't really have seizures much anymore. I don't. I stare at my hand. My bike lurches hard and quick. The front wheel wiggles and I fly over the handlebars, head first. Somehow I relax my body, but curl it, like a ball, and I thud into the dirt on the shoulder of the road.

I jump right up, horrified, embarrassed, even more soaked. I don't care if I'm hurt. I cannot believe I fell off my bike. I never fall off my bike.

Eddie's truck is stopped in the middle of the road. His door's flung wide open and he's right by me, face tight and wet. "Belle…"

He reaches his hand out. His hand is huge and waits in front of me. I follow the line of his arm to his face. His brow crinkles and below it his brown eyes plead for me to take his hand, to take it, to trust him.

"I'm fine."

"Belle, I think you had a seizure."

I pace away from him, pivot back. My shoulder hurts. My ankle hurts. My head feels groggy and funny like it used to after I had a seizure. I did not have a seizure. I only have seizures when I've had caffeine or aspartame. I did not have caffeine or aspartame.

"I'm fine." I grab at my bike, lifting it like I'm going to jump on it and ride home. The frame looks okay, but the front tire is flat. "Crap."

I could patch it, but I don't want to. I unbuckle my helmet and yank it off. Water sloshes into my eyes. I grab the handlebars to walk my bike back home but everything in me feels weak and tired, like all my muscles have been yanked hard and fast.

"I couldn't have had a seizure," I whisper out.

Eddie's meaty hand lands on my wet shoulder, the one that I didn't land on. "Belle, let me bring you home."

I stop walking and breathe in. "I can call Em for a ride. I have my cell."

He does not move his hand and it's all I can do not to run away. It was horrible in the hall that day, the way I couldn't get away from him, the way his eyes hardened like asphalt and he wouldn't listen. I felt helpless.

I did not just have a seizure.

Thunder echoes across the sky. Tom is at practice, but maybe coming home now, because the weather's so bad. My mom is running errands and I am here, on the Bayside Road, standing with Eddie Caron and his hand, his hand is on my shoulder.

Let me go, I say, but it's only in my head. Let me go, Eddie.

When we were little kids we'd play together. We'd do all those little-kid things. We'd hold hands and pull on each other, running in a circle and chanting Ring Around the Rosie. We'd fall down and giggle forever, staring up at the sky. Back in first and second grades, when I was too little to fit in and Jade

Gerard would bully me into giving him my Goldfish snacks, it was Eddie who would beat him up behind the school.

That was the old Eddie. Now there's this Eddie. The hallway Eddie. How can they be the same person? They are. Somehow they are.

His eyes meet my eyes.

Let me go, Eddie.

He lets go. The hand that had rested on my shoulder wipes at the water on his face, rough and impatient.

"I'm sorry, Belle," he says with a voice that doesn't match his hand. "I was a shit. I know I was a shit. You know…back then. I was drunk. That's not an excuse. I'm better now. The old Eddie."

He swallows and I don't say anything.

Something in his eyes flickers and I feel sorry for him somehow. I do not want to feel sorry.

"Please," he says, "let me give you a ride home. It's insane out here. And I really think you had a seizure. You were jerking."

My breath sucks in. "You saw me?"

"Yeah."

I nod, just the tiniest nod, and Eddie grabs my bike and hoists it into the back of the truck. He opens the door for me and makes sure I don't fall getting in his truck. But it was just a seizure. It doesn't make me incapable of getting in a freaking truck.

"I'll get it all wet," I say.

He shrugs. "Like I care. It smells like puke in here, anyway."

I sniff in. It does. My head wobbles back against the seat. There's a crack in the black vinyl shaped like the letter Y.

He starts driving. "It's my dad. He went on a bender one

night and slept it off in my truck. I used Fantastic but you can still smell it."

"Really?" It's hard to imagine Mr. Caron drinking. He's so Bible School with his perfectly creased shirts.

"Fantastic is a pretty good cleaner."

"That's not what I meant."

"Things have kind of sucked at home lately," Eddie says. The wipers swish back and forth, frantically trying to rid the window of water. "Should I be doing something special for you?"

"What?"

"Because you just had a seizure?"

"No."

I rub the wet out of my eyes. Eddie's shirt clings to him. He says, "I'm sorry."

We both know what he's talking about. We both know it's not about his father. We both know it's not because I was jerking on the side of the road.

"So am I."

It takes us less than five minutes to get to my house, even though Eddie has to drive slow through the puddles. My phone beeps. Tom's sent me a text message. It's a picture of him, soaking wet with Shawn. They've got their arms wrapped around each other's shoulders. Then the message: *MISS U.* Why couldn't it have said *LOVE U?*

Great.

The whole way, I keep thinking about how mad Tom would be if he knew I was in here with Eddie. He hates Eddie. He hates when I do what he thinks are stupid things. Like when I forget that Wrigley's Spearmint gum now has aspartame in it and start chewing. Or when I climb on top of the roof of my house so I can be closer to the stars. This ride with Eddie? Tom would count this as an extremely stupid thing. And the seizure would make it worse.

I won't tell him.

U 2, I text back.

Just as Eddie turns the truck into my driveway he says, "Remember Cardigan?"

Cardigan was this eighth grade trip we all had to take. We climbed up a mountain and camped out for three nights with the teachers, and I was a total wimp. My backpack was really heavy. My head was spinning. I'd drunk five Pepsis on the bus ride over. Now, I realize I must have been in pre-seizure mode, but back then I couldn't figure out what was wrong with me. I didn't know why I passed out. I didn't know that caffeine and aspartame gave me seizures. I just felt bad.

Eddie had come all the way back down the mountain to where the teacher and I were resting. He took my pack up the mountain for me. He climbed the mountain twice. I called him my Hero Friend and everyone teased him about it, but it was kind of nice. Eddie's never been popular, and I think he felt kind of popular that weekend, like he fit in, and for once no one cared that he was so huge and not super smart or really good looking. They just cared that he was my Hero Friend.

"Cardigan was crazy," I say, opening the door. The rain attacks us. Eddie just barrels out of the truck anyway, hauling out my bike and carrying it to where it will be safe under the porch.

"Yeah," he says. "But it was fun. Do you know why you had one? A seizure?"

I shake my head, accept the truth. "No. Now? I didn't have anything today that would make me have one. No coffee or gum or anything."

He cracks the knuckles on his right hand. They're scratched up and rugged. "You stressed?"

"Yeah. I'm always stressed."

"Sometimes elevated stress levels can make people who are prone to seizures have seizures. It gets them closer to their threshold levels."

I eye him. Rain beats down. "You sound like a doctor."

"I looked up a lot of stuff up on the 'net, you know." He shifts his weight. His left leg jiggles nervously. "When you first had them."

"Oh."

I don't know what to think. The rain keeps pummeling down, so I just thank him and go inside, slouching, soaked, and not looking very powerful. At all.

HELLO HOUSE.

Goodbye Eddie.

Water falls off of me, puddles by the front door. I rip my clothes off, check out the bruise on my ankle and head upstairs for the bathroom. My cat, Muffin, rubs against me and then hisses.

"I know, I'm wet," I tell her.

She turns her back to me, shows me her kitty bum.

"It's not like it's on purpose."

Why does Tom have to be so cute? It kills me. The white of his teeth against his tree bark skin. The water molding his hair to his skull, dripping down his ear. Stop. Darn it. Stop being so damn cute. God, God, God, hormones just suck.

I throw my wet clothes into the washing machine, turn on the shower and check out his picture one more time. Damn. I won't tell anyone about my seizure. I won't risk it. This will be the one secret that I keep. Yeah, I keep it with Eddie, but nobody's talking to him anyway, and if I tell…. If I tell it means doctor appointments and medications, probably. It means no taking showers or baths without my mom pounding on the door every minute making sure I'm okay. It means no riding my bike and I already can't drive a car.

"It was a fluke," I announce to the bathroom.

The bathroom, I'm happy to say, agrees.

THERE IS NOTHING TO DO tonight, so Em and Shawn and Tom and I, we take off for dinner ourselves. We just go to Pat's Pizza, to sit in the green vinyl booths, to peruse the same coffee cup-stained menus we know by heart. And of course, I peruse Tom's face, the same jaw that's strong and straight but not in some ridiculous Superman way, the lines that crinkle by his eyes when he laughs, the cheek muscle that twitches when he's mad. I know him by heart too, and the longing...It's crazy. I can't believe you can long for someone so much when that person is right there.

Anna and Kara and Crash are at another table with Dylan and Bob. Bob shifts his eyes away when I say hi. The overhead lights glint off his glasses. The sun has burnt the scalp beneath his super short hair.

"You guys want to sit with us?" Anna asks.

Shawn holds his hands out. "You look crowded."

Anna wipes at the corner of her lip, which she's outlined with black, and then says, "We could sit on laps?"

Even she knows it's a stupid idea.

We end up only a couple booths away and while we sit perusing and perusing and perusing, the voices of the other table breeze over. They hum towards us. The fan on the ceiling turns and turns. Each spin of it causes the blades to shake and it reminds me of my hand, of falling on the ground.

Tom shuts his menu.

"You know what you're getting?" Shawn asks.

"Mexican."

"No green pepper?" I ask.

Tom sticks his tongue out, disgusted at the thought.

"Stick that thing back in unless you're going to use it," Em says. "Oh, wait...Bellie, you do want him to use it?"

I kick her underneath the table. She yelps and smiles.

"Sometimes I hate you." I make my voice go hard mean.

"You really love me." She hides behind the menu then pokes her eyes over the top, all little girl sweet. "Right?"

Shawn hauls her into his side, wraps his fingers around her shoulder. He smiles so hard his face muscles must ache, the world is in that smile. "We all love you, Emily-bemily."

She kisses his cheek. "Good."

Tom shakes his head and whispers, "They're disgusting."

"I know."

"We aren't that bad, are we?"

"Worse!" Shawn yells. He jabs his finger at us like some sort of conservative news channel host making a point about the wasting away of American morals. "You are worse."

This is a total lie.

"I'm going to go wash up," I say and scoot out of the booth.

There's a one-person line outside the bathroom at Pat's and it's Anna in front of me. She's got her Palm Pilot thing out like the old-style techno geek she is, figuring out her busy schedule I guess. I tap her on the shoulder. It's wet from the rain. She turns around. "Hey."

"Hey."

"Someone is taking forever in there." She bites the end of her stylus and says in a perfectly normal, unwhispering voice, "I heard you and Em are going to Wal-Mart tomorrow to buy some condoms."

My mouth drops open. "Em told you that?"

She nods. Someone flushes behind the door.

I cannot believe Emily, the girl who can't even buy tampons by herself, has announced this to Anna. This is totally out of character for her.

Anna checks something off on her Palm. "Can I come?"

"To buy condoms?"

"Well," she shrugs. "I need tampons and Emily says it's really fun. That you pretend to be a secret agent person on a recon mission."

"Oh God." I bring my hands up to cover my face. "My life is so embarrassing."

"It's cute!" She taps my shoulder with her stylus. "Don't worry. You'll get to use them soon."

"Is it that obvious?"

"Yeah. Both your faces are all longing like Princess Lea and Han Solo in the original Star Wars trilogy. Or Strider and Arwen in LOTR."

I shake my head. "What?"

"You need to see more movies," Anna laughs. She shows me her LOTR shirt and points to Viggo, the guy who must play Strider. "The want. You guys have the look of want."

"The look of want," I mutter.

"It's too bad it's going to totally suck the first time."

"What?"

"You know, the first time you do it. Boys are all awkward. Especially guys under thirty, not like you should do it with someone that old, because that would be gross and possibly criminal."

"Where do you get this?"

"Have you or have you not read John Green?"

I shake my head.

"*Looking for Alaska*?"

I still have no clue.

"With the whole blow-job scene?" she's shrieking. She stylus-points at me. "Do not tell me you have never read the blow-job scene."

A woman with cropped unbending hair opens the door, awkward, bewildered. Her eyes adjust to the darker light.

"Sorry," she mumbles and skitters away.

I don't recognize her. I whirl on Anna and whisper, "You just said that out loud."

Anna swallows a half-laugh and gives me a little wave, closes the door, gone.

When it's my turn, I study my face in the mirror. I don't see it. I don't see the look of want. But I know it's there and once we're sitting down at the movies, staring at the cartoon about a rat who wants to be a chef, just Tom's leg bumping into my leg makes me shiver.

A rat on the screen cooks something gourmet. Shawn laughs, leans forward clutching his stomach. Tom leans back, too, chuckling like some old grandpa, but his hand lands on my knee. His thumb moves up and down and electric stuff moves with it. His thumb nail is ragged. My whole body goes wiggly and aching and it's too much to handle.

The rat on the screen smiles.

I grab Tom's thumb, just circle my fingers around it and breathe in.

People laugh.

----0----

After the movies, Shawn and Em leave together. I try not to wonder if they're going to have "awkward teenage sex."

Tom brings me home. Almost the whole way I babble about how I wish I didn't dislike Bob, how I'm worried that makes me a bigot somehow and it's true, but it's also because I can't stand to think of Tom's thumb on my knee and how it makes me feel and how I want to have awkward teenage sex, and why was it so unawkward with Dylan, which makes me blab on about Bob again.

When we park Tom just says, "Belle, if you loved all gay people just because they were gay that would be just as bad."

He gets out of the truck and takes my hand to walk me to the door, but I pull on him and bring him around to the back of the house.

"Where we going, Commie?" he asks.

I hold my finger to my lips. "Shhh... and don't call me Commie. I am not a communist. I am just in Amnesty and Students for Social Justice and you are so ruining the mood. Okay?"

Silence.

We walk around the house to the backyard. I bring him to where there's a big oak tree. Its trunk bark is gnarled with age and wisdom, covered with cracks that separate the bark, lichen clinging to it for life and support. I place his hands against the trunk. He lifts up an eyebrow. The moonlight casts shadows against the lines of his face. I don't think he could be any more handsome. I don't want him to not love me.

He turns and leans his back against the tree. I press myself against him. With my eyes closed, there seems to be no distance between us. The world sways beneath my feet. The spring night air lifts my hair gently, rustles through the leaves. *Kiss me. Kiss me. Kiss me.* My eyes open. Tom's face leans down.

I press my hand against his cheek.

"Please," I say, but I don't know what I'm asking for.

His arms enclose around me. Every molecule of my body yearns for this, for him. He's so warm. He moves a little against me.

"Commie," he says.

He whispers it like a moan. "Commie."

We somehow end up on the ground. The roots of the tree bump beneath my back.

He kisses my cheeks, the top of my head, softly, lightly. "You have to stop beating yourself up so much."

"I don't."

"Yes, you do."

I prop myself up onto my elbow. "You didn't always use duct tape."

"Where did that come from?"

"I don't know," I say, running a finger along the top of his shoulder. He shivers in a good way. "I was just thinking that you've changed since middle school."

"People change, Belle."

"Then how do we know who they are? How do we love them if they're always changing?"

He pulls in a breath through his nose and slowly lets it out. "We don't know. We just love them...the parts we know."

"But it's not real then?"

"You don't think you can know the essence of someone without knowing all their details?"

I snort. "Essence of someone?"

"Shut up."

"I want to know why you like duct tape," I say and he flops onto his back. I snuggle into his shoulder and breathe in. There's a faint grass smell and soap. He smells so Tomish. I love that smell.

"Why I like duct tape?"

"Yeah."

"Should I make a Belle list?"

I nod, my head rubbing up and down against the soft cotton of his shirt. "Yep. Good idea. It helps me process, you know."

"I know." He sighs and thinks for a minute. "The Reasons Why Tom Tanner Likes Duct Tape."

"One," I say.

"One. It's sticky and you can make stuff out of it."

"Fine."

"Two. It's hard to rip. Only manly men can rip off duct tape repeatedly."

"So macho," I whisper and try to tickle him. He grabs my fingers in his hand, brings them to his mouth and kisses them.

"It let me have the best Halloween costume ever."

"Duct Tape Man?"

"Yep."

"That was the best Halloween costume ever?"

"Yes," he laughs. He kisses my ring finger. "Four. It holds things together."

"Do you want things to hold together?"

He is silent. His hand isn't as tight around my fingers.

"Tom?" I whisper ask. "Are you afraid of things falling apart?"

"Everybody is."

"I never imagine you afraid."

"Don't tell Shawn." He laughs and his voice quiets into the night. "Guys get scared all the time."

"I won't." A twig snaps in the woods. Muffin trots out of the woods, snuggles into our sides. "What are you afraid of?"

"That I won't be good enough?"

"For what?"

"For you."

He's afraid of awkward? Love is bigger than awkward.

"That's stupid." I prop myself up to kiss him again. He pulls me on top of him. We rock back and forth, rushing towards each other and then he pushes me away, pulling his lips from mine.

"What?" I'm shocked and angry and empty, really empty feeling.

"Not now, Belle," he says, sitting up. His face is empty, blank. "Not like this."

He's already standing up, and he reaches down to help me to my feet. "I'll see you tomorrow?"

Shocked, my lips bruised and aching like my heart, I say the only thing I can think of. "Okay."

If I were Mimi he wouldn't have stopped. If I were Mimi I wouldn't have said, "Okay." Because it wasn't. It wasn't okay.

I WAKE UP WITH THE knowledge that I am going to have to go buy condoms at Wal-Mart. This is not a good thing, but it is a good thing, and there's something funny about it too. A condom shopping spree. I stretch out full on my bed, point my toes, move my arms above my head. Muffin senses that I am alive and well and have survived the night in my lonely bed, so she greets me with a cat butt in the face.

The kitty litter smell so early in the morning is not the greatest thing.

I groan and roll over.

The kitty litter smell follows me.

So I heave the blankets off and will my aching body into a sitting position, drop my bare feet onto the cold floor. My flowers are in a vase on the bookcase, blooming and making everything smell good. The little duct tape guitar Tom made me right after Dylan came out waits nearby. I grab my real guitar from her resting place beside the wall.

"Good morning, Gabriel," I mutter. Shafts of morning sun slide through the window and bounce against Gabriel's shiny blueness. My tired fingers move across her strings, finding the proper positions and then I begin to play. It's a song of longing, a longing that might soon be over. It has no words.

My mom comes and stands at my door. She's already dressed and spiffy-looking. She dresses up even on Saturdays if she's going out and about. She's always wearing skirts that flow around her ankles for her public persona. Of course, at home she schlumps around in slippers. Muffin flops off the bed and twines herself around my mother's legs, popping her head against the red cotton fabric of her skirt.

"Silly cat," my mom says, and bends so that she can scratch Muffin's ears. "Nice song. What do you call it?"

"Buying condoms," I say.

She straightens up, smiling. "Ha. Ha. Ha. Very funny."

"Really."

She lifts her eyebrows. "Mm-hmm. I made you some Postum and some toast."

I strum a final chord and shift off the bed, resting Gabriel against the wall. Then I stretch.

"I see your belly," my mom says, smiling. She puts her fingers out to tickle me. "I see a cute Bellie belly."

"Don't you dare tickle me," I back up, hands out to ward her off. "Don't you dare."

She dares.

Some people's mothers are nice and normal. Mine is not. End of story.

Okay, it's not really the end of story. My mom is a great coper. For years she worked at a dental supply company coping with boredom. This year she got a new job as the human resource director at the hospital. She copes with nurses and doctors having affairs, MRI techs looking at porn on their computer and a million other things. At home, she copes with being a single mom who has a daughter who has a seizure if she drinks coffee or eats anything with the chemical aspartame in it. She does it all alone.

She also messes up song lyrics on purpose, but I'm the only one who knows that it's on purpose. Like even the Happy Birthday song. She'll sing, "Happy torque day, Big Blue."

I think she's just trying to mix people up a little bit.

She's okay, really, for a mom, except for the whole tickling thing.

And the fact that sometimes when I tell her the truth,

44

like about the condom song, she just doesn't seem to hear. Or that I can't tell her some truths, like the seizure thing, because it would make her not sing at all.

Em picks me up first because I am friend number one. Plus, I live closer.

Em sighs as we head to Anna's. "I've been thinking."

"Uh-oh."

"Funny. Do you want to know what I'm thinking?"

"Sure."

"You aren't going to like it."

"Then why tell me?"

"Because you need to hear it."

"Okay…What?"

"You don't love Tom enough."

"What?"

"You don't love him enough. You hold back. You don't let yourself go because you're scared of him loving you. And Tom's a smart boy. He senses it."

"That's crap."

"You do? You love him the way you loved Dylan?"

"That's different, Miss Psychotherapist."

"That's right."

"Dylan was gay."

"That's not why it's different."

"Okay. Why is it different? Tell me, Oh Wise One."

"Don't get snarky."

"Snarky? What kind of word is that? I am not snarky. My mom went on a date last night with a man who collects *horror movies* and you're grilling me about whether I love my perfect boyfriend who does like duct tape way too much…but…whatever…and now you're calling me snarky. What's with you?"

"I'm just trying to help."

"Well don't."

"Fine."

"Good."

We both start laughing because even when we try to fight it comes out stupid, like a bad play script, or a really sucky horror movie, like we're just saying the lines because we're supposed to, not because they mean anything. But Em ruins it because she keeps talking.

"I just think you're afraid to love him because of what happened with Dylan. You're afraid to need him because he might let you down."

I tie the laces of my Snoopy shoes. The canvas started pulling away from the soles awhile ago, so Tom duct taped them for me. He is sweet like that. I do not answer Em.

"It's not easy to open up and trust someone when the last time you did it, it turned out that they were pretending. You're afraid to love Tom because you're afraid he might not be who you think he is. But he is, Belle. He really is and he loves you."

"Yeah, right."

"He does. Shawn told me."

I pull the laces tight. I try not to look too excited but I fail miserably, obviously, because Em is laughing. I say, "He did?"

"Yeah."

"Did he actually use the word 'love'?" I put my other shoe on the dash and work on lacing it. This one doesn't have duct tape on it so I don't like it as much. I hold my breath waiting for her answer.

"Yep."

"Wow. And you're sure he wasn't saying it about Shawn. He was saying it about me?"

"Tom's not gay, Belle."

"I know."

We're silent, then I say, "How'd you get so smart?"

That's a line my mom always pulls on me. Em answers the way I always do with a corny high-society Manhattan accent crossed with a Russian heiress. "Talk shows and years and years of therapy dahling, years and years of therapy, talk shows and tequila."

The thing is that love … love is what is still there after everything, that big, overwhelming love, that's like the glare of snow on a sunny day, when you're riding through that snow and all you see is whiteness, blinding you, obliterating everything, and you still go through it, go into that blinding glare, even though you can't see, even though you don't know where your feet will end up or if you'll fall off the road and into a river or run into a mountain. You still just go.

Love does that to you.

It obliterates you.

I know that. I know. I know. And I know that's how it will be with Tom. I know that too. And I know what it's like when love ends up being a lie, an uncertainty.

Em watches me sink into thought and says, finally, "Thank God we're picking up Anna, because you are no fun today."

"Thanks."

She smiles, shuts off the car and we wait for Anna in the driveway. "No problem."

After a minute, Anna pops in the car.

Em's mouth drops open. "Your hair."

Anna smiles and buckles herself into the backseat. "You likey like it?"

"It's green," Em stutters, still staring.

"A beautiful shade of green," I say. "Like Kermit the Frog or the Geico lizard thing on the commercials."

"That's exactly what it's supposed to be!" Anna pulls her black T-shirt away from her chest all proud. "Read it."

"I heart Miss Piggy," Em reads. "So…you're Kermit?"

"Well, I'm not an amphibian." Anna lets her T-shirt settle back to her chest. Miss Piggy's face smiles out from a star. "Obviously."

"Obviously," Em repeats, starting the car again. "Why did I shut this off?"

I lean in, smell her mandarin orange skin soap. "Because you were good and didn't want to waste gas."

"Right!" Anna says, plucking a water bottle off the floor, opening it and giving it a gulp. "Good Emily. But I like Kermit. Like how he's so crazy awkward that Miss Piggy is chasing him around in a total lust frenzy. It's like a role reversal."

Em zooms out of the driveway. Her car tires kick up dirt, dust, little pebbles jolted out of their place by the movement of wheel and force.

"Role reversal?" I repeat.

"Yeah, because usually it's the guy who's chasing the girl, but the truth is that's so not the truth, you know?" Anna's voice gets all high-pitched excited. "The truth is that it's the girls who usually chase after the guys. Remember middle school?"

I mind flash an image of Mimi latching onto Tom, grabbing his maroon EMS sweatshirt with the duct tape on the elbows, telling him how cute he was. "Oh yeah."

"And in first grade when we had the kissing girls and we played tag but we only chased boys and then we kissed them and got points by how hot they were," Em sighs. "I loved that game."

"Dylan was a hundred points," I say. "Tom and Shawn were like fifty. So, Anna, you dyed your hair to celebrate the role reversal of Muppets from an ancient television show, when it wasn't even a role reversal at all?"

Anna nods. Her hair flops into her face. "It's all about media distortion."

I turn back around to face front, pick up the ripped-off cover of a *Glamour* magazine. The cover says the actual magazine's got an article on how to catch your guy's guy and super hot sizzling secrets in bed. "Is this all related to the teenage boy awkward sex thing you were talking about in Pat's last night?"

Anna's voice echoes through the car. "Yep."

"So, it's like you're just trying to prepare me for bad sex." I fold the magazine cover over and over again until it's just a tiny square of shiny color. "Great."

Em reaches over and pats my arm. There's a tiny cut on her knuckle shaped like a moon. "It will be fine when you guys do it, I swear."

"Colossal," Anna giggles.

"Life changing."

"Monumental."

"Brilliant."

"Miss Piggy inspiring."

"Enough!" I bark at them, turning Em's radio back on. I push the volume up to twenty so I can't hear them anymore. It's on Bangor's one hip-hop station. It's a Justin Timberlake song about consequences, which is great. "Can we put in some Christine Lavin?"

"No. Today is not a Bellie Folk Girl Day." Em points at me. I grab her finger and pretend like I'm going to bite it. She squeals. "Today is a Bad Girl Buying Condoms Day."

Anna manages to yell over the Justin Timberlake muttering. "Onward to condom quest!"

Em floors it. We move forward, faster and faster towards the next piece of road, the next piece of land, the next purchase of latex-covered *awkwardness*.

"Okay," I whisper in a commando voice, nodding with my head at Em and Anna, my back pressed against the end of the Wal-Mart beauty products aisle. "Little Foot you go right. Killing Queen you go left."

Latex-ware? What would Kermie think?

Em nods, starts a stealthy trot right and then says, "Little Foot is a stupid name. That's not a cool name."

I sigh. "Fine. Vampire Slayer."

"Too used." She crosses her arms and her pretend gun, which is really her index finger and thumb, balls up into a fist. Anna snorts and then looks so embarrassed she covers her mouth, which only makes us all laugh harder.

Marge Torrance, who works in the mouse room at the Jackson Lab over in Bar Harbor, pushes a shopping cart past us. Her little girl is hiccupping and asking for a Barbie.

"Maybe," Marge says. The carriage wheel is loose and it makes a jarring noise that's in synch with the hiccups, like it's the bass beat to some generic Wal-Mart hip-hop song.

We wait until she passes, heading into the aisle full of toaster appliances and I offer up, "Okay. How about Sperm Slayer?"

Anna jumps back. "Uck."

"Your guns, girls!" I say and make a fake gun with my fingers. They copy me and start to giggle. "This is serious! Okay."

I point at Em with my gun hand. She ducks and I bark, "No more talking back unless you want to buy your own tampons. You are now the Uterine Avenger. Now go!"

We scatter.

Anna's assignment: three boxes of condoms.

My mission: a box of tampons. Two boxes of condoms, which I will hopefully some day actually get to use.

Em's mission: volumizing shampoo and Cheez-Its—a.k.a. camouflage.

We don't want to make it too obvious what we're really here for.

We rendezvous at the self-checkout lane.

Anna and Em are laughing so hard that they're having a hard time standing up straight, but they're trying to shield their purchases from the eyes of my mother's new boss, Mr. Jones, who is buying a hair dryer and some film with his wife and daughter at the next lane.

"Oh my God," I say as I frantically push the first box of condoms over the bar code scanner. It beeps.

On the screen, in bright blue letters it reads: TROJAN. $4.99.

Em points at it and starts laughing again.

"Shut up!" I tell her.

"The commander commando has lost her cool," Anna says as I scan in the other condoms. Em moves her position to bagging, plopping everything into the plastic Wal-Mart bag with the gigantic yellow smiling face. What is he smiling about?

Mr. Jones strides over. "Hey, Belle. How are you doing?"

I whirl around. Anna takes over with the scanning. The stupid thing beeps in another box of condoms. Then there's the comforting sound of plastic crinkling as Em slams the box into the Wal-Mart bag.

"Oh. Hi, Mr. Jones. I'm great."

I make a big, fake smile and wave at his wife, and Cala, his little girl. She hugs my leg.

"I love gymnastics," she says. "You're my favorite teacher."

The scanner beeps some more, hopefully it's the tampons.

"You're a great gymnast," I say and grab Cala, heave her up and twirl her around in my arms. I pivot so the rest of the

Jones family is no longer facing our checkout with its condom boxes but watching us. Cala tilts her head back and laughs. Then I haul her over my head like she's an airplane. Her little belly sticks out of her shirt and she giggles.

"Prepare for landing. Deploy landing gear," I say and whirl her down, down, down, until she's standing on the floor.

The moment her feet touch, she jumps up again, reaching out her arms and yelling, "More! More!"

Mrs. Jones shakes her head and grabs Cala's hand, while looking at me. "You're a great kid, Belle Philbrick. You're going to be a great mommy some day."

Behind me, Em announces, "We're done with our purchases!"

Anna snorts.

Mr. Jones smiles at them and says to me, "Tell your mom to take it easy. She works herself too hard."

"Okay," I say.

"I heard she went on a date last night," his wife says.

"You heard that?"

She smiles an apology. "It's Eastbrook. Everyone knows everything about everyone. You know that, Belle. Sad but true."

"And if they don't know it they make it up," Anna says, slugging one of her arms around my shoulder while Em starts chasing little Miss Cala Jones in a happy little circle. Em woofs at her, pretending to be a puppy, the blue Wal-Mart bag full of condoms, tampons, Cheez-Its and volumizing shampoo banging against her leg.

Mr. Jones ushers them all out after trying to get Cala to calm down. They wave goodbye. Cala blows kisses and then takes off through the half door that only shopping carts are supposed to use. Her little fanny wiggles in a defiant girl dance. You have to like that kid.

It isn't until the Jones family is safely through all automatic doors and in the parking lot that Anna, Em and I lose it completely, grabbing each other's shoulders, shaking with laughter and the relief of having escaped.

Operation Uterine Safety is complete.

- - - - o - - - -

Anna has stuff to do and leaves us, but she takes her prized box of condoms.

"Anna?" I lean out the car window. "Um. Who are those for?"

"I'm going Boy Scout. You know." She snaps her fingers and cheesy-1970s points at us. "Be prepared."

She salutes and skips up the walk to her house. Em squeals her tires backing out of Anna's driveway, and runs her hands through her hair as we speed down the dirt roads of Hancock back towards Eastbrook.

"Thanks for getting me the tampons," she says.

I clear my throat and wave to Danny Brown, who is biking down the bumpy, windy road. "And…"

"And thanks for getting me the condoms, too," she says.

Danny Brown is shirtless and he clutches a fishing pole in his right hand. He pedals slow, like he's got all the time in the world. Anna's little sister was hit by a car in Hancock. She died. Hancock's always trying to petition the state for money to help them make breakdown lanes. The state keeps putting it off. You have to hate the state for that. Em honks at Danny. He laughs and gives her the finger.

"The Joneses were really cute at Wal-Mart," I say. "They totally love their kid."

"It's disgusting." Em laughs.

"I think it's sweet. People *should* be nice to their kids. Usually people are screaming at their kids in Wal-Mart."

Em turns onto Route 3, by the old cheese house where they used to sell cheese or something, way before we were born. It's got a FOR LEASE sign up on the window.

It makes me sad. "It must've been hard on the cheese-house people when their business closed. It must be so hard to be a business owner, or even a parent, I guess. I mean, like you have to be all *good parent* all the time."

"Right," Em shakes her head. "Like your mom is."

"She tries."

"True."

"She's not a bad parent. At all."

"Also true. I am going to be a sucky parent," Em announces. "The whole diaper thing."

I think of Em woofing at the Jones kid. "You'll be a good parent."

"Yeah, right."

We get stuck behind an RV going twenty miles per hour.

"Swear to me that when I'm old you will not allow me to buy an RV," Em says. "Swear it!"

"I will not allow you to buy an RV."

"Or drive thirty miles under the speed limit."

"I swear."

"Or be one of those screaming mothers at Wal-Mart."

I put my hand up in the air like I'm doing that Boy Scout Pledge thing. "I swear that you will not be one of those mothers, or one of those fathers if you have a sex change or something."

"Belle!" she starts laughing. The RV slows down more. "I don't want to get old and have to drive slow and be all responsible. I don't want blue hair either."

"Downer there, Em. The other day, Tom had this quote—"

"Duct taped?"

"Of course."

"Where? I think I'm going to have to pass the RV."

"Not on the right."

She glares at me. "I promise. I will pass on the left."

She peeks the car out, but there are other cars coming, big cars that are half SUV and half tractor-trailer truck.

"It was taped around his wrist. He has nice wrists."

"And it said?"

"'Freedom is the will to be responsible to ourselves.' It's Nietzsche I think."

"Tom is weird."

We nudge out again. Em's frantic to pass. "I know."

We're clear. She stomps on the gas and her little, red car zips into the other lane, fast, fast, faster. We're free.

"I think a better quote would be, 'Responsibility is the freedom that comes from acting our will,'" I say. "Nice pass."

"You're trying to out-quote Nietzsche. A little pompous there, huh, Bellie?"

I smile. "Just a little."

We go back into our proper lane. Em drives on. "You should probably stick to song lyrics."

"I know."

EMILY HAS TO WORK. I have homework and I have to ride my bike and play Gabriel. Tom and Shawn both have to work too. They do landscaping stuff and always get all smelly.

Our mail comes in the middle of the afternoon on Saturdays. I rush out, hoping there will be info about college. I still haven't gotten the letter that says who my roommate's going to be and all that.

But there's nothing good in there. Just bills and flyers from real estate guys who want to BE OUR BEST FRIEND and MAKE A GOOD SALE because FRIENDS HELP FRIENDS. I start crumpling up the flyer as I walk back down our flat little driveway. I hate how fake people can be.

"Hey Belle!"

Eddie's voice hits me.

I turn around, check to see if anyone's looking and give a weak wave. "Hey, Eddie."

He's wearing long jean shorts that are just above his knees and a black wrestling T-shirt. He's holding his mail.

"What're you up to?"

"Homework. Stuff," I say and turn around again and start back down the driveway. One step. Another step.

His voice stops me. "You feeling okay?"

"Yeah."

"No repeats?"

"I'm good," I shout over my shoulder but my stomach's all cringed up. No repeats. There will be no repeats.

"Hey! You want to hang out?"

I whirl around. The mail drops on the driveway. It scatters across the asphalt. I start picking it up. Eddie darts across the street. I hold out my arm straight like a crossing guard.

"I've got it," I say.

"I just wanted to help," he says, eyes wounded.

"I know."

We just stare at each other and I don't know what I'm supposed to say next.

I'm really mad at you Eddie.

I'm really mad at me for not hating you.

I'm really mad and sad too and embarrassed.

Tom was right, and if you'd done what you did to me to any of my friends or even someone who wasn't my friend I would kill you, even if you were high when it happened. You still were responsible. Right?

But I don't say anything, because my cell phone rings. I open it up really quickly and say, "Hi."

"Hi," says a handsome male voice. "It's me."

"It's Tom," I say to Eddie and wave goodbye, hauling away into the house because it's a safe place to be. I look down at my right hand. It almost feels funny, that jerky feeling. The mail shakes a little. Obviously nerves. Right?

"You want to see a movie tonight?"

"Again?"

"Yeah."

"With Shawn and Em?"

"Nah," he says. "Just you and me."

"Oh, like a real date."

"Yeah, a real date with just two people."

"Are Em and Shawn okay with that?"

His voice hardens up. "Belle. We don't have to ask them permission."

"I know. I just…I don't want them to feel left out."

"They're going contra dancing with Shawn's mom." Amusement makes his voice hoarser.

I giggle, trying to imagine it. "Poor babies."

"So, you and me?"

"Okay, if you really don't want to go contra dancing."

"Commie, you kill me."

I sit on the stairs. "I promised my mom I'd have dinner with her, but after that?"

"The nine o'clock," he says. "It'll give me a chance to shower."

I imagine him all grass-smelling and salty-sweat from mowing lawns and cutting bushes and weed whacking.

"You don't have to."

He chuckles. I imagine his lopsided smile that's a little bit smirk, a little bit dangerous. "Oh, you like me all man-gross."

I bite my lip because I do.

Once I've dropped my mail on the counter and trotted into my room, I decide to procrastinate and make a list. A Tom list. I write it on my computer. This is stupid, but I am stupid and I've obviously read *Sloppy Firsts* too many times. So…

Things That Are Good About Tom Tanner

1. The way he can smell like pine or like mint or like grass, but there's always this sexy Tom smell underneath.
2. The way he calls at just the right moment.
3. The way his cheek twitches when things bother him.
4. Those creases in his legs. I will not think about those muscle lines in his legs because he is not here right now and it is dangerous to think about these things because they make me long for him. Long should be with a capital L. Longing hurts.
5. The way he makes me long for him.
6. Crap.

I take Gabriel out to the backyard and plop myself down between two big spruce trees, leaning my back up against the trunk of Clannad, which is what I named the tree when I was little. The other one I named Guthrie. Muffin follows me out. Her tail twitches because she's looking for something to hunt.

"No killing," I tell her, scratching the top of her head.

She casts me a disdainful look worthy of Mimi Cote, and saunters off. I start working, tune Gabriel up, and practice some legato slides before I get into the heavy stuff. Legato slides are when you hit the note and then slide your finger down the string to the second note. You don't strike the second note. It's a nice noise. Gabriel likes it.

Everything is pretty peaceful, and good for song writing and Gabriel playing except for Muffin, who has noticed something in the grass and pounces on it. Her kitty ears flare back and she looks up at me triumphantly. She's probably attacked an ant.

"Murderer," I tell her and look away. I close my eyes and play for a while.

My foot pounds out a rhythm against the tree root. I don't think Clannad minds.

"Every time you giga-play, you take a pizza pie with you," my mom's voice sings from her bedroom. While butchering the elevator '80s song "Every Time You Go Away" (sung by Paul Young, written by Darryl Hall), she is also packing for her trip and still on her post–Jim Shrembersky date high, which is cute, I guess. Her trip is business-related, but since it's somewhere warm she keeps calling it a vacation. She's never had a vacation or a conference trip before.

I mean, I can't be angry at her for having a life.

A squirrel chatters at me from a tree as I scribble down some lyrics, which are kind of pedestrian, but whatever…

Do you know how much need kills you?
Do you know the price you'll all pay?
And do you regret it, at the eclipse of the day?

God. Eclipse of the day?

Muffin checks out the squirrel, but he's too high. She's a low-impact hit-cat. She doesn't kill things bigger than mosquitoes. The boom-boom of some hip-hop music Eddie's listening to bounces down the street. The squirrel chucks a nut in that direction. It lands near Muffin, who squeals and races away to safety. That big mean squirrel.

"You tell 'em," I say to the rodent.

My mom yanks up the screen on her window and leans out. "Belle?"

"Yep." I finish writing a chord progression that I'll probably change. "What?"

"You sure you're okay with me leaving Tuesday?" Her voice is tiny like the backtrack on a song. "You'll be okay and everything?"

Her face is twisty-sad and expectant.

"I'll be fine," I say. "I'm a big girl."

I toss out a jokey smile to lighten her mood. She nods, just the tiniest inclination of her head, and says, "Okay. Okay."

She closes the screen and then yells out, "I love you, you know."

"I love you too," I say and get back to my song, which sucks, so I flip to a new page and start over, thinking about Tom. I'll write Tom a song. Maybe I'm not good at paying attention at his ball games, but this is something I can give him, something I can do. So, I start writing.

It's immediately you.
When you breathe out my name I know

I can feel all these poems I remember I once
had to know.
I can feel them touch me from ages ago.
It's you. It's immediately you.

Gabriel likes those lyrics better. I think the trees approve but I'm not sure, it's kind of schmarmy. I write down the words before I can forget them. I'm not sure how I feel about the word "immediately," but the world…everything…seems perfect. Everything seems like a promise. Tuesday my mom is leaving. Tuesday, Tom and I will have a house all to ourselves.

"Can it get any better than this?" I ask the squirrel.

He tosses a pine cone at me.

"Punk," I laugh.

He laughs back.

I am so glad we are now buying condoms.

HAPPINESS NEVER LASTS LONG. JUST like people. It drives off. It gets killed overseas by enemy fire. It turns out to not like girls that way. It fades.

That's just what happens. One minute you're making up bad lyrics and talking to squirrels, thinking about your boyfriend's abs and then…Poof. A mortar hits you in the gut.

When Em tells me, she is wearing a Hello Kitty T-shirt and her hair is all scraggled into a ponytail. It's obvious that she has things on her mind. She sits on her bed with her legs crossed, hugging a stuffed turtle. I probably don't look much better. I'd raced over there on my bike the moment her text message flashed on my screen:

U must come over. Now.

When your best friend in the world texts you, you have to come. So I put Gabriel away, stashed my song lyrics and all the rest, then grabbed my bike and hightailed it the mile to Em's.

I did not drive because I do not drive, all part of the occasionally having seizures thing.

Em knows that, of course. Em knows almost everything about me. She knows that I drink Postum instead of coffee. She knows that I like the way Tom's thighs have all these creases in them from the muscles. She knows that I want to be a folk singer and not a lawyer, which is what everyone else in the world wants me to be. She knows that I talk when I sleep, but not too much.

And I know that she likes to take the side of her dog's lips, pinch them together so that they are sort of a mini-mouth and go, "Oh, jowly jowls. Look at them jowly jowls." I know that she takes pictures all the time, not because she wants to be a photographer but because she's afraid of losing people, of losing their faces and expressions, the memories of them, the way she lost her dad.

And I know she hates text messaging because she thinks that it's pivotal to the degradation of human communication, an opinion only shared with people over seventy years old. So, for her to text me, that's big.

I knock on the door to her house, but nobody answers. I let myself in. A dread quiet fills the house. My stomach attacks itself, knotting itself into a nervous ball. Em's dog meets me in the hall and licks my knees. We head down the quiet hall together. It's full of pictures. Em's mom and dad in wedding outfits, smooshing cake into each other's face. Em, in seventh grade, dressed up in rags for the school musical *Oliver!*

"Em?"

"In here."

I tiptoe into her room and perch on the edge of her bed. She's clutching her stuffed turtle, which is not a good sign. I glance up at the wall. The sun glints off her poster of Kermit the Frog, the Muppet, and he's riding a bike under a rainbow. My stomach hits itself again. How does it do that?

"There'll always be rainbows," I say in a too-loud jokey voice, because I can't think of anything else to say and I thought somehow that it would be a good corny first line. It isn't. It bombs and falls flat to the floor, flopping there like a fish on a dock waiting to be put out of its misery.

It does, however, make Em look up.

Her eyes flash. "Don't be stupid."

I shrug. I take the turtle from her and pantomime like it's talking instead of me. I give the turtle a tough New York accent. "So, ya gonna tell me what's troubling ya? Did one of them colleges reject my little princess, 'cause I'll go over there and jack them admissions people crap heads, I tell ya. I will."

The edges of her lips almost creep up.

"You are such an idiot," she says. "It's May. I'm already accepted at St. Joseph's and Turtle Wurtle is southern, not from Brooklyn."

I nod and ease myself further onto her bed so my back rests against the wall. "I should know that."

"Yeah, you should."

She brings Turtle Wurtle up to her face and then places him against a stuffed alligator named Crocky Wocky. Em is not the most inspired stuffed-animal-namer.

I grab Crocky Wocky and clutch him to my chest, somehow resisting the urge to make him talk.

"Your shoes are on my bed," Em says.

I uncross my legs and yank my Snoopy sneakers off. "Sorry."

"Not a big deal," she shrugs. I wait. Crocky Wocky's tag tells me he was made in China. I imagine his journey on a barge in a box full of Crocky Wockies, trying to survive the waves, the wind, the rough seas, the suffocating nature of being a stuffed animal transported in a box on a barge to a foreign land. Poor Crocky Wocky. I hug him.

"Are you going to ask me what's wrong?"

"I was waiting for you to tell me."

Em arches an eyebrow. "You were waiting?"

"I didn't want to be pushy."

She shakes her head. She sighs. "I can't believe you're my best friend."

"You're very lucky," I smile. "I buy you tampons and condoms because you're too wimpy to buy them yourself."

She relaxes a bit, starts trying to fix her crazy ponytail. "I know. You're the best friend ever."

The elastic snaps into place again, and she looks more like Em and says, "I'm sorry I'm being such a witch."

"It's okay," I say and rest Crocky Wocky in my lap. "What's wrong?"

"I missed my thingy."

It takes me a second to figure out what she means by thingy and then the breath snaps into me. "Oh."

She nods and her lip trembles. "Uh-huh."

"It might not mean anything. You've missed it before."

"It's really late."

"But obviously, you think you're going to get it. I mean, you just made me buy you tampons yesterday," I reason out, but I know she and Shawn have done it. I know they've done it a lot.

"Did you use condoms?" I ask her.

She nods and then whispers, "But what if they didn't work?"

"Condoms almost always work unless they slip off or something." I pat her knee like a Grammy or something. "Did it slip off?"

"Belle!"

"Do you really think you are?"

She shrugs. She shakes her head. She grabs Turtle Wurtle again and smooshes him against her like she's trying to hide behind him. Her voice comes out little and small. "I don't know."

I GRAB HER HAND, YANK her up off the bed, then let go so I can slam my shoes back on.

"Let's go."

She turns crazy eyes at me. "What?"

"We're going to Wal-Mart."

I toss shoes at her. She catches them, slides her feet into them, dazed.

She grabs her camera and even though she's all disheveled and befuddled she takes a picture of me. "Why?"

"We're going to buy a pregnancy test and we have to go to Wal-Mart to do that, because even I cannot buy a pregnancy test from Dolly at Rite Aid," I say. "Do you have money?"

She starts to protest, but I clamp my hand over her mouth. "I will go in by myself and buy it. Okay? Let's just go."

"I'M PROBABLY NOT," SHE SAYS in the car.

"I know."

I open her wallet and pull out a twenty dollar bill.

"I mean, I'm probably just being hyper about this."

"Uh-huh."

"Right?" her voice squeaks.

"Right," I say and grab her shoulder. I can feel her bones beneath the thin cotton of her shirt, beneath her skin. She's so skinny. How could a baby ever grow inside of her? "But either way, you just need to know."

We don't play any music.

We don't really talk.

"Do you think it's like that BabyBeMine program in health?" Em asks as she parks the car in the Wal-Mart lot. She hides it between two RVs from Alabama. People with RVs drive all the way up here, using all that gas, to come visit Acadia National Park out on Mount Desert Island, but then they're too cheap to pay for a camping spot so they park at Wal-Mart in Eastbrook. How's that for communing with nature? Still, Em's little Mustang is pretty small and hidden between the monster Winnebago things.

I try to remember the BabyBeMine program where we all had to lug computerized babies around and remember to feed them and not jerk them and stuff.

"No," I say.

She turns off the car, leans back in her seat and slow motion turns her head to look at me. Her eyes are so scared. They are not Em eyes. "Why not?"

"I think all BabyBeMine babies is a big pain. You know? You can't prepare for them. They can't hug you back or smile at you or anything. They're all the bad parts of babies, but none of the good stuff, you know?"

She just keeps looking at me so I add, "Not that there aren't bad parts of real babies, obviously. They're a huge responsibility."

"Thanks, Mom," she cuts in, closes her eyes.

A seagull lands on the hood of her car and stares at us through one eye. He hops around looking for food.

"What do you want me to say, Em? You don't even know if you're pregnant yet. You're just jumping into this depression, end of the world scenario and you have no clue if you're even preggers."

She chokes out a laugh. "Preggers?"

"I don't know? Pregnant sounds too formal. Preggers sounds more like you, like us. It's a good word."

Her eyes shift into something softer. Someone in one of the Alabama RVs turns on a country song about lying men and cheating dogs. The world smells like hot asphalt and dirt. Welcome to Wal-Mart. The seagull takes off. He must have realized there's no nourishment here.

I squeak. "Isn't preggers an okay word to say? What do you want me to say?"

"I want you to say the truth."

"The truth?"

"Yeah."

I grab her hand, squeeze her fingers in mine. "The truth is that I'm really scared for you."

Her lip trembles. "Me too."

I OPEN THE DOOR, SLIDE out my legs and stand up. Then I slam it shut. I lean through the open window space and say, "I'll be right back."

She nods.

She opens her mouth and says, "Okay."

Walking through the Wal-Mart lot is not real. It's like my legs are moving. My heart beats, but my head is somewhere off in this nothing place, up above the clouds, floating and incapable of intelligent thought.

All my brain can do is repeat one little word over and over. With every footfall it comes out, "Shit. Shit. Shit. Shit."

Because I already know the truth. It's been there waiting in the perfect Maine May blue skies, lurking beneath the surface of the Union River. It's been there hiding behind every dread feeling I've had the last two weeks.

I already know.

MAYBE I'M MORE MATURE THAN I pretend to be, or maybe it's just that I'm doing this for Emmie, because I need her, but whatever the reason I just storm right through Wal-Mart, as determined and as casual as if I'm going in to buy a package of 97-bright, 24-lb printing paper.

Maybe I just want to get out of there quickly, I don't know.

Inside, a fine layer of Wal-Mart dust covers the linoleum floor, the consumer goods. From ashes to ashes, dust to dust. We are born from dust and to dust we shall return. Blah. Blah and all that funeral stuff, which is sort of funnily appropriate because, well, this is Wal-Mart, and pretty much represents the death of all things spiritual in our consumer-based society. All bow down and hail the yellow smiley face who bringeth us low, low prices and self-checkout lanes so that we can purchase without actually interacting with another human. Who needs humans? We have slashed prices and smileys and dust.

Sometimes when my mom and I feel goofy, we pretend it's pixie dust and we can make wishes on it. My mom isn't here. Goofiness does not race through my veins, but I run my finger along the top of the pregnancy tests, picking up the dust, and make a wish. Then I grab a test, and carry it in my hand, back through the aisles, past Mrs. Darrow who kisses me on both cheeks but never checks to see what I'm carrying.

"I'm making cookies tomorrow," she says, eyes twinkling, holding up a bag of Nestlé's chocolate morsels.

"Yum," I say, because to not be excited about my next-door neighbor's cookies would be to break my next-door neighbor's heart. My own heart thumps wild in my chest. There is a pregnancy test in my hand. There is a neighbor casting me "Oh, aren't you a good girl?" looks.

Then Mrs. Darrow pulls me into a hug again and whispers into my hair, "You are so much like your father, Belle."

My body goes soft like it's melting into her T-shirt with the puffy flowers on it. I swallow hard and she says in an even softer whisper, "He would be so proud of you."

I nod and wonder about that. I really do.

The self-serve checkout counter will not let me buy the pregnancy test.

It bleeps angry at me each time I pass the test over the scanner and announces to the world, "ITEM NOT RECOGNIZED!"

The first time I am cool with it, but after the third time, people are starting to look over at me. Mr. Dow trots over and says, "Need any help with that, Belle?"

He has big brown eyes like a puppy's and he has a garden hose in his arms. I love Mr. Dow but now is not the time I want to see him.

"No. Nope. I'm okay," I say, holding my hands over the box and trying to scan it again.

"ITEM NOT RECOGNIZED!"

He plops the hose on the counter and reaches out, trying to grab the box from my hand, "Here, let me have a shot. These damn things. I swear they try to—"

"No, that's okay!" I don't let the box go and he jumps back, hands upraised, I guess because he's not used to the hysterical shriek in my voice.

The self-serve checkout monitor barges up to us. She pulls on her blue apron and reaches out her hand for me to give her the box. "Here, let me punch it in."

"No, that's okay."

"*Let* me *see* it."

I swallow and hand it to her. Her name tag instructs the

world that her name is Darlene. She's not from around here. Most people who work at Wal-Mart come from Cherryfield, about an hour away. There are no stores up there. No work except for blueberrying in August, crab picking occasionally, and making pine wreaths in December.

Checkout Darlene stares at the box. She glares at Mr. Dow like he's a dirty old man. Her mascara clumps around her eyelashes, which is not something I should be noticing right now, but it's hard not to notice. Poor Mr. Dow has eyes like a deer about to be run over by a logging truck with the name *Darlene* painted in loopy letters across the front.

"No," I say, trying to rescue him. "It's not him. I mean, it's not even for me. It's for…"

I can't say that though. I can't say it's not for me because then everyone will know it's for Em. Well, not Darlene, who doesn't know us at all, but Mr. Dow. Because he'd tell his wife who is on the school board and…

Darlene turns her back and starts pressing in numbers. Her fingernails have dolphin decals over rainbows.

Mr. Dow's face turns white because the fact that I'm buying a home pregnancy test has finally registered.

"I'll just mosey on back here," he says. "Good seeing you Belle."

"Uh-huh," I say, heart falling into my stomach.

"Yeah, figures you'd just up and *leave her* to do this *herself*," Darlene says. *"Some man you are!"*

Mr. Dow clutches his hose. "What? What? I don't know what you're talking about."

"Taking *advantage* of a pretty *young* girl like this," she shoves the pregnancy test into a blue bag and then tosses the bag at me, still spitting at Mr. Dow. "You should know better."

"I—I—You've got the wrong idea," Mr. Dow says. He

turns, frantic, looking at me for help. He shoves the hose over the scanner at the next aisle. I do my best to press the *finish and pay* button and shove the twenty dollar bill in the machine. It takes forever. "She has a boyfriend."

"It wasn't him!" I say, meaning Mr. Dow not Tom.

Darlene pulls me into her chest, squishing the pregnancy test box in between us. "It's okay, honey. You *don't* have to protect *him*."

"It's not even me," I squeak out into her super huge boobie things.

She puts me an arm's length away. "You're a good girl, don't you forget that. One mistake does not make you bad. Okay? You promise me you'll remember that."

I nod.

"Say it, say, 'I am a *worthy person*,'" she demands, her dolphin fingernails cutting into my upper arms.

Mr. Dow shoves his credit card into the machine. I glance at him for help. He does not look my way and I can't blame him.

"You can say it, sweetie," Darlene says. She has obviously watched too many women-centered talk shows featuring low self-esteemed guests and the book-writing, publicity-adoring psychologists who love them. "I'll say it with you, 'I *am* a *worthy person*.'"

"I am a worthy person," I mumble, because right now I'm willing to mumble anything. Right now I would mumble "I have sex with gophers" if it would get me out of Darlene's clutches.

"Good. Good girl," she kisses me on the top of the head like she knows me, like she's Mrs. Darrow or my mom and not some random Wal-Mart worker from Cherryfield. "You say that every day, every hour, until you believe it. Words have power you know. You repeat them enough they come true. "

She lets me go.

I run as fast as I can through the automatic doors, but Mr. Dow beats me by twenty seconds and flies into his truck.

I swear, right now we could both run three-minute miles.

IN BETWEEN THE ALABAMA RVs waits a giant empty space where Em's car once was. And I have no idea what to think about that. I stare at the space. I stare at the backs of the Alabama RVs and the little maps of America on them. Every place they've gone is colored in. They haven't hit Utah or Arizona. They haven't hit Idaho.

I whirl around.

Mr. Dow's truck comes thundering down the lane and zooms by. He doesn't wave. This is the first time in my entire life that Mr. Dow has not waved at me.

I start walking down the rows of cars. One row after another. Mrs. Darrow offers me a ride home in her Subaru with the bumper sticker, NOT MY PRESIDENT.

"Thanks anyways," I say and keep walking.

Tom's dad stops in his cruiser and asks me what I'm doing. He knows I don't drive. He smiles at me.

"Looking for Em," I say. "She parked in between the RVs while I ran in and now she's gone."

"Practical joke?" he asks.

For a second, I think maybe it is, maybe she's just being a total jerk-off and this is some elaborate scheme, but I know it isn't. Still I say, "Maybe."

He leans over and opens the passenger door. "Hop in. I'll help you look."

The inside of the police car smells like Subway's Italian subs and pine tree air freshener. Is this the smell Tom associates with his dad? Would my dad smell like this? I hope not. How about Shawn, what if he's a dad? Will his smell change?

Chief Tanner waits while I pull on my seat belt. "Thanks."

"No problem," he cruises slow like we have all the time in the world. "Tommy treating you okay?"

I nod. I put the Wal-Mart bag between me and the door, so Chief Tanner can't see what's in it. "Yep."

"You tell me if he gives you any trouble," Chief Tanner says. He lifts his hand up to wave to Mr. Jones, who is back at Wal-Mart again. He's as bad as I am this weekend, Wal-Mart regulars. "Tanner men have a reputation of being good to their ladies. He's got to uphold that, you know. It's a big responsibility."

"Uh-huh."

We cruise down another aisle at a super slow pace. Some seagulls hop out of our way. They were munching on something that was in a McDonald's bag.

"How are you doing, Belle? You and your mom getting on okay?"

"Yep. We're good."

"She must be sad about you leaving her and going off to college next year."

I'm not sure what to say. I hate to think about that, hate to think about that part of college, just like I hate to think about the whole financial aspect of college, so I just go, "Yeah. She is."

"She's had a hard time, your mom."

I swallow. He turns down another aisle. He drives with one hand, just like Tom. Would my dad drive like that? I don't know. I imagine he would. I like it, sort of casual. I am obviously trying to not think about what is in my bag. I am obviously trying to not think about where Em went off to. Damn Em.

"Your dad was a good man, a little wild at times, but good."

I lift my eyebrows up. This is the first time I've ever heard anyone say that about my dad. "Wild?"

He laughs. "Nothing big. A little like Shawn, you know,

a little bit of the devil in him, just enough to keep life interesting, but his heart...that was all good."

He points to a glimpse of red car that's peeking out from behind the back corner of Wal-Mart. "Looks like Emily."

He drops me off and pretends like he doesn't see her head bent over the steering wheel, her shoulders moving up and down as she sobs.

He grabs my hand as I open the door and says, "You're a good kid, Belle. Don't try to handle too much on your own. Remember you've got Tom. You've got your mom. And me and Mrs. Tanner, anytime you need us, you just give a holler, okay?"

I nod and resist the urge to kiss him on his super clean shaven cheek. "Okay."

- - - -o- - - -

Em doesn't lift up her head when I get in the car, but her voice, weak and broken from crying says, "I'm sorry. I just couldn't stay there. Between those RVs. I felt like everyone could see me. Like everyone knows."

I tuck the plastic bag in between my feet on the floor and rest my hand on her shaking back. "It's okay."

"I'm sorry," she hiccups, lifts up her head from the steering wheel, straightens her back. "I'm such a bad friend."

"You're the best friend I'll ever have," I say.

She pulls her hair out of her face. "I'm just so scared."

I nod. "Me too."

WE GO BACK TO MY house.

Not hers.

We go back to my house and she pees in the bathroom, runs the wand under it. My mom is in oblivious boyfriend talking land with the phone attached to her ear. I do not witness Emily in the bathroom with the wand. I stay in my room, strumming Gabriel, a thoughtless song, just chords progressing from one to another, endless variations on the same notes.

There are ways to play the chords that always sound good. There are progressions that are meant to flow. You don't resolve a V7 into a IV. It just doesn't work. There's an order to chords. It matters.

That's what life is isn't it? We all deal with the same things—love, death, need, babies, failure, hope, leavings—just in different orders and in different ways. Sometimes we strum hard, loud and fast, sometimes quiet and slow, sometimes so softly we don't even realize we're playing the notes.

We look at the results together. Two lines.

Her face whitens and blanks like the ghosts of people we barely knew, like chords that are all played out. "I knew."

"I know."

I toss the stick in the trash.

knowing

CB said: Sex is kicking
kicking death
in the ass
It's a kick in the ass
It's a kick
Ass
Ass
Ass
But it's all kinds
all kinds of death
It causes all kinds of death
Crap.

EM AND I TAKE OFF because my mom's there.

I wave goodbye to her, this woman who used to be my mother. She's painting her mom toenails black (!) while chatting to Mr. Jim Shrembersky. She never paints her toenails. We live in Maine. Only people my age and TV anchor people paint their toenails in Maine. Most of the year our feet are hidden in wool socks. She is not the sort of person who paints her toenails.

And black?

Black!

She's over forty years old. People in Maine over forty do not paint their toenails black, unless it's Halloween or unless they're that cool lady at the shoe store.

Everything in my life is shifting into another key. It's like I think everything is all C major, and common and normal and then—boom—we're in B-flat minor, and life is full of crazy.

My mother's shoulder and head wedge the phone in place. She looks like me. She should not look like me. She should look like her.

My mom grabs the phone, pulls it away from her mouth and says, "You girls okay?"

"Yep, just taking a walk. Be back soon." I try not to shudder, pushing Em along.

"You want to stay for dinner, Em? We're having chicken dinner," my mom says. The nail polish applicator dangles from her finger.

"No, thanks though," Em says.

My mom doesn't stop. The polish drips onto her thigh. "We could invite your mom."

Em puts on a fake smile but backs away towards the stairs, twisting her fingers. "Oh, thanks. But we can't. Big plans."

My mom nods and puts the phone back to her mouth. "Well, maybe next time."

Muffin scoots in the door when we open it. She runs inside the house like a horde of angry squirrels are chasing her with radioactive acorn bombs. We rush out, the same way, but not the same, because nothing is the same now.

Emily's just earned herself a new label: pregnant teenager.

Or better yet: unwed mother.

I do not like how that sounds.

THERE'S THIS OLD CEMETERY THAT Dylan and I used to go to. It's just down the road from my house, an easy walk. It's not the one my dad is buried in. It's a lot closer.

"I can't believe this is happening," Em says as we wander amid the headstones. Some have sunk into the earth. Some, like Faith Alley's, are half covered with lush green moss that seems to expand over the stark white of the old stone. It covers half of the writing, so we can only read the date of Faith's birth and not her death.

"I'm not ready to have a baby," Em says. Her eyes are blank like the back of gravestones. I think she's in shock. What do you do for people in emotional shock? Do you make them plop down on the ground, elevate their feet, give them blankets? "I'm really not ready."

"I know."

Blue sky gives way to clouds. Stone gives way to moss. Em keeps wandering lazily in between the graves, stopping every once in a while. She hands me her camera and lifts her shirt up a little bit. "Take a picture of my stomach, okay?"

It's still flat and smooth. Her belly button is an outie. I forgot about that even though I've seen it a million times. I zoom in, take a picture of just her stomach then I zoom out and take a picture of her small hand holding up her shirt, a dark gravestone next to her, the fear on her face. The wind lifts her hair and blows it out.

I hand her back the camera.

"I want to remember my pre-pregnancy belly," she says. She checks the shots. "These are good. You could be a photographer."

"I could never be as good as you," I say and I swallow, touch the cold granite headstone of Charity Meyers. I'm afraid to ask the question, but I have to. "You're going to have the baby?"

She nods. Tears come to her eyes but her mouth is a line, a determined straight line. Above our heads is a jet trail that is just as straight.

"You don't want to think about it?"

"Sometimes people just know what they're meant to do," she says.

Emily has already decided what chords she's going to play.

A million questions rush through my head like what she'll do about college, what she'll tell her mom, what she'll tell Shawn. But I know Em, and I know she doesn't really have those answers yet.

I bend down and finger a tiny white flower. My mom and I used to call these fairy flowers and when I was friends with Mimi Cote back in grade school, we'd pick them, weave them into delicate rings and wear them around our heads pretending to be princesses. We'd leave the fairies notes on tiny pink paper and my mom would write us back, disguising her handwriting. She just wanted us to believe in magic, to believe in fairies, to believe in dreams.

I pick up a flower and hand it to Em. She smiles, a slow, sweet Em smile that makes me smile back.

Then I bend down and say to her stomach, "Hello little baby."

My words make her choke or sob or laugh or some sorrow-heavy combination of all three. My words make it real, maybe. Three little words. Hello. Little. Baby.

Everything has changed. I was so worried about graduating, and the seizure thing, and losing Tom to anybody and the whole Problem. I was so worried about needing anyone. And here it is...true need, total dependence, full and real.

I stand up again and tell her, "We'll do this. We'll do this together."

May + nine months = February = first year of school.

I can't see my lips, but I know what they look like. They are a determined line.

- - - - o - - - -

When I get home my mom tells me dinner's ready.

She has made a huge dinner full of stuffing and potatoes and eight hundred million vegetables. We place the leftovers in containers, seal them up and put them in the fridge. Everything is controlled, has a place.

"There," she says, rubbing her hands together. "That should do it. You should have enough to eat."

"Mom," I say, stacking a broccoli casserole container on top of a mashed potatoes container. "You're only going away for a couple of days."

She rubs at her face with her hands. "I know that. I just want to take care of you. Be a good mom."

"You are a good mom," I say for the five hundredth time. "We've gone through this."

I reach out and take a piece of mashed potato out of her hair. I run my fingers under the water trying to imagine Em having this conversation in eighteen years. My stomach lurches and I bend over the sink for a second, just staring into the shiny metal.

"I know we've gone through it." My mom pulls in a big breath as I wipe off my hands. "I'm a little worried about that condom mention this morning."

I do not turn around even though I am done wiping my hands. If she only knew…

"Really?" I manage.

"Yes, really."

She waits for me to say something. I don't. Muffin jumps onto the counter. I take her off and set her on the floor. She wraps herself between my ankles.

"Are you going to have Tom over when I'm gone?"

"Mom!" I turn around, cross my arms over my chest.

"Wanting to have sex is normal, Belle. I just want you to be careful," she says in a clipped, even, rehearsed tone.

I roll my eyes, not literally, obviously. I can't just pluck my eyes out.

"Sex is a big thing," she says. "Not a bad thing, but big."

Can she really not have known I was having sex with Dylan? This is so hard to believe. Or is this because she's somehow psychically figured out about Emmie. Oh, God.

I decide to deflect her whole "topic of conversation."

"Have you had sex with Jim?"

"Belle!" Her cheeks pink right up. She grabs the dish towel and snaps me with it. "You're changing the subject and you think I'm stupid enough not to notice."

"Yep."

She takes a big breath. "Have you ever thought about how old Tom's mom was when she had him?"

I shake my head. "Why would I?"

"I don't know. Tom hasn't talked about it?"

"No."

"She was sixteen when she got pregnant. Tom's dad married her, of course, but she had to give a lot of things up. Not that she's regretted it. But she'd been a smart, smart girl. Straight-A student. Everyone thought she'd end up at Harvard or some-where. But now she's stuck."

My hands shake. Em's face flashes in my head, her danc-ing down the hall. "Tom never told me that."

"Maybe he's embarrassed," my mom says, reaching out to hug me. I let her. My mom is big into hugging and it's kind of nice sometimes and kind of embarrassing other times. Right now it's kind of nice. She smells like cooked chicken and warmth.

"Chief Tanner had to give up his dreams too. He didn't always want to be a cop, but the criminal justice academy was an easier swing than college," my mom continues. "He some-times still feels guilty that Jenny didn't get to go off to school, to reach her potential."

"She's a great mom," I say. "She really loves Tom."

My mom nods. "But she's full of sadness."

If my mom were Em I'd ask her if this is the real reason why Tom hasn't had sex with me yet, but my mom isn't Em, and I don't ask her.

"Do you think everyone who has a baby when they're young is sad?"

She shakes her head. "No. But it's hard."

I consider telling her. Just for a second, I really think about it, but instead I grab a movie she's rented. It was on the counter.

"What is this?" I hold it in her face.

She shrugs. "Night of the Living Dead Zombie Mutant Cannibals?"

"You are someone who watches love stories."

She bites her lip.

I stare at her. "Oh my God. You're in love."

"Like."

I shake my head. "Pitiful."

THERE ARE TIMES WHEN I think that my mom isn't sad any-more. Like when she's just sitting at her computer, chewing on her nails, or maybe trying to peel off the sticker that says DESIGNED FOR WINDOWS XP. Or when she's talking about Jim and his horror movies and his 3-D photography and all that stuff.

But the truth is that she's stuck, too.

The moment my dad died she became a war widow, a single mother. Her life story changed from a happy ending to a CNN three-minute human interest story on Memorial Day.

Once, I asked her, "Did you ever regret getting married?"

And she sipped her coffee and then she stopped. She set the mug down. It was white and blue and had pictures of Asian flowers on it, pictures of things we'll probably never see in real life, but can only just know about.

She said, "No. Because then I wouldn't have you."

I didn't say anything, but my eyes must have moved because she said, "Don't you roll your eyes at me."

"You have to say that," I said. "You're my mother."

She pulled in deep breath. She stared into her coffee like it had answers in there. "I don't have to say anything."

I waited. The thing is, with my mom, if you give her enough time, she'll eventually say something. It's like she can't stand the silence. She has to fill it up.

"It's hard," she finally said. "When you love someone that much and then they're gone. You're stuck. Because you still love them. But you aren't with them. You get stuck with the sadness, with the plans that won't ever happen, with the dreams that don't come true. Just stuck."

MAINE IS WHITE. THE WHITEST state in the nation. And Eastbrook does not do much to combat that. For decades and decades, there were no black families here, no people originally from Latin America or whose ancestors came from Asia. You don't hear Spanish spoken at the Shop 'n Save. There aren't any Asian markets, any hair dye kits for hair that isn't naturally blonde, brown or red.

Eastbrook is bland, full of Tuna Helper casserole and white-bread hamburger buns. The people who live here know it and don't care, most of them. For generations we have dealt with the blandness, and just let it be.

"It's not like we can recruit black people to come here." My mom says this after dinner, after I shove the *Eastbrook American* article in her face. Jim wrote it, so she probably already knows it by heart.

The headline reads, "Racial Diversity Proves Elusive in Nation's Whitest State."

"Why not? There's still a lot of people from Somalia looking for places to live. How about people running from Darfur? We could totally set something up. "

She pulls a hand through her hair and turns away. "You're going to be late for your date."

Then she casts me her "I'm a single mother and have some mercy on me" look.

I gulp down my post-dinner Postum and stay quiet.

For a second.

"I just think it's ridiculous," I say. "It's like if you have a guitar and you only play D7 chords on it. You know? Maine is the guitar and races are the chords."

She doesn't even look up from the paper because obviously my analogy stinks. She just waves her hand at me.

"You're so cute when you're all riled up," she says.

This makes me swallow, because the truth is, I am riled up, but it's not just about this. It's about Em, too. The world seems to sway in front of me, the newspaper letters lose their meaning.

My mom blurts, "Kara Raymond's black."

I get back into it. "That's one person."

"Better than nothing." She scrapes some stuffing from a plate and then announces, "Dylan's gay."

"That doesn't count. I'm talking about racial diversity." I slam my mug down on the table and Muffin skitters away, looking at me over her shoulder like I'm some sort of fiend. The truth is I've scared myself.

My mom? She just smiles and pulls some extra crescent rolls out of the stove. "Forgot these were in there. I'll wrap them up for you."

She drops the cookie sheet on the stove top because it's too hot and executes a perfect change-the-topic maneuver. "There's Rajeesh."

"Crash?" I forgot about him. Maybe I just don't notice. That's not right either, though, is it? To not notice people's race? That's like ignoring their difference instead of rejoicing in it. What would Angela Davis say about that? Audre Lorde? God, it's all complicated. And now Em...Em's going to be the one who is different, not because of sexuality or race or religion but because she's pregnant. She's the pregnant teen, the unwed mother. Dinner hardens in my stomach.

My mom doesn't notice. "Right. Crash. Whatever he calls himself now. Are you getting a headache?"

I shrug. "I'm thinking too hard."

"You doing anything super special tonight?" She smiles. She grabs a bread knife out of the drawer.

"Nothing as hot and heavy as you."

"Belle!"

My mom has a date with Jim again tonight. As much as I don't want to admit it, it's very unlikely that she is tormented by The Problem. I will not think about this.

"Not a big deal," I say, but I'm not sure what I'm talking about. The date? Maine? Guitars? What is wrong with me? I throw my arms around her shoulders. "I love you anyways."

She kisses my wrist. Her hair smells like burnt twelve-grain toast and vanilla. "Good."

Then she adds an extra-loud smack on the top of my head and says, "I love you too. I just worry about you, that's all."

"There's no reason to worry," I say and I don't know if it's a lie.

While I wait for Mr. Thomas Tanner, my mom's screwing up the lyrics to this ancient Beatles song, "Love, Love Me Do." She's really belting it out, screaming, "Love, love my poo. You know it's on my shoe. Oh, what am I to do. It's smelll–ell-elly…smelly poo."

"Mom!" I throw some biking socks that are on the couch waiting to be put away. They plop her in the head.

"It's funny," she sing-song says just to annoy me. "You know it's funny. I think your boyfriend is here."

She has bizarrely good hearing. Mothers should not be allowed ridiculously good hearing. I move the curtain in the living room window and peek out. Tom's truck idles in the driveway and he doesn't knock on the door, just rushes in the house.

"Good evening, Thomas," my mother says, smiling. She loved Dylan, my last boyfriend, but she gets all giggly when she sees Tom.

"Good evening, Mrs. Philbrick," he says and runs a hand through his dark hair. He smiles at my mom, but his smile shifts when he sees me into something bigger, something fuller.

"You are one ridiculously good-looking young man," my mom announces. Tom flushes. She keeps going. "Just a sigh-inducer."

"Mom!" I kiss her cheek and rush past her down the stairs.

"He is!" she says, pulling her purse over her shoulder. "You both know it. He has to be to keep up with you."

I hug Tom, press my face into his T-shirt and then turn around to glare at my mother.

"How about Tom? He's not too white-bread," she says.

"He's still white," I say, grabbing Gabriel's gig bag and slinging it over my shoulder. Tom, being the well-trained boyfriend that he is, takes her instead.

My mom prances down the steps and touches Tom's forearm. "But the sun's made him even darker than he normally is. Look at him. He could pass."

"Pass? What kind of thing is that to say? Isn't that what they used to say about African Americans who were really pale?" I wait for an answer. "That is not a cool thing to say."

Nobody answers.

Then Tom just smiles and says, "French blood. Penobscot too."

"Really?" I did not know that. How could I not know that?

He nods. "My dad's mom was from Indian Township."

"Not as white-bread as you think, eh, Bellie?" my mom captures my face in her hands. "Have fun at the movies tonight. Do not come home too late. You look stressed."

I would nod, but my head is stuck in her thin hands. Someday Emmie will be doing this.

"Don't be too late, Bellie baby," she says like I'm two years old. Her eyes go all misty.

"Don't be too late tonight on your date," I wiggle my eyebrows at her, in a lascivious way, I hope. Tom and I sprint out the door.

"Hurry up, sort-of-white boy," I tell him, "before she T-bones the truck and apologizes for dating again."

"Okay Bellie Baby," he teases and wiggles his eyebrows. He puts the truck into reverse. His head looks over his left shoulder as he backs out, a precaution Em doesn't always take. The cords on his neck pop out and I get some sort of weird vampire urge to bite them, or nibble on them, or at least lick them. I groan.

"What?" Tom asks, shifting. His big brown hand holds the stick.

My cheeks flame. They burn. "Nothing."

"Belle Philbrick, don't lie to me. You just groaned."

"No, I didn't."

"Liar."

"The stars are out tonight."

"You're changing the subject."

"Yep."

He laughs. What would happen if he knew? If he knew about Emmie? Would he never even kiss me again because he'd be so afraid that it would happen to us, that he'd get either:

1. Stuck with me forever
2. Stuck with the ego-reducing knowledge that he is no hero man and ditched me
3. Explode
4. Cry

What will Shawn do? That's the real question, isn't it? What will Shawn do? Will he go away? Will he just be a memory and no longer a connection? What will Em call him? Just *Shawn, that guy who made my baby*?

Sometimes in the morning on our way to school I imagine these elaborate fantasy scenarios of Tom and I finally doing it. I imagine him hauling the truck into the breakdown lane by Billy Ray's house. Billy Ray's wife, Rena, stares out the window of their clapboard house as Tom pulls me into an embrace. She gasps in shock as the truck rocks back and forth as Tom and I finally consummate our relationship. Or maybe would it turn her on? When arms meet skin. When legs entwine and thrust. When lips nibble on necks. When tongues…

I close my eyes. And for a second I imagine it isn't me and Tom, it's Shawn and Emmie. It's…Oh God.

"You groaned again," Tom announces.

"I'm achy," I say, which is a half truth.

"Why?"

"I fell off my bike yesterday."

The truck slows down. "You did what?"

"Nothing big."

"Are you hurt?" he says, grabbing at my hand and holding it in his. His eyes are worried, scared.

"Just scraped. It's not a big deal."

"Commie, that's just not cool." His hand lets go of my hand and moves up to graze my face. It's strong and rough and smooth. "I don't know what I'd do if something happened to you."

My fingers find the on button of his radio, somehow, without my mind telling them to. Slow, soulful music comes on. The music is about love and need and getting it on. God. Godgodgod.

Nobody ever talks about women's sexual desires, except in *Cosmopolitan* magazine. And here it is, my best friend's pregnant and I'm completely in the desire zone. What would Tom think if he knew?

1. That I'm ridiculous and shallow.

2. That I'm a slut, which is a horrible word, but it's the word that people slam on girls who want to have sex, even if it is perfectly monogamous sex and they are a senior in high school, with a ridiculously attractive boyfriend.

3. Yes. Yes! Yes! Yes!

- - - - o - - - -

I change the station to public radio where the guest commentator talks about losing his son to a heroin overdose. His kid was seventeen.

"My dad's worried Eddie Caron is using," Tom says, his voice a grumble low and penetrating.

"Really?" I pull at my gig bag, resist the urge to try to pull her out and play. My pulse starts to race like I'm biking up McGown's Hill and I don't tell Tom about Eddie giving me a ride because I can't. I can't tell him. He'd be flipped out worried over the seizure thing, but the part about me being alone with Eddie would push him over the edge. I can't tell him about Em because it's not mine to tell. I am full of hollow sounds, secrets, words that don't resonate, empty notes. I try again. "Really?"

"Yeah."

Eddie has to go to school in another town because of what he did. When we were little, Eddie was always my protector-knight, my hero friend. Then I thought he was like a book bad guy in a thriller novel, just muscle and meanness. Now, after the ride home yesterday, I don't know. I don't know who he is. I think that the only thing I know is that being certain about something is impossible. We take things for granted.

Exhibit One: Em is pregnant.

Exhibit Two: Tom's not even white, technically, I don't think. Did I have a clue? No, I did not.

Exhibit Three: My last boyfriend was actually gay.

We think people are a certain way and we build our whole lives on that, and then…bing…we were wrong. We thought we were certain, but certain is pretty much impossible.

Okay. Not everything. I am certain that Tom hates Eddie Caron, but I ask the question anyway.

"Using what?"

"Heroin."

"Oh."

I shiver. A lot of people have gotten into Oxycontin and eventually heroin. This is, of course, not what people think of when they think of Maine. Not me. Not my friends. But Eastbrook is small. We all know somebody. Nate Clarkson, who's just three years older than us overdosed on heroin when he was at school at USM this winter; they named a basketball tournament after him. Another guy, Austin Hubbell, is in treatment because his mom caught him down behind Shop 'n Save surrounded by syringes. He weighed about a hundred pounds. He used to wrestle in the 180-pound weight class, so that gives you an idea. White conquered his skin making him look as if he was already a ghost. Austin had run away a week before she found him. Now his mom's eyes are blank, grassy lawns and her hands shake when I see her at the Y. I want to hug her and tell her that it's alright, that her love would save him, but that would be a lie. I don't think love can save anyone.

It didn't save my dad. It didn't save Nate.

I imagine Austin Hubbell sprawled out behind the dumpster, needles in his arm. I imagine Nate the last time I saw him in his casket. The funeral home people put lipstick on his lips. It was too pink. I close my eyes and imagine beefy Eddie Caron face down on his lawn. His mother screams and runs out in her bathrobe. His crisp-shirted father staggers back against the rose bush, not noticing the thorns.

That's not going to happen.

I pull in a breath, try to make my pulse slow down.

"Eddie's not on drugs," I finally announce to Tom, his duct tape figurines on the dashboard, and to the world in general. "He can't be."

"Belle. This is the same freak who attacked you in the hall first semester, remember?" Tom says. His dirt-road voice melts into something harsher than normal.

I pull my gig bag a little closer to me, but it requires me opening my eyes. Sometimes it's easier to just keep your eyes closed.

"People can change," I say thinking about Em. "People change all the time. I mean, if they have a chance to. It's not like people's personalities are set in stone."

Tom's cheek twitches like it does when he's angry. I start playing out the chord progressions in my head. I finger a little duct tape soccer player Tom's made. The soccer player has his leg up, ready to pummel a little duct tape ball.

"Eddie Caron's going to school in Bar Harbor now," I tell him.

"I know that."

"I know," I inhale and exhale slowly and put the soccer player back on the dash board. "I just don't want you to start obsessing about him."

"It's hard not to obsess about him when he lives right across the street from you."

"Diagonally."

"Fine. Diagonally."

We drive past the Beechland Road. Some highland cattle graze in the twilight-lit field. They belong to Ben and Sue Piazza. Just as we drive past, the boy cow mounts the girl cow, I think. I'm no good with cattle gender identification. Actually, I don't know if you even call boy cattle, cows. Anyway, the boy starts getting pretty active up there.

"Oh God," I say.

Tom looks over and starts laughing.

"Don't get any ideas," I say and hit him in the thigh.

The girl cattle doesn't seem to be having a good time. She swings her head slowly so that she watches the truck past. Our eyes lock.

We drive past and the view of fornicating farm animals is blocked by pine trees. Great green limbs afford the couple a special Maine privacy, I guess.

"When we do it, it's not going to be like that," Tom says, grabbing my hand. "I swear."

"Oh," I mumble. "When we do it."

"Yeah." His hand squeezes mine.

"Promises. Promises." I squeeze his hand back but it hurts to move my fingers; there's just this ache. So, instead, I take my hand away and rip off one of the stupid duct tape quotes stuck to his dash: *"Sexual intercourse is kicking death in the ass while singing"—Charles Bukowski.*

Em's belly is still so flat.

I try to shred the tape into little pieces but I'm no good with duct tape. Instead, I fold it into itself, crumpling itself into a little ball so the words mean nothing anymore, nothing at all.

"Belle? What is up with you?"

I pocket the duct tape. "Don't ask."

Mimi is in line ahead of us at the movies. I stare at her and then at the glass front of Wild Styles, where there are all these pictures of women with short spiked-up hair. That will be Mimi some day. She turns around and sees us. She smiles big and waves. Tom waves back. She mouths the word, "Pathetic."

"Great," I say, looking at the Formica floor of the Maine Side Mall. "Can we go?"

Tom gets this stunned look. "What?"

"Mimi's here," I whisper.

"So?"

I try not to schlump. I don't succeed. "You waved at Mimi."

"It was instinctive," Tom hugs me to him, puts his head on top of my head and rests it there. "Do not let her intimidate you."

"Right. Everything intimidates me."

He pulls away. "Belle? You okay? You haven't been acting right."

I swallow. I breathe. I stare up at his eyes and get caught there. "I'm just…I just…I'm worrying about things."

"Do not worry about Mimi."

"Okay."

We move forward in line. Mimi enters the theater. She has good legs and you can see almost all of them in her skirt. She winks our way when she enters.

Tom doesn't see. He takes out his duct tape wallet. Then he takes my hand and squeezes it. "And do not worry about me."

TOM PICKS ME UP AND takes me to breakfast, just the two of us. No Emily. No Shawn. No Andrew or Kara or Anna or Crash. Just us and my secrets.

Everyone stares at Tom and me as we walk into the Riverside Café. This is not because we have blood on our teeth or because my skirt is tucked into my underwear because that is not the case. They stare because this is Eastbrook and in Eastbrook everything is stare-worthy. Something in the edges of my jaws simmers and tightens. Maybe it's tension. I'm not sure.

Larry Shaw, the town mayor, slaps Tom on the back. "Taking the little lady out on a big date, Tommy boy?"

Tom grimaces. "Yep. Big date. Breakfast at the Riverside."

I step on his foot. He laughs.

Larry's eyes move up and down me. I shiver and sniff in the smell of frying bacon. "And how's life treating you, Belle?"

"Good."

"And your mom?"

"She's good too."

It's proper to say "well" instead of "good" but Larry's not that smart and I don't want to confuse him. His eyes drift over Tom's shoulder to the Dows who are hustling in the door. They are more important than us in the political world of voting and land use ordinances it seems, so he drops his hand off Tom's back and moves on. Cringing, I turn away before Mr. Dow sees me.

Jessica, the *Eastbrook American* reporter, waves to us. "Any hot high school news?"

"Nope," Tom says in a friendly way and then the hostess, who is Mimi Cote's mom, hustles over to sit us down.

"Hey Tom. Hey Belle," Mimi Cote's mom smiles real big at us. I forgot that she was working here now instead of Denny's. How could I forget that? "You two have a seat."

She settles us into a booth and gives us menus, fussing over us like we're celebrities. She leans down and exposes some cleavage, which is a Mimi-type move, although she's much nicer than Mimi. "You two know what you want? Or you want me to give you a minute?"

I smile at her. "Maybe a minute?"

She winks and wheels around, grabbing a couple of plates off the booth behind us, which is where our kindergarten teacher, Mrs. Phipps, is sitting with her husband, who is also a city councilor, though he quit for a while. Mrs. Phipps gives me a friendly little wave. Mr. Phipps nods. Tom nods back.

This is how life is in Eastbrook.

Tom and I peruse the menus and the silence between us is deep. Then he leans over and whispers, "I heard Mimi hooked up with Andrew after the movie last night."

After the movie.

"How would you know that already?"

"Andrew texted me."

"After he did it?"

Tom shrugs. "Andrew has no class."

I let that settle for a second, but it doesn't settle well. It's annoying that Andrew would send Tom a rooster message, but it's almost worse that Mimi gets more action than I do, despite the fact that I have a boyfriend.

"She gave him hickeys in a line all the way down his chest

and each hickey is in the shape of a cross," Tom tells me all deadpan serious.

I spit out my water. Tom starts laughing. He gets a napkin and starts mopping the table.

"That's disgusting," I manage to say.

He shrugs like it's maybe not so bad. Something ugly settles into me.

"Am I not lustable?" I ask him over the menu.

He sputters and puts the napkin down. "Where did that come from?"

I pluck the lemon off the edge of my water glass and drop it in. "Am I not the kind of person people lust after? You know, am I like the girl-you-want-to-marry or am I the girl-you-want-to-copulate-her-brains out and have her give you a line of hickeys?"

"Copulate?"

"I'm not going to say the f-word in the middle of the Riverside." I grab the salt shaker. "So? Which is it?"

He pulls some duct tape out of his pocket and starts looping it around. I don't know what he's making. He doesn't seem to know either. "You can't be both?"

"I don't know."

"I think you can be both."

"Emmie's probably both," I manage. I close my eyes. I don't know what Emmie is now. "Well, what am I?"

He sticks the tape in his mouth to make some tension so he can rip it. "Both."

"Right," I push my lemon to the bottom of my glass, trying to make it sink faster. "I'm both. Seizure Girl is both."

"Don't call yourself that."

Over at another table Alison Merrill dumps her orange juice. It splatters on the floor. Her mother shrieks. Mimi's mom rushes over with a big cloth, smiling, saying everything is alright. I want so badly for everything to be alright. But it isn't. Anger and fear are tornadoing up through my body because everything is so unright and I can't talk about it.

"I think you're both," Tom whispers and he puts a little duct tape ring on my finger. All its edges are turned in and smooth. There's a little duct tape simulated diamond on it.

A ring.

I'm not sure what to think so I smell instead. Why does bacon frying smell so good? It's so wrong. The poor pigs. And why does a duct tape engagement ring look so good? It's so gray, and sweet and…Tom's fingers brush across mine. I hold my hand up and admire the ring like it's the real thing.

"Oh. That's so nice. Thanks. That's really good…Um…It's a really good ring replica," I say.

My smile meets his. His hand touches mine. I lean in, warm and toasty in the morning sunlight, smelling coffee and bacon, surrounded by the chatter of people I've known forever.

So, I just say it. "Tom, are we ever going to…you know…"

His eyes go wide.

I whisper and hold up the menu in case someone wants to read my lips. "I mean, it's okay if you don't find me attractive that way."

"I just said you were both."

"I know, but why…"

His hand leaves mine. He slams his back into the booth cushion. "That's not it, Belle."

"What is it, then?"

"Do you really want to discuss this here?"

I nod. "Yeah."

He doesn't say anything. He starts ripping pieces of duct tape off the roll. I bet he's not making another ring.

"Tom?"

My voice is pleading.

He doesn't say anything, just rips the tape, loud and fast. I put out a hand to stop him. "Tom?"

"I'm not gay," he whispers. "If that's what you're thinking."

"I'm not thinking that."

"Right. You think everyone is gay."

"No I don't."

"I just don't want you to think I'm using you. There's this quote by Stacy Nelkin. It goes, 'For me, love is very deep, but sex only has to go a few inches.'"

I tip the pepper shaker sideways, on purpose, just to see if any will fall out. "Do you have to talk in quotes?"

A grain falls out. Another. Tom puts the pepper shaker right side up. "I don't want you to think it doesn't matter to me."

"Why would I think that?"

He shrugs.

"That's absolutely stupid," I say.

"No, it's not." He rips more duct tape. People are looking. Duct tape ripping is a noisy thing. "Dylan is gay. I used to be friends with him in eighth grade…People might think."

"Tom, enough with the tape."

I clamp my hand over the tape, take it away. He glares at me.

"Okay. So, you're not gay. Great. I think we knew that. What is it then? Are you not ready?" I ask.

He groans, looks one way, then another, pulls his hand

through his hair. "I've been ready forever. I've been ready since kindergarten."

My eyebrows seem to raise all by themselves. I pull them back down. Tom in kindergarten was super cute especially when he yelled at Shawn for eating paste. "Then why not?"

I rock the pepper shaker back and forth. I want to ask if he's afraid I'll get pregnant like his mom, like Emmie, but I can't quite do it.

"I told you." He gulps his water. "I don't want you to think I'm using you."

I scrunch the sticky tape into a ball. "That's a stupid reason. And I think you're lying because you're afraid to hurt me."

He puts his glass down, picks it up, puts it down again and finally says, "You're not Mimi, Belle."

"Oh, that's a good one. What? I'm not hot enough to have sex with, is that what you're saying? I'm not a hickey queen." I spit it out quiet so the world won't hear but then I stand up. My brain feels like bacon sizzling in a too-hot pan, crunching up into itself, drying out. "Or is it I'm too delicate because I had stupid seizures and you don't want to do it with a freak? Is that it?"

"Jesus, Belle, what the hell are—You don't even have seizures any more."

He looks around to see if people are listening. Everyone is pretending to not notice.

"Or are you going to pretend like I'm too good to do it with? Is that it? Sort of like a mommy–good girl complex issue thing? Well, that's bullshit. Listen to me, Thomas Tanner. I'm not a virgin. Dylan may have been gay but we had sex. All. The. Time. Okay? So, obviously, I'm not like the good little super virgin you're making me out to be in some sort of duct tape induced macho frenzy? Alright?"

"I'm not my dad."

I don't even know what that means. My feet start marching me out of the restaurant before my brain can figure out what's going on and right in that instant I hate Tom. I hate Tom for not even trying to have sex with me. I hate him for making me want to have sex with him. I hate him for not magically knowing about Emmie. I hate Mimi who doesn't seem to have my problems. I hate me for being such a psychotic idiot about this when this is not my main problem anymore. This is no longer *The Problem* but it's something I can lash out about. Even when I'm walking away I know I'm doing the wrong thing, the melodramatic thing, but that doesn't stop me.

Mimi's mom puts out her hand and touches my arm. "Belle, sweetheart, you okay?"

"Yep."

But I keep on marching away from her hand, away from Tom, away from everybody in the whole damn place. They are all staring at me.

As I bang through the door Larry Shaw gives a low whistle and tells somebody, "Looks like Tommy Tanner's got himself a little trouble in the love department."

The door slams behind me.

This is a stupid, stupid town.

The door slams behind me again. One second passes. Another. Then my stupidity hits me. All the muscles in my face push up towards my eyes so I don't cry, but it doesn't work. My feet shuffle forward on the cold cement sidewalk. I buckle, grab my stomach and let out one sob. Just one. That's all.

And I don't know if I'm crying because I'm stupid or I'm frustrated or I'm worried about Em or because I already miss my pre-college life or because I'm finally really missing my dad. I just know it comes. One sob.

I swallow. My lips press into each other. I straighten. I want someone who'll always love me even when I'm stupid like dads are supposed to. Crap. I want my guitar. I left it in the truck. Damn.

Tom catches up to me in less than twenty seconds, swings me around by the arm and makes me face him. "Belle…"

I stare at the sidewalk, ignore the pleading in his voice. Tom is not the sort of guy who pleads.

"Belle, you know I love you."

"This does not count as saying the l-word. That is saying it under duress," I announce, moving my shoulder forward a little to show him I hear him, but I'm not about to answer back the way I'm supposed to, all lovey-dovey.

The sidewalk has a big crack in it that is shaped like New Hampshire. New Hampshire is called the Granite State. It borders Maine. This is not important, but this is what I think. This is what I think because I don't want to think about anything important.

Tom drops his hands. I stand there. He stands there. Somebody drives by and toots, but I don't look up. I don't wave. I am tired of waving.

"I'm tired of waiting, Tom," I say, slow. Words are quiet, like a sidewalk, like a piece of toast waiting to pop up.

His feet shift. He's written my name on the duct tape that surrounds his shoe. "Me too."

His eyes are tree bark brown and deep, deep, solid something I could lean on forever. "Yeah?"

"Yeah."

"The other night…having you go…it was so hard."

He smirks and says an Andrew line, "Yeah, it was really hard."

I punch him. He doesn't even cringe.

"I hate that feeling."

"What feeling?"

"The missing-you feeling. It hurts." I squeeze his fingers with mine.

He rubs the back of my head with his free hand, supports my neck with it and smiles down into my eyes. "I know. I hate that feeling too, but you can't be afraid of it. It goes with liking someone."

"You said love before."

He rests his forehead against mine. Our noses touch. "You said that didn't count."

"I'm stupid sometimes."

He kisses me lightly.

Just then, just when everything gets back to bacon sizzling perfect, Jim Shrembersky hops by. He's smiling and happy. His black shirt is tucked into his black jeans too tightly and it makes him look zombie pale, but his smile is nice when he says, "Hey, Belle. How's your mom?"

Like he didn't just see her last night? I bite back a smile. He looks like a little kid talking about a Caterpillar excavator toy he just got for his birthday. "She's good."

Jim nods at Tom. Tom nods back. He's got the same amused smile I have, I know.

"She had fun on your date," I tell Jim because I am a nice person.

He bounces up on his toes. "Really?"

"Uh-huh," I say and lean against Tom, who puts his arm around me.

Jim stands there bouncing and beaming for a second

and then he says, "I saw you out on your bike the other day, when it was pouring. I'd just picked up my car from the garage. I was about to give you a ride, but I saw you get into Tom's truck. I can't believe you can bike in that. That's amazing. It was good of you to bring her home, Tom."

"Oh..." I don't know what to say. Tom's body tightens next to me and Jim bounces away and into the Riverside.

The moment Jim's gone, Tom says, voice rough, "Who gave you a ride home?"

"Um..." I move my Snoopy shoes a little further away from Tom, towards the Citgo gas station. "Eddie Caron."

He reacts just like I thought he would. His cheek twitches. His lips tighten. "Belle, what were you thinking?"

"It was pouring out."

"It. Was. Eddie. Caron," he groans. "Belle, do you remember what he did to you?"

"No. I forgot."

My voice sounds as snarky as I feel.

Tom shakes his head at me and looks away, starts ripping up duct tape, his motions fierce. "I can't believe you got in a truck with him."

"It was fine. It was raining, I'd crashed," I say. I breathe in deep, touch Tom's arm with my hand. My touch makes him jerk. "I don't think he's all evil-bad bad. I think he just screwed up."

Tom grabs my hand in his. A piece of duct tape gets lost in the movement and sticks to both of us. One end clings to the back of my hand; the middle part wraps itself against Tom's finger. Tom does not try to move it. He wills my eyes to his. I can feel it, all this will power coming out of him and I bristle, but I look. His voice comes out the color of duct tape. "You're always thinking everyone is good, Belle. Not all people are good."

I pull away. The duct tape rips at my skin, arguing. "You're being an ass."

"You're being stupid."

"Whatever."

"Shawn's right," he says, hard and mean.

My hands go to my hips. "Right about what?"

His cheek twitches, pulses really.

"Right about what?" my voice is all demanding but I don't care.

"That you don't know who you are. You're the most reluctant 'popular' person in the universe. And you try to ignore it, but you are. You are popular. Then you're all anti-label and then you put everyone in categories: Mimi is evil. Dylan is a good, gay man. Eddie is okay. Emmie is the perfect best friend. Your mom is naïve. Jim is whacked. It's like you make that all they are. You ignore everything that contradicts your image of people." Tom slams out these words, hard, like they're baseballs coming right in the center of the strike zone, right over home plate. He smacks me out of the park.

I bullet into myself because even though I am mad, mad, mad, I know this is true. At least a little bit. My heart flinches. I don't want to hear this, not now, not from him. He's supposed to care about me, not shove me down, not now, not when there are problems going on, major problems.

"So, I'm wrong about you? You're really not a good boyfriend. You're really a combative ass."

"I deserve that."

"Yep, you do."

He puts his hand on my shoulder. I shrug it off. He grabs my wrist.

"I currently hate you," I say, and my words come out soft and weak.

His fingers let go. "I know. But I don't hate you, Belle."

"You don't?"

"I don't."

I can't swallow. There's a gulp caught in my throat but I get the words out. "You think I'm pathetic, shallow and pathetic."

The Citgo station waits on the corner lot, abandoned because it's Sunday. There are just a couple tanks for gas, a door for the body shop. It's filthy and oil stains the pavement.

My feet, with a will of their own, start taking me over there. Tom grabs my arm again.

"Why didn't you call me when it was raining?" he says. "Why didn't you call?"

I keep walking away. "I don't know."

He strides right next to me. "It's okay to need people, Belle, you know? It's okay if you have to call me or something. Even if I'm at practice. It's okay. You don't have to be so afraid of needing me all the time."

I stop walking. "What do you know about need?"

No answer.

No answer.

"A lot," he says and then bites the corner of his lip and the grip on my arm eases up.

We face each other, standing right outside Main Street Citgo, which fortunately is closed. Still, a tourist in a Florida car drives in, right over the line that dings to tell the attendant that someone needs service. Only there is no attendant. There is nobody to help them check their oil, fill their tank with gas.

Tom turns his head to talk to the gray-haired man with

the perfectly creased khaki pants and a pink shirt too bright to ever let him pass as a Mainer.

The guy barks at him. "You work here or you flirt here?"

Tom gets one of his shit-eating grins; that's what Shawn calls them. "It's closed on Sundays."

"I just need some gas," the old man says, tapping the nozzle on the pump.

"Sir, I don't work here."

The old man stops tapping, glares at Tom, shakes his head. "Can't even help out an old man. Kids these days."

He slams back into his sedan. Tom yells after him, "There's an Irving Main Way up on High Street. Just turn left."

The man motors out of the parking lot. He turns right.

"No one listens to me," Tom says, smiling. Then he frowns again, remembering what it is we were doing, which is, of course, fighting.

"I'm not afraid to need people," I say trying to finish the discussion, but even I can recognize the weakness in my voice.

Tom's hand reaches up to my face and there's still duct tape hanging off it. "Belle, you are. You're afraid we'll leave you if you're not perfect, like your dad or like Dylan."

"That has nothing to do with this." I grab his hand, pull it down level and rip off the tape. He doesn't even flinch.

A seagull screams over us.

"The river's over there," I tell it, pointing down Main Street towards the Hale and Hamlin building and the little bridge.

The gull lands on the roof of the Grand Auditorium.

Squeezing Tom's hand I say, "Nobody listens to me either."

"That's probably why we're together, huh?"

"Yeah, probably."

I move closer to him, pulled by my pelvis it seems. My hips have better ideas than I do. Swallowing, I get up my nerve. This is a safer topic. This is a safer way to get back on track. So I say, "I don't mean to pressure you about sex."

His hands grab my hips. "You aren't pressuring me."

"Promise?"

His lips find mind, touch, linger, break away. "Promise. I just don't want to be like my mom and dad, you know."

Or Emmie and Shawn.

He keeps talking. "My mom gave up everything, you know, because…"

My hand cusps his cheek. "Because she was pregnant with you."

Someone blares their horn. It's Crash, who finally got his driver's license. He's sticking his head out of his new Saab. It's red. I love his car even though it's much better environmentally to drive a hybrid.

He yells at us, "Get a room and invite me over!"

Tom flips him the finger, but keeps me close with his other hand.

"That's embarrassing," I say, leaning my head into his chest. "People are going to church and we're making out in the Citgo lot."

"We do need to find a room," Tom murmurs into my ear. "When's your mom leaving?"

"Tuesday," I say into his chest that smells like trees and wood and man and…

Ack.

It is not a good idea to smell hot boys' chests in public. The backs of my knees wiggle.

"Tell me that you need me, Belle," he says.

I pull away, examine his face, those lines of jaw and cheek. "Why?"

His eyes crinkle at the corners. His lips are smooth and not too wet, but not dry. They are perfect when they move. I wish that I could make a song like Tom's lips. "Just say it."

"I need you," I say, but I don't want to mean it. Not at all.

But the truth is, I do. I do need him and I can't even tell him why. And the bigger truth is Tom needs me to need him. I do not know what that means, but it means something, something more than words or duct tape rings or lines of hickeys down your chest.

TOM HAS TO WORK MOST of the morning so he brings me home after breakfast. Em doesn't get off from Dairy Joy until noon, so I take a ride on my bike, do my homework and then make a list about why giving seniors homework in the last week of May is stupid.

The list is also stupid so I leave it on my computer, along with my mostly finished paper of didacticism and decide to work on some songs.

I wait.

I think the word: Baby.

I curl up in a little ball and try to figure out what to do, try to figure out how to be the best friend I can be. But I don't know. I don't know the actions I'm supposed to take. I don't know anything.

EM INSISTS WE STILL GO afternoon kayaking with Tom and Shawn just like we planned.

"I am not telling him now, okay?" she glares at me.

"Okay."

I do not ask why.

She sort of tells me anyway. "I just want today to be nice, okay? One more nice day."

The river agrees, sparkles blue, thank God. In the winter it's a rodent-colored river, drab and almost metallic, dangerous looking and cold. Tom's dad bought two tandem kayaks a few years ago.

"All part of his pledge to never be a fat cop," Tom explains as we unclip the kayaks from the dock. I slide in first, in the front and he gets the back so he can steer. Em and Shawn clamber into the other one and we're off.

Tom's mom waves to us from the window and then she goes farther inside. She is ghost-like. I cringe because it's like I'm flash-forwarding to Em.

"She wishes she was going out," Tom says.

This doesn't help my stomach, which sinks into my hips or something. Still, I nod. I wonder what it's like to be Tom's mother, constantly watching her men going out there, having adventures. I wonder what it's like to be the one left behind, waving goodbye. I won't let that happen to Em, no matter what. It will not happen to Em.

We glide and slice through the water, our paddles pushing us along. With kayaking it's almost like a push-up movement when you paddle, unlike canoeing where you dip and dive into the water.

It's peaceful. The smell of sun-warmed skin mixes with salt and pine.

An osprey circles over us looking for fish in the water.

I think about my new package of condoms, all closed up tightly in my purse. It feels like some sort of Christmas present, like some kind of unexpected surprise. I am so ridiculous. I pull the paddle through the water. I pull the other side.

The osprey screeches and normally I love osprey and their soaring circles, the dark Vs that pattern their wings. Today, though, it makes me think of babies crying, angry mothers in Wal-Mart. I sneak a look at Em. Her face is still so white, so blank.

Tom and I paddle in tandem. Our strokes are in unison and the only way we can do that is by him watching me, matching my paddling stroke for stroke, which if I think about it is a really sexual thing. So I do not think about it because I am in a kayak, because of what's in Em's belly. I shiver even though the sun is warm.

The osprey dives into the water, a football-field length ahead of us. One quick splash and he's gone.

I stop paddling for a second, wait for him to surface.

The osprey reappears, his beak empty.

"Lucky fish," Tom mutters and we start forward again, past a swirling eddy, almost up to Em and Shawn.

The osprey retreats to the sky, begins circling again.

Shawn's paddle clanks against Em's. They are hopelessly out of synch. She grunts at him and shakes her fist so her paddle is lopsided and flailing. She grabs on again, leans back, bending herself backwards on the kayak. Shawn leans his giant trunk forward to give her a kiss, but they can't quite reach.

"I owe you," he says as the osprey dives again.

Tom and I pass them and stop. We have to keep stopping and let them get ahead because they are such horrible paddlers.

"Teamwork," Tom taunts. Both Em and Shawn glare at him. Tom splashes them with his paddle. They try to splash us back, but we're too quick and strong. Tom knows the currents, knows how to slice through the river.

"Poop head!" Em yells.

Tom laughs. "Did she just call me a poop head?"

"Yep," I tell him.

Em isn't done yet. "Tom! You going to wear a duct tape tuxedo to the prom?"

"Do not give him ideas," I say. She is being so brave. I can be brave, too.

"You could have a matching gown," Shawn laughs. "You could make it inside out and just stick to each other the whole night."

"Good suggestion," Tom says.

The osprey emerges, a fish in its beak. He struggles back to the air, heavied down by his prize. It's funny how what he needs makes him heavier, how it keeps him from his graceful-wing flights.

"You know what I want," Shawn says, stretching and reaching his paddle high above his head. "I want it to stay like this forever, you know. Just us, floating around."

"What about change?" Em asks as I unpop my water bottle and slug some down. If I thought she'd notice, I'd shoot her a "shut up" look, because Shawn is right this time and she knows it. She has to know it; she just also has to challenge everything.

Shawn dips his paddle straight into the water. The tides take us closer to the bay even without us working at all. "Change is good and everything, and I'm excited about college and freedom and life and all that shit, but…I don't know. This is so good right now. Here with you guys."

He shrugs an apology.

Tom lifts his paddle high above his head. "*To friends!*" he yells.

We all lift up our paddles, touch Tom's yellow blade tip with our own.

"*To friends!*"

Our voices echo down the river. Shawn yells the loudest. It's so incredibly corny but also, somehow, incredibly good here under the sun with the blue sky and the water.

Tom pulls back his paddle and smacks into all of ours. "*To freedom!*"

We echo him, but my voice is softer. So is Em's. Shawn and Tom smile big and bold, but…Em and me…our faces are a little different.

What exactly does freedom mean? Whatever it means, Em will not be free again. And probably not Shawn either.

Our kayaks rock from our movement but we do not tip over. We stay afloat, heading down the river to the wide open sea.

We pull in at our picnic place, a tiny patch of sand with big rocks near Newbury Neck. This patch of rocky sand is what we Mainers call a beach. As soon as we haul the kayaks in far enough so that they won't float off, Em and Shawn start arguing again. This time it's about war. I bury my toes in the sand and sit down next to Tom.

"At least they aren't arguing about canned peas this time. Remember? 'Are they grosser than canned spinach or not?'" Tom whispers to me.

His breath cools itself against my hot skin. I wiggle closer to him, one inch, another, until our stretched-out legs touch. I dip my fingers into the sand, shifting through it, looking for sea glass, trying not to think about what Em needs.

Emily continues on. "How can I support all soldiers when not all soldiers are good?"

"Because they're at war!" Shawn throws up his hands, looks at us with pleading eyes.

"But some of them are bad. Some torture people in prison. Some massacre others."

Shawn's hands come back down. "Jesus, Em. You know, Belle's dad died in a war."

Em looks at me. Her voice quiets. "I know."

My hands find something in the sand that's bigger than a tiny granule. I pull it out.

"I found some plate," I tell everyone. It's blue and white, a piece of an old plate, just about the size of my pinky finger. There's a tiny picture of a house on it. You can just see half of it, a roof and a window. I hand it to Tom.

He examines it and hands it back. "Cool."

He tilts his head, wondering about things, I guess. When I don't say anything he yanks some duct tape off his shoe and starts fiddling with it, folding it, ripping it.

The river and sea have washed the jaggedness away from the plate. The edges aren't sharp anymore. "I hate the war. I don't hate the troops as a whole. You should never hate any group as a whole, isn't that the point? That people are individuals. Like sand. I mean every single grain of sand is different, different colors, textures, but it's all sand."

"She is such a poet," Em announces.

I give her the finger. She tosses sand at me. It only makes it to my feet.

"Commie, you are too cute," Tom says and kisses me on the top of the head while I pocket the plate.

Em takes a picture. Then for a long time nobody says anything. Tom stops with his duct tape long enough to pass a

Gatorade bottle to Shawn. Shawn hauls some in. He swallows hard. He shakes his head and glares at Em. He cannot let it end.

"They're fighting for you," he says.

Em's voice raises to seagull pitch. "They're fighting for oil, for the president, for American imperialism, not for me!"

"They don't have a choice," Shawn says. He slams another gulp down his throat and whips up to stand over all of us. "They're signed up. They have a duty."

Tom glances at me. A muscle in his cheek twitches. Then he grabs Shawn's ankle. "Settle down, Bubba."

Shawn stops, stares down at Tom lounging on the beach. Shawn looms over us, so big. A second passes. Another. "Who the hell is Bubba?"

Tom shrugs and smiles. He's diffused the situation, the way he always does. He just always knows what to do. I nudge even closer to him, then lie back, resting my head on his hip. The sun warms my skin. Emily shakes her head and she starts laughing. Tom laughs too and soon that's what we're all doing, laughing, laughing, laughing under the sun and it seems like nothing in the world could be wrong at all, like everything is right and good. And nobody's dad is killing somebody else's in a desert half a world away. And nobody's having seizures again. And nobody's pregnant way too soon. It feels like the whole world is just us, right here, on a river-bank in Eastbrook.

Shawn plops himself down next to Em and bear hugs her. His arm accidentally pulls up her shirt in the back, exposing pale, delicate skin. She hugs him back, nestling in and he says loud enough for us all to hear him, "I don't know why I love you so much."

She pulls away, searches his face. "But you do?"

"But I do."

The heat hitting my bare legs isn't just coming from the sun, so even though I'm super comfortable and ready for a nap, I grab Tom's hand and yank him up. "Let's go take a walk."

"But..." Tom motions towards the sun and the river and the comfortable place we are at, his duct tape work-in-progress. He's lounging and happy and so cute that jumping on him right then and there is the biggest urge I've ever had. Still, Em and Shawn.... I shake my head and indicate that this would be a good time to leave Em and Shawn alone, especially since their lips are already locked together. Luckily for both of us, Tom is smart enough to understand. So we walk. We leave the lovebirds alone.

Tom leaves his duct tape roll on the kayaks. I'm proud of him. Maybe instead of fiddling with the duct tape, he'll fiddle with me.

I hold his hand.

He holds mine.

The air holds the smell of warm grass.

"People say my dad was a hero," I tell him.

Tom nods. "My dad says he was a great guy, had a wicked jumper."

No matter how hard I try, I can't imagine the man in the photograph in the living room pounding down a basketball court, stopping on a piece of straw wrapper someone's thrown from the bleachers, launching into the air, and gracefully lofting the ball over all the other players. I can't imagine how he'd smell when he climbed into a helicopter, dealt with a mortar wound. I can't imagine how his throat would gulp down a cold Pepsi after spending a hot summer day on the river. Maybe,

Em's been right taking pictures of us all doing random ordinary things, as a sort of insurance plan in case we lose each other.

I pluck a dandelion out of the ground. "I don't remember him."

The dandelion is bright yellow and so pretty.

"I don't know why people call them weeds instead of flowers," I say to Tom. "Is it just because they're everywhere?"

"Maybe."

"Just because something's common doesn't make it less beautiful," I tell him and realize that I'm talking like a poet again, which is embarrassing.

I hand him the flower. He smells it and sneezes, then blushes like sneezing is somehow not manly.

"Bless you," I say.

He tucks the dandelion behind my ear. "Thanks."

"Do you think it's weird if I miss him?"

He knows that I'm talking about my dad. "No."

"No?"

"No."

We stop walking and flop down on the ground. I snuggle into Tom's chest, wrap my arms around him. The cell phone in his pocket bumps against my leg. A bee buzzes nearby. "Even if I don't remember him?"

Tom rests his chin on the top of my head. "Even then."

"I mean I never knew him," I say. "Do you think we ever really know anybody?"

He moves away and my head tilts up towards his, ready for the kiss that I know is about to come.

"Yeah," he says. "I think we do. Shakespeare said something in *Hamlet,* which I won't quote the right way, because I don't remember it, but it was something like: The heart knows what the head doesn't."

"You should put that on some duct tape."

"I should."

"You're going to leave me some day?"

He cocks his head. His hand slides down my arm. "Commie…"

"You are."

"Belle."

I don't answer.

"Belle, look at me."

I don't look.

"Belle, your dad died. I'm not going to die."

"But you could leave."

I think, You could leave if you realize I've had another seizure, or how dorky I really am, or that I know about Em and you don't.

"I'm not going to leave, I swear."

My head manages to turn towards him. There are tiny pores of skin, so tiny you have to be super close to see them. His eyes are brown beautiful. I want so badly for his words to be true.

"If I were pregnant would you leave me?"

"That's insulting."

I gulp. I've gone too close to the truth, Em's truth. I could say sorry, but that would make it too serious.

"If I was having Eddie Caron's baby would you leave me?"

"I'd kill you."

"Because you'd be jealous?"

"No, because you would be so stupid you wouldn't deserve to live."

I twitch my nose at him. "Nice. How about if I had seizures all the time, and they were the really bad kind, the grand mal kind where you wet yourself and everything?"

"What is up with you, Commie?"

"I don't know," I lie. "Senioritis, I guess…Hormones?"

He nods. Guys always fall for the hormones line. Tom is just like the rest.

I STARE.

Em and Shawn run across the field laughing. Their bodies move together. Shawn must have adjusted his pace so that he doesn't go too fast for Em to keep up. You can't tell that, though. It just seems like they're running through the long grass together. The sky blues above them. The wind blows the grass into river ripples. Their laughs reach their eyes and they stop, slam themselves down on the beach a little ways from us. Shawn's hand reaches out to Em's face and his fingers cup her cheeks. She tosses her hair back and smiles. How can she be laughing? How can her laughs be so believable?

Tom's voice touches my ear, carries with it the smell of the sea. "Belle? What is it?"

I shrug. I am not a shrugger, but I shrug. "I don't know."

He waits. I lean back against him, rest my head against his thigh, so that all my eyes meet is the blue sky with the puffy clouds that form into shapes. One resembles a sailboat. Em's laugh drifts down to us.

"They're so happy," I say.

Tom's fingers rake through my hair, gently lifting it from beneath my head and spreading it out across his legs. "That's not good?"

I gulp. "Oh, it's good. It's really good. It's just…"

"Just what?"

Winds shift the sailboat cloud into another shape, blowing it into a giant frog sitting by a cat-o'-nine-tails.

I manage to say it. "I'm afraid it's going to end, you know. I don't know. The whole graduating thing. That I'm going to lose everybody."

"Like you lost Dylan?"

"No. More like I lost my dad. I'm afraid of losing you. What if there's a draft? What if you have a car accident?

What if you just get sick of me and leave? I'm afraid of losing Emmie." I breathe in. God. "I'm sorry, I'm being stupid."

He doesn't laugh at me. "So that's what you were talking about before?"

My eyes close. The sun makes patterns on them.

Tom's fingers move through my hair and I say, "You're a good boyfriend."

Now he laughs. The muscles in his thighs flex beneath my head. The sun warms my skin. His lips touch my forehead. I open my eyes to see his face moving away. "I'm not going to leave you, Belle."

I turn onto my side, stare up at him, past his tan stomach, to his chin line and then his eyes. "How do you know?"

"I know."

The heart knows what the head....Whatever. Sitting up I blurt it out. "Everybody leaves me, Tom. My dad. Dylan."

He moves my hair over one of my shoulders. Down the beach Shawn starts laughing again. "I won't."

"How do you know?"

He leans in to kiss me. His cheek twitches. I touch it with my finger and he lets me and then he says, "I just know."

But this whole conversation? It's true, but it's also a lie because on my worry list it's not Tom leaving that gets the #1 spot: It's Shawn leaving Emmie. That's now spots #1, 2, 3, 5, and 7.

RIGHT BEFORE WE GET BACK in the kayaks, I pull Emily aside and ask, "Are you okay?"

"Why?" She pulls her hair into a pony, because the wind on the water will twist it all up into tangles.

"Because you're acting really happy."

"Belle, did I not tell you this already?"

"Tell me again."

"You always make me repeat things. It's like you get stuck on stuff."

"Humor me?"

"Whatever. I just want this one last day, okay? One last day with him not worried."

"With him loving you?"

She twists the elastic in. Her arms come back to her sides. She stares at me like I'm an idiot.

"He'll keep loving you," I say.

She doesn't answer.

I push on. "You'll tell him tomorrow?"

"Just let me have this, Bellie. Okay?"

"Okay."

ON OUR WAY BACK, A little silver fishing boat slices by us in the water.

"Jesus," Tom hisses.

I keep paddling. "What?"

Shawn puts a hand over his eyes, gazing at the boat and then he looks at us and says to Tom, "Is that who I think it is?"

Tom's voice comes from behind me. "Yep."

I keep paddling, my hands hold the black pole between the yellow blades. In and out up and down. "Who is it?"

I don't have bad eyes, I just don't have super good eyes.

"Eddie," Tom says.

I stop paddling and wave.

"Belle!" Tom yells my name as Eddie waves back. "What do you think you're doing?"

"Waving?"

"To Eddie Caron?"

"Yeah."

"Jesus," Tom says, because this seems to be his curse for the day. "Sometimes I just don't know about you."

"What?" I say, anger edging up into my throat. "I can't wave hi? You waved hi to Mimi at the movies."

"Belle, if Eddie did what he did to you to Emily or Anna or anybody else you'd be all over him, you'd be organizing marches. You'd hate him," he says. "And I didn't realize that I was waving to Mimi. It was a reflex."

"Right." Something inside me snaps. I paddle harder, like I can escape him somehow, but he's right behind me and he won't stop talking.

"You'd hate him and it would be right to hate him, but since it's you, it's okay. It's okay that he violated you."

"He didn't violate me," I mutter, but I'm not sure if he can hear because I'm facing away from him.

"I hate that you don't like yourself enough to be pissed off at him. You should hate him, Belle. I hate him." Tom's voice raises up so that even Shawn and Em can hear.

I glance over at them. Shawn looks embarrassed for me. Em doesn't. She looks mad.

I say, "First off, you shouldn't hate people. And…and…I like myself."

"She's too good for her own good," Em shouts over, which is so helpful of her.

A seal pops up, breaking the surface of the water. His big brown eyes stare into mine. I wonder how long he's been watching us. Anger solids up in my stomach. I don't tell anyone he's there.

"No, I'm not," I announce to everyone. "I'm not good."

Tom splashes me with the paddle as Eddie's boat gets smaller as he heads past us towards the bay. "Yeah, Commie, you are."

The seal nods at me. He sinks down, way below the water. I tell no one I saw him and feel a little happy and a little guilty.

"I just saw a seal and I didn't tell you," I say, slicing my paddle in and out, pulling through. "See? A good person wouldn't do that?"

"Oh my God, Belle, that's the worst you can do?" Shawn laughs.

Em's looking for the seal and doesn't see it.

"Oh, bad girl, I'm scared," Shawn says, making a stupid twisted-up face.

I close my eyes and paddle, grumpiness pushing my arms, making me paddle faster. Tom keeps pace behind me, but I doubt that anyone else can keep up.

Eddie's wake hits us. The kayaks bounce up and down in the water, but we still don't capsize. Somehow we are still above water.

EDDIE WAS JUST A BOY in my life, not a boyfriend, just a neighbor so I don't know why it feels like I've lost him somehow, too.

When we were little we would make jumps in the woods behind his house, pounding down the earth and then soaring our bikes over them, darting between the trees. I remember.

One time we made this super-high jump out of dirt built up and two-by-fours we'd filched off a construction site for a house nearby. The light filtered through the trees and slanted at things and I though he was just crazy and cool, because he could build a mound so high.

He got on his bike, but he didn't pedal. He didn't go. His feet planted themselves, flat on the ground. I waited. He didn't go.

"You want me to go first?" I said.

"You want to?"

"Sure," I said.

I pedaled hard and fast and I flew over that jump. I just soared up and up and then I landed. Bam. I wiped out. The spokes jabbed into my calf. I rolled over and over, trying not to smash against a tree.

Eddie ran to me. He ran. And he lifted me up, even though we were only in first grade or something. He lifted me up and said, "You okay? You okay? You have to be okay."

I was bleeding all over him, but I pushed him away and said, "That was really cool."

"You looked like you were flying," he said. "I could never fly like that."

"Sure you could," I told him, but I don't know. I don't know if that's the truth. Eddie seems stuck, stuck to the ground, to the earth, to his life. Especially now, ever since the "hallway incident." I don't think he'll ever have a chance to fly now. At all.

And Em…It'll be so hard for her, for Shawn. She's the one stuck to the ground.

And the truth is, I'm afraid that we'll drift away, drift apart like Eddie and I did, like Mimi and I. That someday we'll be so different we won't know how we were ever friends, and this whole baby thing…that's got to accelerate the process. It means I have to try so much harder not to let her go.

ONCE I GET BACK MY mother apologizes 264 times during dinner. She just keeps apologizing about leaving. I swear, she thinks I'm five or something. Then the phone rings and it is one Mr. Jim Shrembersky, AGAIN, so I decide to take off on my bike before I have to listen to her giggle too much.

I check the tires, put on some bug spray and head to the cemetery, not the old one close by that I brought Em to, but the one on Bayside, the one where my dad is.

With Gabriel strapped to my back, I pedal up the hills and coast down, listening to the wind make melodies in my ears, strange lyrics that I want to decipher.

It seems morbid to go to another cemetery; I know that. But I still go.

The weekend's sun has dried out all the grass from Friday night's rain. Birds sing in the trees. I lean my bike by a tree, put down the kickstand, and walk over to his grave.

"I wish you were here," I tell the stone. "I don't know what to do about Em."

The stone doesn't answer.

"She's pregnant," I say out loud, testing the words. "She's having a baby. Em. Em's having a baby."

A pine needle falls from a tree, pulled by gravity to the earth. I sit down with Gabriel, lean my back against the tombstone. The coldness of it hits my skin, even though I'm wearing a shirt.

I've always wanted a dad.

That's the truth right there.

I've always wanted a dad to help me learn to throw a softball, which I can't do at all. I've wanted a dad to teach me guitar chords, and hug me when boys were stupid and tell me I'm beautiful when I'm getting ready for a prom or something. I've always wanted a dad to sneak me twenty dollars when my mom's said no, or to kiss me on the top of the head when I don't feel well. I've always wanted a dad to help make things better, because that's what dads are supposed to do, isn't it? Dads are supposed to fix things.

I want a dad to fix this, to fix this Emily thing.

I want a dad to tell me he loves me, to hug me and fart on the couch when we're watching CNN or something. I want a dad whose snore noises echo through the house. Will Shawn be that kind of dad? He better be.

"Emily's pregnant," I say again.

The world keeps spinning around. I can feel it, sitting next to my dad's stone. The trees sway in the wind. Another pine needle journeys to the ground. My father is still dead. Emily is still pregnant.

"I want you," I whisper.

He doesn't answer. So, I pull out Gabriel and do the only thing I can think to do, because nothing I do can change what's happening to Em and nothing I do can make me have a dad, living, breathing, right here with me, right now. I pull out Gabriel and I start to play.

Tom comes over after I get back to the house and we do homework together, plunked down at the kitchen table, our books and papers strewn all over the place. My mom's off at Jim's "coordinating things," she says. Ha.

Tom's jaw is strong lines. I want to tell him about Emmie and the fear that gnaws at my stomach. I can't.

Muffin keeps jumping up and trying to get in the middle of things. She shoves her kitty bottom in Tom's face and lifts it up high.

"Nice view," he says, crinkling up his nose. He scratches her back at the base of her tail, which is a good kitty-friendly thing to do.

"She just wants some lovin'," I say in a pseudo-sexy soul-singer-from-the-1970s voice, instantly hating myself for sounding so stupid when Em's having a crisis.

Tom smiles, but his eyes stay serious and intense. "Don't we all."

Then he starts humming this song from West Side Story, the musical Dylan and I were in last year. It has the words "tomorrow night" in it. The song is like a promise. I swallow and try not to think about how my body is warm all over. It is. Warm all over. Even with the Em thing.

I stare at my law book.

> In Roe v. Wade, 410 U. S. 113 (1973), it was determined by the United States Supreme Court that a woman's judgment to terminate her pregnancy is protected by the Constitution.

My stomach flip-flops. We are covering abortion, which figures. Em must be studying this too, right now. If she's okay enough to study anything at all. Tom's going through some advanced math logarithm-type stuff. He's put duct tape around his pencil like a finger stop, which is really cute. Muffin bats at the pencil with her paw. She wants attention.

I want to tell him.

I can't tell him.

I slide my feet across the bare floor, back and forth beneath the table. There are eyes in the wood, brown circles where the boards had knots, where tree limbs once grew. Now, they are just flat, shiny boards, a hardwood floor.

> In Doe v. Bolton, 410 U. S. 179 (1973), the Supreme Court ruled that states could not prohibit or limit a woman's right to an abortion. It held that a state

could not limit access to ways for her to understand
her own judgment to terminate her pregnancy.

Emily could have an abortion. She hasn't even really mentioned
it. Of course, she's only known she's pregnant for what? Thirty
hours? I close my eyes and try to imagine what the baby
would look like if she had it: Emily's duck lips and Shawn's big
shoulders and blue eyes. I imagine a baby swinging on a plastic
toddler swing, hair blowing in the breeze. That's all romantic
though, that's a romanticized television version. Instead I should
imagine Em haggard and stressed, spit-up crusted on her shirt,
screaming at Shawn because he forgot to bring home diapers.

But even that's romantic, really. I mean, what if Shawn
doesn't stay with her? And what about college? They're both
supposed to go to college.

I groan out loud and don't even realize it until after the
fact.

"Belle?"

Tom's staring at me. Muffin's staring at me.

"You okay?" he asks.

I nod. I lie. "Yeah. Bad law stuff."

Tom's eyes flash. "You don't want to tell me what's wrong."

I flip the page in my law book. "It's nothing."

"Belle…"

I do not want to fight with Tom. We never fight. Well,
not until this week. I swallow hard and look up at him, into
his about-to-be-mad eyes and say, "I can't tell you. It's not
mine to tell."

He lets out a long, slow breath. He lets out a long, slow
silence. And then he reaches over and grabs my hand in his.
Electricity and warmth charge right through me. He says,
"Belle, you can trust me, you know. I'm right here for you."

"I know."

My feet slide beneath the table. I wonder how we ever walk on this floor, it's so slippery. I've never realized it was so slippery before.

Tom sucks in a long breath. He lets go of my hand. Then he presses the base of both his hands into his eyes like he's got a headache or something.

"Tom?"

He nods. He doesn't move his hands.

"Tom?"

My fingers wrap around his wrists and I pull his hands away, gently. He is not crying. He is almost crying.

"I need you to be here for me," I tell him. "I really do."

He nods and smiles, not a joyous smile, but a tiny one.

"I just don't want to screw it all up," his voice cracks. He pulls his hands away and then changes his mind, grabbing on instead. "You know? We could screw everything up."

Like Em and Shawn have. But that's not who he's thinking about. He's thinking about his parents.

What can I say?

"I know."

I start a stupid list because it's all too much. I can't just figure it out thinking. I have to write it down.

What It Means to Be Responsible:

1. To always do the right thing? That sounds dull.
2. To always try to do the right thing? That sounds worse. And what is the right thing anyway?
3. To do the things you're supposed to do to try to make things better when everything goes bad because you've already screwed everything up super famously bad.

4. To pay a mortgage, show up to school, blah, blah, blah.

5. Doing what society expects is right. And how does society determine that? And who in society determines that? Crud.

6. Being accountable.

7. Not every girl who has sex is a slut. Not every girl who has sex gets pregnant. But everyone always makes it out like they do. It happens sometimes, right. It's less likely to happen if you use condoms or the pill or the patch or something. But if it does happen you are accountable.

Oh, this sucks. Responsible? This word just sucks. It all basically just sucks. Especially this list. Where is the delete button? I have to press delete.

Tom's almost leaving. We're standing outside by his truck. My mom's come home. She's singing love songs in her bedroom.

I lean towards Tom. My eyeballs hurt I'm so stressed out about Emmie. He wraps his arms around my waist, lets his hands dangle, stares at me. It's dark out, but not too dark.

"Commie?"

I bend my back so I can get my face far enough away from him so I can actually see him.

I try to remember how to talk.

"Commie?"

Something is wrong. My hand shakes.

His mouth makes a word. I can't tell what it is and then I am gone.

----o----

We are sitting on the driveway. Tom's legs stick out straight.

He's holding me sideways against him. My body aches. Oh God…

Pine needles crinkle beneath my legs. I should have swept the driveway.

"Belle?" he whispers. "Honey, you okay?"

He called me honey.

I nod. I do not speak. I'm trying to remember how.

He pulls me closer to him, hugging me. He rocks me there for a second. I can hear my mom's voice singing in the bedroom.

"I plead you. I read you. I feed you, I feed you," she sings. It's a country duet song. It's suppose to just go "I need you" over and over again.

I swallow. "Did I…?"

"Yeah," he says as I pull away, try to sit up by myself.

"I'm so sorry."

"What?"

I start crying, not sobs, just tears. "I'm sorry I had a thing."

"A seizure?"

I nod.

"Belle, I don't care. I don't care if you did. I just want you to be okay," he says. He takes my face in his hands. "Is that what you've been freaking about? Is it because you've been having seizures?"

"Just one, the other day, " I whisper. A truck rumbles down the road. "It's Eddie."

"Great." Tom swears. Eddie pulls into his driveway, sees us all lit up from the light of Tom's open truck door. "He's coming over."

Eddie doesn't even shut his door, just runs across the street, right up to us. He is monster huge, standing over us, and then he crouches. "Belle? You okay?"

I nod.

He turns to Tom. "Did she have another seizure?"

Tom stiffens. He doesn't address Eddie. He says his words to me. "He knows?"

"I…" Oh, it's so hard to talk.

"She had one Friday. I saw her on the road and she fell off her bike. I gave her a ride home," Eddie says. "God, Belle. Are you okay? You want help up?"

He starts to reach out towards me.

"Don't touch her," Tom snaps. "Don't put one freaking finger on her or I'll kill you."

Eddie's hand stops and hovers in mid-air.

"Jesus, Tom. Don't talk about me like I'm not here," I manage, struggling away from him. Everything is so hazy, confused. I put my hands on my head.

"She's stressed," Eddie says. "I think she's having seizures because she's stressed."

"She has seizures because she's had caffeine or aspartame," Tom says as I struggle to stand up.

"But all those seizures she had before have made her more prone to seizures now," Eddie says. "That's how it happens sometimes, and stress makes it more likely."

"Right. Like you're an expert," Tom says, sounding like he's eight.

"Guys. I'm right here," I say, wobbling in between them. They are both tense and rigid, like goats ready to fight, to slash their horns into each other's chests. Eddie's all dressed up like he's been at church. I only just notice this. "I'm going inside."

Eddie nods, turns, leaves.

"I'll walk you in," Tom says.

"No. If you walk me in my mom will know something is up and I am not telling her."

"Belle…" Tom glares at me.

"I mean it," I say. "She's all excited about her vacation. If I tell her she'll stay home."

I grab for Tom's hand, miss, then really get it. "I'm not going to let this ruin her time, okay? She gets back, then I'll tell her. There's enough stuff everybody has to deal with right now, okay?"

He stares hard at me. "Okay."

Once I'm in my bedroom, I go to the window, lean against it. Tom's truck backs out of the driveway, super slowly. Eddie goes and shuts his truck's door. He turns around, stares up at the house and sees me at the bedroom window. He waves. I give him the thumbs-up sign to show him that everything is okay. But everything is not okay. Emmie is pregnant.

I stumble into my bed, stroke Muffin's back and try to figure out everything, but I can't. I can't figure it out at all.

I call Em's cell.

"Hey," I say.

Her voice is tired. "Hi."

I don't know what to say.

Muffin squirms on top of my lap, above the sheets. She starts kneading them, trying to make a nest.

"You okay?" I say.

She sniffs in. "Yep."

"I love you."

Silence.

Muffin repositions herself, turning in circles until she finds the perfect place. The room is so dark. I can't see anything, just have to go by sound and feel.

"Em?"

"I love you, too."

----0----

I finally fall asleep and later in the middle of the night my mom's voice startles me back awake.

"Jim!" she yells. "Help me! Jim!"

I stumble into her bedroom. She thrashes and turns in her sleep. Muffin skitters down the hall, like this is too much for her kitty nerves to handle. I know how she feels.

"Mom," I whisper. "It's okay. You're having a bad dream."

I place my hand on the top of her head and soothe her. She sits up straight like she's possessed and stares at me with big, frightened, still pretty much asleep eyes.

"Belle?"

"You're dreaming, Mom. It's okay," I tell her. "I'm right here."

She flops back down on her bed and covers her face with her hands, which shake.

"I was having a nightmare," she says, all sleep-voiced.

"Mm-hmmm. It was just a dream." I tell her the same thing she's told me a million times.

She grabs my wrist gently in her hand. "Thanks for taking care of me, sweetie. I'm okay, now. You go back to bed."

She gives my hand a little squeeze and lets go.

I turn through her dark room and she says, "Can you put up the shade for me? Let a little starlight in."

I trudge over to the window because all my adrenaline is gone and I'm back in sleep zombie mode. I give the shade a little tug. It doesn't move. Normally it flips up. I try another little tug.

"Stuck?" my mom asks.

I don't answer. Something burns in my throat. This stupid shade. I tug again a little harder and it pops right off the roller things that hold it up and slams down onto my foot.

"Crap," I say. "I broke it."

"We'll fix it in the morning, honey," my mom says, all sleepy again and calm. "At least now the starlight is coming in."

"It's moonlight," I grump and trudge out of the room.

"I love you," she murmurs.

"Yep."

I bury myself in my covers.

She was calling for help from Jim. Jim. Like he's her hero. What kind of hero name is Jim? And that's not his job. It's my dad's. He's supposed to be her hero. It's his name she's supposed to yell when she has a nightmare.

There are roles for people, places they are supposed to be.

My jocky boyfriend = Tom

My unpregnant best friend = Emmie

My best friend's boyfriend = Shawn

My gay ex-boyfriend = Dylan

His annoying boyfriend = Bob

My arch enemy = Mimi

My mother = Mom

My mother's hero man in nightmare times ≠ Jim

My childhood friend/difficult neighbor with aggression
    issues = Eddie

My father =

- - - - o - - - -

I can't sleep. I pick up Gabriel and start to strum this old Van Morrison song about being a motherless child, only in my head it's fatherless, too. And maybe it is motherless, because who the hell is my mother if she's yelling out the name of a newspaper reporter in her sleep?

He collects horror movies. God.

I'm fooling myself. It's not about Jim, or my mom moving on. I switch off my lamp.

I look out the window. Eddie's truck is gone again. I stare at the trees, green, leafy, full of life. Somewhere out there in the Eastbrook night people's lives are changing. Someone is being saved at Maine Coast Memorial Hospital. Someone is being beaten up in their house. Someone is crying alone in their bedroom, hiding their sobs into a pillow. Someone else is snoring away thinking that everything is okay, but tomorrow—tomorrow their world will be ripped apart by news they have no control over.

They've made a life.

A life.

I yank open the window, pop out the screen and slide it in. It's still too early for black flies, so this is okay. I sit on the sill, dangle my feet out and look into the oak tree branches. The leaves are hiding the world from me, but I know the world is there, right past those leaves. It stretches on and on.

Pretty soon Em won't be Em any more. She'll be the pregnant teenager, the unwed mother. Maybe Dr. Mahoney will deliver her baby. Maybe Tom's mom will offer her advice, buy her some onesies, or a card. Maybe people will look at her differently, I don't know.

Maybe they'll say, "There's that sweet, Emily girl."

They'll say, "…her dad died of cancer. Shawn Young got her pregnant, did you know? She's decided to keep the baby."

They'll say, "One fool mistake and her life's ruined."

It doesn't have to be ruined and sex itself is not a mistake.

I swing my legs into the blackness. If I jumped, I wonder if I'd land easy on the grass, or if the fall is too much. I wonder if I'd hit limbs on my way down, if anything would try to catch me. I wonder if anyone will try to catch Emmie, anyone other than me, and I wonder if I'm strong enough to break her fall.

Eddie's truck storms up the road. I listen to the bass beats of the music playing too loud. The engine shuts off. The seat belt unbuckles and the car beeps warnings. Then the door opens. I can't see it through the trees, but I can hear it.

"I'm home!" yells Eddie's dad. His words smoosh together with booze. "I'm freaking home, you assholes! What kind of shit have you been up to?"

He slams the door shut.

"Hello!?! I'm home."

The house door opens. Eddie's voice urgent-whispers through the dark, "Dad, keep it down. You'll wake everyone up."

"Jesus Christ. Don't you go telling me what to do."

"Dad..."

"No goddamn son of mine—"

There's this noise. I don't know what it is and Eddie gasps.

I suck in my breath. I pull myself out of the window, rush through the house and out the door before I can think. In two seconds I'm across the street. Eddie's standing in his driveway, alone. He's hunched over like he's going to throw up.

I stand on the edge of his driveway, whisper his name. "Eddie?"

He doesn't answer.

"You want me to call the police, Eddie?"

He moves slowly, lifting up his body and then his head. He stares at me like he doesn't recognize me.

"If anyone needs to call, I'll call," he says.

"He hit you."

This is so obvious. I don't know why I say it.

"It's against the law, Eddie. It's assault."

Night noises blend into a hum, crickets and tiny birds, predators stalking their prey, mice hunker down and hide, breathing in and out as quietly as they can while their hearts race away inside their tiny chests.

"You don't need to save me, Belle," he finally says. "Go home. Text Tom or something. Tell everybody about the latest idiot truth about Eddie Caron. Alcoholic. Abuser. Abused. Right? Everyone'll love that."

"Eddie…"

"I mean it, Belle. You can't save me, okay? I'm not one of your stupid causes."

I turn away. I go back inside, fix my window, hold my cell phone in my hand, listening for sounds from Eddie's house, but I hear nothing. I push my head against the window pane, remember to breathe.

"I can't fix anything," I say to the window, to Eddie, to Em.

Nobody hears.

after I know

Em's Song
i did all the good girl things
since I was three years old
i love him so we did it
over and over again
and it wasn't a good girl thing
but it wasn't a bad girl thing
it was a thing bodies do
and then it was all about urine
and cells and change
and i'm stuck here in this body
that's getting ready to implode
and i'm stuck here in this body

that's getting ready to exercise
its rights and it's my body
it's my body
but it's not just mine right now
but it is
i did all the good girl things
since I was three years old
and i don't know what
those good girl things are anymore
i don't know what I am anymore
i don't know
i am running down a river field
i am slicing through the water
i am refusing to talk about it
about my choice, about my choice
about a play set in a yard, a law book on a
table
about my choice, my choice

"TELL ME MORE ABOUT YESTERDAY?" my mom asks me, watching me sip my Postum, even though she has to leave for work soon.

"We went kayaking."

"Did you wear life jackets?"

"PFDs, Mom. No one calls them life jackets."

"Fine. PFDs?"

"Personal flotation devices."

"Whatever. I just want you to be safe." She eyes me. "Did you really buy condoms with Emily and Anna, Saturday?"

"Mom. What do you think?"

The Postum is too hot to swallow easily.

My mom grabs my hand in hers. "If you are going to have sex, which I hope you aren't, I want you to be careful, that's all. It's a big commitment and it's a big risk. You could get pregnant. You could get a disease."

"Mom!" I pull my hand away and stare at my toast which is burnt black on one side and tell her the truth, which I wish was actually a lie. "I'm not having sex."

I can't believe I've just said that and it was the truth. This is not how I see myself. I've always been a girl who had sex, protected sex, of course, monogamous sex with a committed partner and blah, blah, blah, but definitely a girl who has sex. It's really hard to suddenly be Belle, the girl who doesn't have sex. It's hard to go back to that. I now understand the whole term "born-again virgin." I do not want to be a born-again virgin. Although, it's better than being an unwed teenage mother, I guess. Oh God…

My head hurts again. I can't even think anymore without my head hurting.

My mother snorts and crosses her arms over her chest. "Right. You aren't having sex. But if you are, I want you to use condoms. I could make an appointment and you could go on the pill."

"Mom!!!" God, what would she say if she knew about Em?

"I just want you to be careful, honey. Losing your virginity is a big deal."

I stand up before I even know I'm standing. All I want to do is get out, get away. "I know Mom. Okay? I know."

I book out of there and slip into the bathroom to take a shower. I lost my virginity a while ago with Dylan, my ex-boyfriend. Yes, the gay one. Yes, we had sex. Yes, he was capable of having sex with girls, specifically me. Yes, to all those questions. Yes. Yes. Yes.

Ripping off my pajamas, I step into the shower stall without getting the water temperature right first. It goes from hot to cold to scalding to okay, just like my life.

Mr. Duffy taught us about how in literature authors use the "objective correlative" to show the character's emotion. Something like a wilted flower becomes a symbol for the character's emotional state. I don't think it's only in literature by T. S. Eliot or other old dead guys that there are objective correlatives or endowed objects or whatever you want to call them. I think they follow us through life.

The shower becomes lukewarm.

I do not want the shower to be my objective correlative. I do not want to be Hamlet, the hero who could not act. Not that I'm a hero since I seem absolutely unable to fix anything for anyone. But we do both have dead fathers, and mothers who are now getting randy. And issues about words and certainty.

Crap.

Hopefully, we'll move out of our Shakespeare unit in English soon. It's only like we have a Shakespeare unit every single year. I am so sick of Shakespeare.

I press my head against the tiles and try not to think about condoms and sex and objective correlatives. I try not to think about how much I want to have sex with someone again, to feel Tom next to me. I try not to think about my mother and her modest eyebrow lifts. I try not to think about Em being pregnant, Eddie being smacked around.

"I am a blank slate," I announce to the hair in the drain that is clumped and disgusting, full of soap residue and shampoo. "I am thinking of nothing."

But I do think of someone. I think of my dad. What would he say?

Probably something like, *Suck it up, Sweetheart. Stop your bitching and moaning.*

I almost laugh, because it's funny to imagine him like that. I give him a wicked Maine accent where he drops the "g"s off the ends of his words and draws out his "a" sounds into "ah" sounds.

Suck it up, Sweethaht. Stop yah bitchin' and moanin' deah.

The water pressure spritzes into something weak and then comes on full force and as it does my grin morphs into something else. I miss my dad, after how many years? I really, really miss him.

Daddy.

It's a word I've never called anyone.

Daddy.

It's a secret club that I can't get in.

When my dad died, I was just a baby, not even in school yet. My mom didn't have a job. People in town had bake sales at the First Congregational Church and raffles at the Knowlton

School and penny drives at the Tideway and Mike's to make sure that we had enough to get us through the funeral. Then the dental supply company hired my mom into the human resources department/secretary stuff, even though all she had was a college degree and no work experience.

People call my dad a war hero, but it was never officially a "war." It was a "conflict," the first one, in Iraq. He was a paramedic for the Eastbrook Fire Department, which translates to being a medic in the National Guard. Those are the things he was. Those are the words that describe him: war hero, paramedic.

Every time I see the fire chief, he pulls me into this big hug and says, "Your dad was a hero, Belle. You know that, right?"

I pull away and nod. He gets tears in his eyes and always says something like, "He'd be so proud of you."

I smile and then I say something like, "He'd be proud of you too."

That always makes people, especially Chief McKenney, turn away and wipe at their face.

My dad was kind of a superstar in this town. He grew up here, played basketball for the Class B Boys State Champions, went on to college, and became a paramedic. When he died, they named the gym at the high school after him. There was a big ceremony and everything, but I don't remember that. I was just a baby.

When people die they put their names on things. If they weren't famous or "popular" or if their death wasn't tragic, it's just a gravestone. If they were famous, or rich, or tragic, it's a building at a university, an emergency room at a hospital, a gymnasium. Then eventually people forget the person the thing was named after. Years and years and years pass and the name means nothing anymore, it carries no memory of the person. It becomes just words, meaningless, empty.

Since my mom never married again, people still look out for us. Mr. Dow mows our lawn, trims our lilacs and helps us with our taxes. Eddie Caron's dad plows out our driveway. Mr. Jones invites us out on his sailboat at least once a summer, and he secretly paid for my cheerleading camp in middle school, and always asks about my grades.

"It's like every man in town is your daddy," my mom always laughs.

"That does not sound good," I always tell her. "That sounds like you're the town slut."

She always laughs more. "I wish."

The shower water rushes down on me and I try to not think about my mom out on the town with reporter Jim Shrembersky. Still, I see her giggling over the salad bowl at Olive Garden up in Bangor. I see Jim Shrembersky wiggling his eyebrows lasciviously and making some stupid jokes. I see my mother reaching out to touch his hand with her finger. His heartbeat quickens. So does hers. Thumpity. Thump. Thump.

My mother knocks on the bathroom door when I'm toweling off and from the break in her voice I can tell she's been crying.

"I'm going to miss you," she says. "I'm going to miss you when you go."

I scrunch on a bathrobe and pull open the door. The cold doorknob is like peace after the hot steam of the shower. My mom waits on the other side, trying to look brave, but her bottom lip trembles. Mine does the same thing when I try not to be sad.

Up on the ceiling, a spider crawls towards its web. My mom's face straightens itself.

"I'm not going far. It's just college," I say and pull her against me.

"It's life," she says. "You're going into life without me."

I nod and pat her back. The cloth is dry and thin. I whisper to her, "I won't be far."

She shakes her head, pulls away, smiles at me. "You already are. You're doing the typical teenage self-involved thing."

We wait a second. We wait another second, just standing there with each other and then I point above her head at the hallway ceiling. "There's a spider up there."

"Let's let him be," she says, and then reaches and pulls my hair out of the collar on my bathrobe. "You go get dressed before you catch pneumonia."

"It's May," I say and then bite my lip, because I've realized my mistake.

Her hand wanders to my cheek. "Let me mother you while I still can, okay?"

I nod. "Okay."

----o----

A second passes. Another goes by. I grab at the doorframe of the bathroom, looking for something to help hold me up. It's dusty. I should dust.

"Mom?"

She turns around.

"What, sweetie?"

"I'm glad you have a good time with Jim."

She smiles, slow and sweet. It spreads its calm joy across her face. "Thanks, honey."

Her bottom does an extra wiggle as she tiptoes down the

hall and she starts singing. The wrong lyrics come out, like always. She does this on purpose. I have no idea why.

"I'm not slow in a Vette," she sings.

I think she means to say, "I'm not so innocent," which is an ancient Britney Spears song, but I will not ask.

"NO!!!" she croons. "I'm not slow in a Vette."

"No more, Mom," I yell.

"Sorry," her voice comes back up the stairs, but the rest of her has already disappeared.

I start a list.

Self-involved? My mom said I was. I'm not. Am I?

Am I primarily interested in things that only have to do with me?

What do I care about?

1. Em.
2. Tom.
3. My mom.
4. Mimi's evil ways.
5. My dad.
6. My guitar.
7. The fact that I'll be $40,000 in debt when I graduate college even though I'm getting work study, two dinky scholarships and a grant. Oh, God. Oh God. God. God.
8. Being a good person and not obsessively worrying about my in-debt future.
9. Amnesty International, racism, sexism, homophobia.
10. The fact that Eddie's dad came home drunk and hit Eddie last night. Just hit him.
11. Ha!

EMILY'S SECRET DOESN'T MAKE ME feel any heavier, although I guess it shouldn't yet. The secret is only one month old, we think, locked inside of her, waiting until it won't be a secret anymore. It is not my secret to hold, but I hold it with her as if it is my own.

That's what best friends do. They hold each other's pain inside their womb as if it were their own. I am going to be a good friend for Em. That's my role now, my label.

Emily usually drives me to school instead of Tom on Mondays, Wednesdays and Fridays. They made an agreement when Tom and I first started dating. I think it's kind of cute that they fight over me, but in a way it makes me feel like a kid stuck in a custody battle, only the parents actually like each other.

We don't all ride together because Tom has a truck and Em has a little red car that makes Tom sweat the moment she starts pumping it over sixty. Tom drives crazy too, so it makes no sense.

"Control issues," Em explained once. She's probably right. His dad *is* a cop.

When I get in the car, Em does not turn on any music. We do not sing like we normally do. I've stashed Gabriel in the backseat and buckled up my seat belt, because Em drives like a wild woman and she is not so good at paying attention to the road. This is why Tom perspires. Me? I'm used to it.

"Are you going to tell me what's bothering you?" she says like she doesn't know that I couldn't sleep at all last night because I was too busy worrying about her. Her hands clench the steering wheel getting ready for my answer, I guess. The neon green fuzzy dice that Shawn gave her as a joke jiggle as she backs out of my driveway.

I wait a bit. I stare down at the ant crawling across my shoe. "There's an ant in your car."

She screams and slams on the brakes. My hands come out in time to smack into the dashboard.

"Oh my God!"

"It's just an ant," I say, sitting back up and looking around. We're stopped in the middle of the road. Em's hand rakes through her hair. For a minute, I forget all about her secret and smile at her, because her eyes are crazy and she's almost stuttering.

"Shawn said I was a slob. He said it and I was all, like, 'No, I am not a slob, you ass.' But I am. Aren't I?"

I shrug and worry for a second that I've smooshed the ant during Em's forced stop. Em smacks her hand into her forehead. "I am such a slob. I'm disgusting."

"No, you aren't."

The ant heaves an old half-green French fry onto his back and trucks it in a path parallel to my Snoopy shoe.

"You're lying," Em pouts. "I'm worthless. Just worthless."

"No, you aren't," I say again, "but you are stopped in the middle of the road."

"Crap," Em mutters and picks her foot up off the brake and we start rolling down the Bayside Road. Lucky for us, not a lot of people live out here. "I'm a wreck. I cannot believe it."

"You're okay," I say. "Just think that your car is single-handedly sustaining an entire colony of ants. It's an environmentally conscious thing to do."

"Ha."

"Ha back."

"Some friend you are," she teases, pretending to be mad, but her long duck lips turn up at the corners.

The ant disappears under the seat, heading for the rear of the car, I guess.

"I'm the best friend you'll ever have," I tell her.

She sighs. "I know."

And just like that the secret settles in over us, muffling our happy hearts, silencing our smiles. That's what secrets do, they silence us.

WE HAVE A SECRET THAT we haven't even told anyone. We haven't told our boyfriends. We haven't told our moms. We have a secret that we do not want. That we do not want to be true.

Tom finds me by my locker.

He looks at me.

I look at him. His jeans are ripped at the knee. I can see his dark skin through the hole. I want to put my fingers in there, pull him closer.

His voice is husky and quiet at the same time. "You doing okay?"

For a second I think he's asking me about Emmie, but then I realize it's about my seizure.

"Yeah," I say. "Stressed about the talent show tonight, but that's it."

He reaches across and pulls the hair from my face, tucks it behind my ear. "I worry about you. I'll try not to. I can't help it."

People slam by us. Shawn yells, "You're going to be late for Law, Belle."

"I'm coming," I say, grabbing Tom's hand.

"You seen Em?" Shawn asks, hovering above us. He's so tall and clean looking. Oh God…and innocent looking and he's about to learn he's a father.

"She's at her locker," I tell him and he takes off. Tom's hand squeezes mine. "I just don't want you to think I'm a freak."

"Belle, I know you've had seizures."

"But not all the time. They were pretty controlled," I say, letting go of his hand so I can shut my locker. The warning bell rings. "I've got to go."

I rush away from him without looking at his face, without letting him say anything. I rush away because I'm afraid I might see what he thinks. I grab Em at her locker and we book it to Law. Neither of us says anything, but I know both our brains are racing.

----o----

When we get to law class, I squeeze Em's hand, which makes Mimi lift up her eyebrows, smirk, and whisper something to Brittney who sits in front of her. Brittney did not grow up here. She moved in, so I forgive her for being stupid enough to hang out with Mimi.

Mr. Richter mock applauds Em and me for making it before the bell, something we have a hard time doing. Then, he announces that we're going to discuss abortion today.

Somebody groans. I pull out my notebook. Brittney opens up her laptop. Mimi cracks some gum and announces, "It smells like puke in here."

Mr. Richter sighs and says, "Well, open a window then, Mimi."

"It didn't smell until Belle came in," she says, moving over to the window and yanking it open.

I gulp.

Shawn chucks a pen at her and goes, "Shut up, Mimi."

"Mr. Young!" Mr. Richter stands up tall, his face reddens.

"She was insulting Belle," Shawn says, all relaxed, leaning back in his chair as casual as if he were sunning after a ball game.

"It doesn't matter, Shawn. I will deal with Mimi. I am the teacher," he points at us all, "and you are the students."

Mimi saunters back into her chair and hikes her skirt up to show a little more thigh.

"Mimi. See me after class."

She pouts, leans forward and says, "Why? I didn't throw anything."

"You know why." Mr. Richter shuffles back to his desk.

I think that both he and I want to start the day over. I start sniffing while he opens up a book. Kara shoots a note at me. I open it. It says: *You do not smell like puke. Mimi is puke.*

I smile back at Kara. She gives me a thumbs-up. I love Kara. I write that to her: *I love you.* Then I shoot her the note. It's sad that we have to waste so much paper writing notes. They should just let us text, which is much more environmentally friendly, although I guess we aren't supposed to write notes either. But it's not like teachers confiscate your paper if you get caught the way they confiscate cells.

Mr. Richter stops fiddling around with his book and says out of nowhere, "This class is not going to be about what you believe or what I believe about abortion. It's about the law. Got it? No big political debates? No religion. Just the law. That's it. Anything else and you're out of here. I'm serious."

He gives us a glare down. I start doodling in my notebook, trying to draw Tom's face. I sneak a sideways glance at Em. She's fiddling with her fingers in her lap, which is something she only does when she's super nervous. I'd give anything to go over there and just grab her hands and hold them still, to lie to her and tell her everything is going to be fine.

"Okay." Mr. Richter clears his throat and leans back against his big metal desk. This means things are getting serious. "Who can tell me the first state that began the march towards legalized abortion?"

Kara shoots her hand up. "Colorado. 1967."

"Good," he says. He looks at me. "Belle? What did Colorado base its legislation on?"

My hand keeps doodling Tom, but I make eye contact with Mr. Law Teacher, try to ignore Mimi's snort and say, "The Model Penal Code. It allowed abortions in instances where the mother's life was at stake. It was adopted by more than one third of all the states by 1973."

Mimi coughs. "Suck up."

Shawn mutters, "Shut up, Mimi."

"Belle's an abortion gone bad," she says and smirks, because for Mimi this is brilliant. She looks over at Andrew for approval. He's staring out the window. His shirt is buttoned all the way up. I force myself to not imagine the hickey line hiding under there.

Shawn glares at Mimi and says it again, only way more menacing. "Shut. Up."

Mr. Law Teacher's head snaps on his neck in a nice version of teacher-possessed and he says, "Mr. Young, are you at it again?"

Shawn shrugs.

Mimi whispers really loudly to Brittney, "It's funny that Belle would know all about abortion. It's not like she and Tommy are ever going to have sex. She's so frigid."

Everyone's heard that. Even Mr. Richter. He turns bright red and starts sputtering. He has no idea what to do. Neither do I. I start writing *I hate Mimi* in the margins of my notebook. I flash a glance up at Em, but she's schlumped in her chair looking like she's going to cry, which is not normal Em behavior. She's normally the one who screams at Mimi for me; that's my Em, defender of all underdogs.

She's not paying any attention.

She's thinking about babies.

It's all I can do not to get up and hug her.

Mr. Law Teacher is now pulling Mimi out of the classroom by her elbow. She has to quick-walk in her juicy outfit to keep up. The heels are a killer. People titter. I don't care. Em looks up like she's finally back in this universe.

"You okay?" I say to her while Kara simultaneously announces to the world that Mimi's a bitch.

"No, you are," Brittney says to Kara.

Kara lifts her eyebrows. "You do not want to go there."

"Abortion is stupid," Shawn announces to the world like an idiot. I'm not sure why he does this. Maybe to change the subject off of whether or not Tom and I are ever going to have sex, I don't know.

He keeps going on. "I mean, it's stupid to get pregnant in the first place, but unless you're raped or going to die, I don't think you should ever get an abortion. You have to be responsible for your actions. Without responsibility you don't have nothing. You have no self-respect. You have nothing. You can't just run away from the costs of your choices."

Em sinks lower in her chair.

"Never?" Kara's eyebrows raise and she's into super feminist woman mode. "What if Em got pregnant? You'd want her to throw away the rest of her life? Would you?"

The world freezes. One century passes. Another.

"Of course," Shawn says. "If we were stupid enough to make a baby."

Kara shakes her head. "Your entire life would change. You'd have no freedom. All your dreams would be gone. And it wouldn't be your decision, Shawn. It would be Emily's. Right Em?"

Kara expects Em to rally beside her like normal, but Em just nods and looks down again. She takes out her camera, snaps pictures of all of us in the room. Kara quiets.

Even Shawn notices and his voice comes out sweet and kind. "Emmie? You okay?"

She nods and takes a picture of him but doesn't say anything.

Shawn stares at me for help, for a clue. I raise my shoulders in a big lie, pretending I don't know anything, pretending that Em doesn't have a secret.

"Mimi's an idiot," Em announces. Everyone stares at her because she didn't answer Kara.

When we were little every time there was a concert for chorus or an assembly where we had to go up and have our names called for honor roll, Emily would get really nervous. She'd start wiggling her long fingers together, moving one then the others. My mom called it "fidgeting." Mimi used to call Em "freaky fingers." I thought Emily had grown out of it, but the moment Mr. Richter comes back into class she has to put her camera away and her freaking fingers start.

"Between 1968 and 1973 how did people challenge abortion laws? On what grounds?" Mr. Richter says, striding back to the front of the class, pretending like nothing happened. Mimi returns to her seat a second later, pretending to be a good girl but flashes me a look of pure evil.

Andrew raises his hand. "Vagueness."

"Good. Good." Mr. Richter keeps lecturing and asking questions. We keep answering and life goes on in our first period law class. Em barely looks up. It's going to be a long day.

----o----

It's later in the morning when I'm walking to Advanced Math that Shawn finds me in the hall. His eyes plead. "Belle. Can I talk to you for a sec?"

We duck into a corner of the stairway. Freshmen skitter by on their way to the foreign languages section of the building. They look at Shawn with awe. He's tall with big shoulders to match his voice and he walks like the jock he is. He's a good guy though.

That jock stereotype is wrong when it comes to Tom, and

Shawn. Most stereotypes are wrong, if you think about it. For example, since I'm a liberal high school feminist folk singer some people might assume that I do not shave my armpits. Those people would be misinformed and nasty. Those same people would assume Shawn was a sexist idiot because he's good at baseball and soccer. They would also be wrong. Shawn is sweet and funny and he's really good with kids and his mom. He cooks a great spaghetti casserole, which is corny, but true. My stomach grumbles. Thinking about all this labeling stuff is hard work.

Still, though I love Shawn and his spaghetti casserole, I do not want to talk to him, especially not about Em.

"I'm going to be late for Math," I say.

He pulls a pout. "It'll only take a second."

I lean against the wall with one shoulder. The light flickers over us. From the smell of it, it seems lasagna is being made in the teachers' lounge. Shawn smiles at a sophomore junior varsity baseball player, Josh something or other. Then, Shawn focuses.

"Is Em mad at me?"

Everything in my body relaxes. He has no idea. He doesn't suspect.

"No," I answer, honestly.

"You sure?"

"Positive."

He exhales big and long. "Good. 'Cause she's been acting funny all day."

Andrew trots by and hits Shawn on the shoulder. They start talking baseball and I push off the wall, my feet ready to take me to Math. Shawn grabs my elbow, lightly, not in some he-man aggressive way and he says to Andrew, "I'll catch up."

Andrew hustles down the stairs.

Shawn blue-eyes me and says, "Do you know what's wrong with Em?"

I shake my head.

"You should ask her," I say. The light flickers again and starts buzzing.

"But she's not mad at me?"

"I swear."

He nods, lets me go, flashes me a smile and says, "I just really love her, you know?"

He takes the stairs three at a time, ascending towards the top of the school, moving fast and sure, like he knows just who he is and where he's going, a confident guy, a popular guy with a beautiful girlfriend, a college acceptance letter, and possibly some Eastern Maine baseball playoff action in his future. I watch him go and mourn him, the Shawn I am about to lose to fear the same way I just lost my best friend, Emily.

Our math teacher is missing in action.

"He's meeting with the vice principal," Anna explains when I sit down. She gestures at the board.

It says in big white crooked letters: *You have 20 minutes to amuse yourselves. Do not break any laws. Do not commit murder. Do not fornicate. Think about math.*

"Wow," I say.

Anna nods and her still-green hair swishes around. "Yeah. I know it. You up for the bike ride Wednesday?"

"I'll be there," I tell her.

She smiles. "Good."

"I'm not bringing any tampons though."

"Condoms?"

"Nope."

She laughs and then she starts asking everybody else. She just goes up and down the rows, reminding people. Sweet

Dylan says hi and we talk about music for a minute. He tells me he thinks Bob gets too jealous about everything.

Dylan's leg bounces up and down, jingling change or keys in his pocket. "He's all nervous about colleges."

"Because you're going to Carnegie Mellon and he's going to UMaine?"

"Yeah."

"Dylan," I gulp in air and rush the words out. "Are most guys awkward about sex?"

"You and Tom still haven't done it."

"Shut up."

I hit him in the shoulder. He laughs and doesn't even rub at it. "Powerful fist there, Belle."

I lower my voice, "I mean it because…"

I should not be going there.

"Because I wasn't?" he starts mega-watt smiling. "Thanks, I'm honored."

My hands cover my face. Dylan plucks them off. "I think we weren't awkward because it was a natural progression of our love, you know? Like we were exploring who we were and we felt so safe with each other. God. Did I just say natural progression?"

"Yep."

He cracks up. Then he gets it under control. "I just mean. It wasn't like we built it up into a big thing so it wasn't like I had the chance to be awkward."

"Okay. Right."

"It will be fine," Dylan says. "Tom will be fine."

Crash be-bops in and pounds Dylan's big shoulder with his small hand hard enough for Dylan to jerk forward. Crash is only carrying a notebook. I bet he'll ask to borrow a pencil. He always does. "Dylan, how's my favorite gay-man friend?"

Dylan laughs, but does not rub at his shoulder. "Good, how's my favorite Pakistani-descended American friend with an appropriate name?"

Crash bashes his hip into the desk and smiles at us. He says to me, "Sometimes that boy just wants me to flip him off, you know? It's like he's calling for it. Belle, you got a pencil?"

"I know," I say, handing him a pencil and Crash has already turned his attention to Anna, his newest ideal girlfriend. Anna, oblivious, starts talking to him about the bike ride Wednesday. Crash almost drools.

"Will you be wearing spandex?" he asks. "Little biking shorts? Sports bra?"

Dylan shakes his head, sits down and starts texting Bob a note, which will earn him three nights' detention if he gets caught. I know he's doing this because I, being nosy, ask. I start working on a song and then get distracted because Andrew and Mimi are having a shout-down. I'd forgotten they hooked up Saturday night. I shudder. I'm not sure how I'll look at either of them again.

"We are going out," Mimi says.

Andrew opens up his math book. "You wish."

Mimi's head flips back. Her eyes narrow and for a second, she looks, gasp, vulnerable. "What?"

Andrew totally ignores her and turns a page in his math book. Nobody ever looks at our math books. Mimi is not stupid. She knows this. "Andrew!"

Still nothing.

She comes back at him, standing up now, shoving her breasts near his face. "What?"

Andrew leans away. "I said, 'You wish.'"

Mimi's voice lowers to a whisper but everyone else in class is quiet now, listening, just like me, watching the five-car-motorcycle pileup that is known as Mimi Cote. "You said I was awesome."

"Having sex was awesome but that doesn't mean you are awesome," Andrew says in a quiet voice for Andrew, which really isn't saying anything. "But you and I are definitely not going out."

"Yes, we are."

"You're in love with Tom anyway."

Everyone looks at me. I wave but my blood stops moving, I think, just freezes there in my arteries and veins.

Mimi puffs herself up. "I don't have one-night stands."

"Right." Andrew stands, eyes hard and mouth stuck in a fake smile. He spreads his arms wide. "Everybody hear that? Mimi and I are not going out. We are not a couple."

Mimi stares stunned, shocked.

"Sit down, Andrew," Dylan says.

Anna gulps. I can actually see her swallow.

Mimi's lips twitch like they used to do when we were little and she didn't get to be the flyer anymore on the eighth-grade cheering team, or when she didn't make it to the geography bee in sixth grade. Her lips twitch like that because she is trying not to cry. And one horrible little part of me kind of likes it, because she's such a jerk-head to me all the time, but this other part can't stand it, and remembers us practicing cheers together and giggling while we ate popcorn with mustard on it and our fingers turned yellow like a Muppet's.

So I say, "Leave her alone, Andrew. Don't be such a user."

Andrew's mouth loses his happy look and it becomes a hole in a guitar, nothing comes out, nothing goes in.

I say more softly, "Mimi, everything's okay."

She power pivots and stares at me. "Shut up, Belle."

All the hate in the universe is in those three words.

"I don't need a pity party from Frigid Girl and her do-gooder friends," Mimi announces and slams out of the room.

"Frigid Girl?" I cough out my new superhero name. "I'm Frigid Girl?" I start giggling. If I'm Frigid Girl, what would my super powers be? I will not answer that.

Dylan pats my shoulder. My stomach does a back tuck and settles somewhere near my kidneys.

Andrew sits down and announces, "Belle's not a frigid girl. Maybe a Do-Gooder Girl, and Mimi's just a bitch. Right, Dylan? I mean before you came out you were banging Belle all the time."

This, as my mother would say, is not a helpful comment. My hand shakes and I use it to cover my eyes, like I can hide or something, incredibly mature of me, I know.

"Andrew," Dylan says with his deep voice and killer eyes, "don't you think you've been a big enough ass today? Why don't you just shut up?"

Andrew does.

- - - - o - - - -

Dylan and I leave class together. We walk down linoleum halls following the black scuff marks left from all the people who have walked here before us. We plod past lockers with stickers on them, past windows that show a beautiful May day outside, while we are stuck in here.

"Why does high school suck so much?" I ask him.

He bumps me with his hip. "It's people who suck."

"Very positive."

"I know," he beams a smile at me. That smile with all those white teeth used to light up my world. It still does, although obviously not in a sexual way. "Call me Pollyanna."

"Doesn't suit you. Are people giving you crap anymore?"

"Belle, I'm gay. People are always going to give me crap...but it's not too bad right now."

"Swear?"

"Swear."

"'Cause I don't want to have to go punch anyone."

He laughs. Em stands at the end of the hall and clicks a picture of us.

"Hey, Em. Wait up!" I say.

She turns and disappears into the throngs of students we here at Eastbrook High School call "classmates."

Dylan raises his eyebrows. "What's up with Em?"

"Nothing." I unlock my locker and get out my books. "Everything. You worried about the talent show?"

"A little. Bob's out of his mind, though."

"He'll do great. He's got great chops."

"I know."

I shake my head, because, well...How do you respond to that? Then I tell Dylan, "I'm having seizures again."

"Oh, honey. That sucks," he says. "Why? Does your mom know? You want me to go to the neurologist with you?"

I shake my head. Dylan went to the neurologist all the time with me when the seizures started. "I think Bob would get jealous."

He nods. "Like Tom wouldn't?"

Two hands swoop around my waist and someone's warm lips kiss my neck beneath my ear, which causes me to instantly melt against my locker and almost drop my books.

"Hey, Commie," Tom whispers in my ear.

I turn around. My arms circle around his neck and the side of my head rests against his chest. It smells so good and safe.

Dylan coughs. "See you later, Belle."

"Bye."

I feel bad for a second, because I don't even look up from Tom to say goodbye to Dylan. Instead, I just snuggle in closer to Tom, despite the fact that public displays of affection are "severely frowned upon" at Eastbrook High School. Tom's hand weaves through my hair. He smiles. "Miss me?"

I nod, but don't let go. "Uh-huh."

He nuzzles my ear and whispers into it, "Want to get out of here?"

I pull away a little bit so I can see him. Crash saunters by and stops. "Man, where's Emily when I need a picture? I think they're going to fornicate in the hallway."

"Fornicate" is such a funny word, but Tom apparently doesn't think so. He glares at Crash, making him back up while forming peace signs with his hands, a look of happy plastered on his face, like we're the biggest joke and he just got it.

"Peace. Peace. Got to live vicariously, you know?"

"So, you want lunch?" Tom asks me.

"I have to rehearse," I say but even as I say it something twinges. "You'll tell Em where I am though, okay…If, um, she needs me?"

He cocks his head. "Yeah, sure."

So, I skip lunch, which is normally when I see Tom and Shawn and Em and everybody. I am not avoiding them. I just have to practice for the talent show tonight. Really.

In the room where I practice, desks line up in rows like good military troops waiting for battle.

"Whose side are you on?" I ask them. "The sexually frustrated Belle? The sexually noncommittal Tom?"

Then I get stupid and say in a fake French accent, "Or perhapz you are on ze side of luve?"

The desks don't answer.

"Fine. Be Switzerland. Like I care."

I move a couple out of line and plop myself down with Gabriel. Tuning her is easy today. Perfect: We are in synch. Content, I settle in and play. Note after note comes out, soft and loud and true.

> *I ride towards you*
> *Like I don't have anywhere else to go*
> *No mother, no bed, no comforter, no home.*

A mosquito lands on my right wrist. I stop playing to smack it, juggling the balance of Gabriel so that I can do it without breaking her. A string protests.

Even though she's outside, in the hall, Mimi Cote's ultra-loud voice penetrates the room. Soundproofing in our school does not exist.

"I mean, really," Mimi says to someone else, "I've heard they still haven't done it. I mean…What? Why not? Tom's such a muffin. You know it has to be Belle. She did date Dylan, gay boy, for how long? Like two years?"

Smack, I kill the mosquito. For a second, I feel guilty, but the bug was sucking my blood.

"Sorry," I whisper to it. But really, I'm not paying that much attention to my act of murder, because I care more about what Mimi's saying about me than I do about the dead bug, which was really only trying to survive by sucking me dry. Kind of like Mimi.

"I mean that whole socially conscious, pretty, granola, hippie girl crap can only go so far. Right? I mean, my God. She must be frigid like the refrigerator, or gay," Mimi says and lets out this piercing giggle. "Or maybe Tom's just freaked by the whole seizure thing, like she'll bite off his tongue when they're doing it."

Is that why?

She must be standing right outside the door. She must want me to hear her. My insides burn.

She keeps going on. "Have you seen the way Tom looks at me? Pure lust. I swear. That poor baby. I know he wants me. He stares at me all during World History. I bet he's popping wood under the desk. He's way more of a man than Andrew."

I flick the crushed mosquito carcass off my wrist and start to play, louder this time, better.

> *I ride towards you*
> *And I wanna sneak in your house*
> *I don't know if you know how I feel*
> *But I want you to feel that way too*
> *I keep riding closer to you.*

Mimi's voice is just a background buzz, a mosquito looking for some nice soft patch of skin where she can land and suck.

It won't be on me. I've already given up too much blood.

Gabriel rests against me and I keep playing her. When I finish my song, I start an old one by Dar Williams, then segue into a Cliff Eberhardt song about want and need, which is appropriate.

That done, I check the clock. It's almost time for the bell, but I don't want to leave until it rings, and there's not enough time left to practice another song. So, I just sit there and vibrate the string by bending and releasing the note. Then I give it up and try some tremolo picking, which is when you take a note and pick it as fast and constant as your fingers can handle.

It sounds a little bit like a mosquito.

I hate mosquitoes.

Walking down the hall, I see Mimi. She sees me. She says just one word: pathetic.

It's the right word her mosquito mouth makes. It's true.

Gabriel smacks against my back as I stop walking. I am out of step, out of tune. I am a fatherless child, a sexless woman, a seizure girl with a guitar who is afraid to play.

ALL DURING BIO EM STARES at her notebook. She is pasty white. Her lips lack gloss. Sometimes her hand shakes holding her pencil. It kills me to look at her.

"You okay?" I whisper. I rest my elbows on the cold, black top of the science lab table and then think better of it. Things get dissected here.

"Will you stop asking me that?" she grumps back.

"Sorry."

She pulls her hand up, tucks some hair behind her ear, makes her earring swing. "I'm sorry. It's just not okay, you know?"

"I know."

She will do it today, she says. She will tell him after school.

When we're leaving Bio she says again, "So, you scared about tonight?"

"It'll be fine."

"Because you're more scared about me."

I shrug.

We hustle past Mr. Zeki who calls out in his super effeminate voice, "Be good, girls."

Once we're through the door and into the hallway, I tell her again, because I want to tell her again. I want to tell the world, over and over again. "I would do anything for you."

Em nods sagely. "Like I didn't know that."

"It's still nice to hear the words."

She hauls in a breath, and pulls her arm around my shoulder. "I'm sorry I'm so moody."

"You've got reasons."

Our sides bump together and I think about telling her about Tom's mom and dad and how Tom was born unplanned and unprepared for, but now is not the time. Even I know that.

We get to our lockers, switch books, wave to Anna and Kara who are talking down Crash who is explaining that everyone thinks he's black but he's Pakistani and it's totally different and why do all white people think all people of color are of African descent and so on. He nods at me and then goes back into his sad, angry face until Kara hugs him and Anna shouts, "White people suck."

White people do tend to suck, but it's pretty funny because Anna is, well, you know, white. Her hair does make her look a little amphibious, though.

Em doesn't even notice what's going on and instead she says, "Do you think Shawn will hate me?"

Her voice is a little girl's. Her fingers twist. She grabs her camera, but doesn't take a picture.

"No." I fill my lungs up with air. "He'll be shocked. And it'll take him a while to figure out what to do and everything."

She stares into the viewfinder. "But what about all that stuff he said in law class?"

"He was just talking," I say. "You know how Shawn is."

She shakes her head. People look at us strangely almost like they already know. Bob hustles by and stares without saying hi. Andrew makes big eyes that are sort of condescending.

She stops looking through the camera, uses her free hand to smash shut her locker door. "I don't know if I can do this. I just don't know."

I hug her because she looks so pathetic, and I can't think of anything else to do. Crash zooms over, steals Em's camera out of her hand and takes a picture of us. I hold her up. Our hair tangles into each other. We look like sisters. We look like best friends. We look like women who have secrets.

TELLING YOUR BOYFRIEND THAT YOU'RE pregnant is not the easiest thing in the world. Except for girls in country music videos, for them the words just seem to pop out of their mouths. The guy walks off the baseball field, throws down his bat, and she blurts it out. Freeze frame the image. Commit it to memory. Fast forward seven years and there are happy family faces magnet-stuck on the fridge.

That's not how it is for Emmie.

Because the truth of it is, Shawn loves her now, and she doesn't want to change that.

And even if a baby doesn't actually change the love part it changes everything else. Everything.

Em's stomach makes a noise that even I can hear. There's an embryo inside there. There is a tiny heart that beats.

I grab her hand and squeeze it. She squeezes back and then we leave each other, heading for classes, trying not to be late, like good girls, good students, good citizens, people who abide by the rules and the expectations. We march to our places, secrets inside us. We go where we are supposed to.

I'M ALMOST TO GERMAN CLASS when Mimi meets me in the hall. She stops in front of me, blocking my way. Brittney, her puppy, stands beside her. Mimi rocks back on her heels, eyeing me and then says in this whoopee pie voice, "Why, Belle, you're absolutely glowing."

I stare at her.

"Isn't she glowing, Brittney?" the evil Mimi says.

This is the first time she's ever said anything nice to me in four years, which means that she isn't actually saying anything nice. I give her an eyebrow raise, just one eyebrow lifts up. I save this move for special condescending occasions and I prefer not to use it because it's so powerful.

It doesn't affect her. Mimi stares me down. Brittney just lets out a snarky smile.

Brittney says, "She's definitely glowing."

"And her skin looks so smooth. Belle, your skin looks so smooth and pretty…all peaches and cream," Mimi says. She reaches out to touch my cheek. I jerk away. She laughs.

I try to figure out if I should just say thank you and walk on.

I start to form a word but Mimi cuts me off. "I hear those hormones will do that to you."

"What?"

She leans in closer and talks at the top of her voice without technically yelling. "I hear that the hormones make *women in your condition* have nice, glowing skin. *Congratulations!*"

She smiles and stands up straight again. My eyebrow falls back down to its proper place. I sputter. I think about Em.

"You don't know what you're talking about, Mimi."

She bites the corner of her lip. "It's okay to want to keep it a secret, Belle. I understand. It's so terribly embarrassing."

I rigid up. "You're such an idiot."

She giggles.

"First, you say that I'm frigid and that Tom and I don't have sex because I'm an ice cube or something, but now, suddenly, I'm pregnant," I say. "God, you need a life."

Andrew stops. A crowd starts gathering. Kara gives me big eyes.

"I know what you bought at Wal-Mart this weekend," she says.

I freeze for a second. My stomach leaves my body, runs away like the wimp it is.

"Ye-ah," Brittney chimes in.

"You're spying on me?" I say. "That's pitiful. You don't have anything better to do than spy on me? Get out of my way, I'm going to be late for German."

Something wobbles in Mimi's eyes. Something shifts. "You can't hide the truth, Belle. Everybody's going to know sooner or later. You are starting to round out a little, already, aren't you? Poor you, I heard pregnancy makes your boobs even bigger."

She touches my stomach with two fingers. I jerk away.

"I bought tampons. Go ask Anna."

"What else?" she crosses her arms across her chest. Her arms have no hair on them. She must have waxed them. Her arms always used to be hairy. This is a stupid thing to register with me, but it still does.

"Condoms, okay?" Pushing by her I mutter, "God, you're a pathetic bitch. It's no wonder Tom dumped you."

Andrew starts laughing. I just keep walking away, pretending I'm all calm and cool and nothing is affecting me, but my heart is trying to escape my body. My hands tingle something fierce and my head keeps chanting *Emily, Emily,*

Emily. Because Mimi-people are cruel people and they'll be cruel to Emmie. This I absolutely know.

Then, I do something that I know will keep Mimi thinking about me, keep her from figuring out that it's Em I bought that pregnancy test for. I place my hand against my stomach, like I'm protecting a baby that's inside me.

I bite my lip and try to look worried.

Behind me, Mimi gasps and whispers, "I am so right. Ohmygod, I can't believe Tom actually did it with her. Pathetic."

I hunch my shoulders and try to look defeated, because I don't care. I don't care that Mimi thinks I'm the one who is pregnant as long as she doesn't think it's Emily. I can handle Mimi, but Emmie...Emmie's already got enough to deal with. She doesn't need more.

I head up the stairs to the foreign language wing. That's when I realize it. There is something wrong with me.

Even though Mimi is evil.

Even though Mimi stole Tom from me back in eighth grade and then took Dylan for some romp when I started liking him before he came out.

Even though I think she is horrible, horrible, horrible.

I still feel bad.

I still feel like crap because I said, "No wonder Tom dumped you."

And I could have said worse things.

But I still feel bad.

I feel bad because I hate her. I hate hating her. I hate being as bitchy and as fake as she is.

My stomach, which seems to have returned to my body, kicks at itself. I put my hand over it as I walk to German. This is sort of what Em will feel, when the baby moves. A kick. A flutter. Pain.

When we were little Mimi used to cry in her bedroom sometimes, late at night, when I was sleeping over. Her dad had left her mom for Nicole, this girl who was like sixteen or something and worked at the drive-thru at McDonald's. He'd go to McDonald's about eighteen times during her shifts, and buy a small French fry, or a small coffee or an apple pie, just going in there over and over again. Then one day he went to that drive-thru window in his beat-up Ford pickup truck, a real old, rusted-out one, navy blue, and he said, "How about I order you?"

She must have been stupid or romantic or just sick of McDonald's and high school, because she crawled out that window, sat on his lap and drove off into the sunset. Well, really to Machias, which is just a bit up the coast.

It was the talk of the town.

Sometimes at night when I was sleeping over I'd hear Mimi cry and one time I got brave enough to not just sit there and to actually hug her. One time my middle school self was brave enough to ask her what was wrong.

And she was brave enough to answer.

She wiped her nose and her face. The moonlight coming through her window made her tears glisten like they were magic. I remember thinking that.

She sniffed in real good and said, "If he loved me he wouldn't have left."

I knew she was talking about her dad. Of course, I knew.

It's funny we spend so much of our lives worrying about men leaving us, about men not loving us, about what that might mean.

So, even though Mimi is evil, I feel badly for making her

hurt more. She's evil, but I feel for her. I know what it's like, missing a dad. I know what it's like feeling like if he loved me he wouldn't have left, but that's stupid. Men aren't good at staying, I don't think. They always leave people they love behind. Of course, sometimes it isn't their fault. Sometimes they die.

Thoughts of Mimi, and Em, and Shawn, and Tom, and even about my mom flying off to her conference tomorrow, clutter up my head when I get to German class, only a mere twenty seconds after the bell has rung, which isn't bad.

Tom winks at me as I get in my seat. I stare at his lips. This is pathetic, but he has really nice lips.

Herr Reitz doesn't mind that I'm twenty seconds late. He loves me now. Ever since I passed out in his class after Eddie attacked me, he's all, "Can I do anything for you, liebchen?"

Every week we have the same exact German geography quiz. It's the same quiz for German 1 and German 4. I've gotten 110 on it every week.

Herr Reitz hands mine back before I even get a chance to sit down. He smiles to reveal something green stuck between his front teeth. Spinach? Broccoli?

"Sehr gut, Belle," he says.

It's 110.

"Danke," I say and make a motion with my fingers that something is in his teeth. He claps his hand over his mouth and looks horrified. He runs out of the class so he can go pick it out. I feel bad.

"Someone had to tell him," Tom says.

Crash wiggles his eyebrows and he leans over towards me. "Do you think Anna will ever fall madly in love with me and want to twist my body into torturous positions while having insane, unquenchable, heart-stopping sex?"

"Probably," I say.

He smiles and gives himself a high five. Then he gives Bob a high five. Bob doesn't look pleased. His hand only made it halfway up, so Crash smacked his fingers. Bob's uptight about his fingers. He's a total nudge, which I'm not supposed to think because he's gay and therefore oppressed, but he's still a nugget of yuck. He doesn't care about anyone or anything except his saxophone and Dylan.

Bob is not my priority, though. Emily is. I try to imagine her in her Spanish class, stressing about things. Her hand touches her still flat stomach. Her heart beats faster because of the load of supporting two bodies. Ah, God, my own heart beats faster, I'm so worried. What is she going to do? I imagine her in a cruddy little apartment with stains on the ceiling. There are roaches on the stove and brown stains in the sink. Her baby's crying and has crud plastered to his nose. She's ignoring him, schlumped in the corner, sobbing, rocking back and forth. I will not let that happen to her.

And God help me, I am so glad that it's not happening to me.

I sit down, press my hands into my eyes so I won't cry. What kind of person am I? Relieved?

"Belle?" Tom's touch on my shoulder jars me back into reality. "You okay? Something wrong?"

I shake my head and wipe my eyes.

Tom's voice gets a little harder. He rips off some duct tape. "I was talking to you."

"I'm sorry."

I am. I am sorry. Tom is so sweet and good and I love the way he smells, or when his hand touches my shoulder. I love the warmth of him when I stand next to him in the hall.

"You want to tell me what you were thinking about?" he asks.

"Nothing."

I shrug. It is a forced shrug. Tom can tell and his face shifts, because he is not stupid. He knows I'm keeping something from him. "You worried about tonight?"

I leap up and sit up straight. "A little."

He laughs and twists some duct tape into a man. He starts on a new piece. What about him? What am I doing to him when I worry about Em?

"Are you doing okay?"

I lower my voice. "I'm sorry about my thing in the driveway last night."

"Have you told Em?"

"No."

"You should probably tell her."

I grab my pencil, click it so the lead comes out. "Yeah."

He smiles. He pulls something out of his backpack. He's made a duct tape woman holding a guitar. He must've been working on it all day. "Really?"

"Yeah."

I take the man and woman and make them embrace on Tom's desk.

Tom laughs. "Us?"

I nod. My heart turns all warm and gooey, except for the part that's stuck worrying about Em. That part is just hard and cold.

Crash turns back to me and says, "Mimi's telling everyone you're pregnant. You don't look pregnant."

"What?" Tom and Bob both focus on poor Crash. He holds his hands up in the air like he's surrendering.

"I didn't say it. Mimi said it," he says. "Mimi is so not as hot as Anna."

Tom's cheek twitches and his face turns darker than normal. He leans in and says, "Why didn't you tell me she was saying that about you?"

"I only just found out," I say and abandon the amorous duct tape couple to start tying my shoes. I can feel all his anger and I can't blame him. It's stupid.

"God, she's a bitch."

"Yep," I look up and his eyes are pained. "I'm not pregnant."

There, I said it, I said the words. There's a label that's true for me. I am not pregnant. I am a girl who hasn't had sex in months. I am a person who is trying to deal with things and not doing very well. I suck. That's it. I suck. I suck and I'm not pregnant.

That's about the only stupid thing I know about myself as an absolute. Am I a good friend? I don't know. A good girlfriend? Do I understand anything? No. Am I popular? I don't know. Am I anything? I don't know. I don't know. I just know I'm not pregnant.

I smash my hand back up to my eyes again and cover them. My hand shakes. Tom grabs it and pulls it away from my eyes.

"I'm not pregnant," I say again.

"Obviously."

"And it's not a sign or anything prophetic like that, okay?"

He nods.

We sit there for a second and he says, "I hate that she hurts you."

"She doesn't hurt me," I say, feeling a little stronger and

it's true. "She's only hurting herself when she does that. Every-one thinks she's an idiot."

"True."

I squeeze Tom's hand and let go.

"Mimi is evil," Crash announces to the room. "Do you want me to go jack her?"

I shake my head.

"She doesn't hurt me at all," I add, but Emily…It's Emily that I'm worried about. I can't imagine what it'll be like tell-ing Shawn. I can't imagine what she's dealing with.

I suck in a huge breath. It hurts my lungs to breathe that deeply. What do I want? What do I need?

"Will you pick me up from gymnastics? Then we can go to my house and I can get ready for the show?" I ask Tom as Herr Reitz prances back in.

"I'd be honored."

His voice melts my insides. I stare right into his eyes, which look a little frightened, a little excited and a lot intense and I shiver in a very good way.

"Oh, yeah."

He makes sexy eyes. "Yeah?"

"Yeah."

Crash starts giggling, "Herr Reitz, Tomen and Bellen are geflirten again."

Herr Reitz smiles to reveal perfect un-food-infested teeth. "Well, that's a news flash right there."

I blush but everyone else just laughs.

I meet Em in the hall before I head to the Y to teach gym-nastics. She's kissing Shawn goodbye. He has baseball practice, just like Tom. They look so sweet kissing. I wish I had Em's camera so I could take a picture of them. I try to freeze their image in my head, anyways.

Tall Shawn, short Em, both of them beautiful, both of them clinging to each other.

Em whirls around and sees me. She shakes her hair out, and reaches through it checking for tangles.

"I can't tell him here," she whispers once he's walked away. "Not in school."

I nod and get my books to go home. I adjust Gabriel on my shoulder.

Em clears her throat and says, "I heard about what Mimi's doing."

"Someone must've seen me at Wal-Mart."

"I'm so sorry, Belle."

Shrugging, I touch her arm. "It's Mimi. Nobody's going to believe her."

Anna plops by all spunky and happy, completely oblivious to our melodrama. "Hey guys."

We smile at her. We make small talk. We act like everything is absolutely normal. I'm feeling loaded down so I lean Gabriel's case up against the locker. Kara stops by too and starts indicting Mimi on crimes of sheer idiocy. Then we say goodbye.

"I'm going to try to tell him after practice," Em says, her voice small as we head down the stairs. They're pretty much deserted.

"Okay," I say. "What do you want me to do?"

"I don't know," she says. "I don't know."

Em drops me off at the Y and I start jamming towards the doors because I'm late and it's not good to only have one teacher in there with thirty kids and balance beams. It just isn't.

I'm past the graffiti-covered picnic table and almost to the door when I hear my name.

I pivot, figuring it's one of the mothers.

But it isn't. It's Mimi.

She totters across the parking lot in her heels. She steps into a crack in the asphalt and swears, yanking her shoes off. Weariness slugs my muscles down. I have no energy for Mimi Cote right now.

She carries Gabriel on her back and reaches her out to me. "You left this in the hall."

"Crap." I grab Gabriel from her and sling my guitar over my shoulder. I don't know what to say. How could I have forgotten Gabriel? Am I that preoccupied? And Mimi? Mimi actually returned her to me? I swallow and say, "Thanks."

She nods. We both stand there. A gust of wind blows Mimi's perfectly straight, sleek hair towards me. She doesn't move to fix it like she normally would.

"I'm sorry about Emily," she says.

"Emily?"

"I know it's not you," she says. "I know it's Emily. I think she'll be okay. I've got a feeling."

I can't understand this.

"Then why did you say that to me?"

She shrugs. "I don't know, Belle. You just drive me crazy. You have everything. You always have everything. You're all talented. You had Dylan. You have Tom. You're smart. You've always been smarter than me."

"No, I haven't," I lie.

She arches an eyebrow. "Don't lie. It just drives me crazy. You're so lucky and you're so oblivious. It makes me hate you."

Okay.

She keeps going. "And you're the good girl. You're always the good girl. You can be the horniest person in the universe and still be the good one. And me? Me? I'm the slut. I'm always the slut."

She's right. I don't know why it is, but she's right. If Andrew treated me the way he treated Mimi people would be all over him, but with Mimi, it's like it's expected.

I can't look at her, so I look down at my shoes. I've painted flowers on them. I painted shoes like this for Mimi in eighth grade. I painted some for Emmie freshman year. Emmie.

"I'll kill you if you tell people about Emily," I say, looking up so I can stare her down.

Mimi clears her throat. Her face is pained and she says, "I was always super jealous of Emily."

Eddie Caron drives his truck into the parking lot. He parks. We both watch him leap out, lugging his duffel bag. He waves hi and smiles when he passes, but he looks curious, because, let's face it, how often do Mimi and I talk?

I'm late.

They will have to manage another minute without me.

I readjust Gabriel and ask Mimi, "Why? Why are you jealous of Emmie?"

Even I don't recognize my voice. It sounds so tired. It is almost easier to be enemies with Mimi than have this random, sudden "heart-to-heart," which is worthy of a feel-good talk show, When Cheerleaders and Folk Singers Make Amends.

Mimi flexes her naked toes. "She took you away from me."

I shift Gabriel's weight on my back. The sky has no clouds in it. It's a beautiful sky but it should be raining to match my heart. It should be pouring and gray with no chance of warmth. With all the patience I can gather up, which isn't much, I say, "Mimi you knew I liked Tom and then you stole him away from me. Remember? Eighth grade?"

She shakes her head. "I only did that because you started hanging around Emily."

I think for a second. "No, that was after."

"No," she insists. "It was before."

I don't think that could be true, but I'll let her believe it. "Whatever. You can be really bitchy, Mimi."

She nods. A tear falls out of her eye, just one. She shrugs. "Anyway, I wanted to tell you I'm sorry about Emily. And I can see why you chose her instead of me."

She's crying. Sort of. Mimi is crying.

"Mimi?" I ask her. "Is this about Andrew? Because I can talk to him if you want?"

"Don't bother." She pivots like the amazingly good cheerleader she is and marches off inside. I could go after her, but I don't. I could think about what she just said, but I don't. Instead, I take off inside and head to gymnastics.

You know that super-adrenalinized rush that people have when their loved one is stuck under a car? The emergency surges extra hormones through them and tiny women can heave up SUVs to save their children. That whole thing.

This is what teaching gymnastics is like.

I am in a state of panic the entire three hours. Children wobble on beams. They try to hang upside down with just their toes hanging on to the bars. They attempt to perform back bends and they'll land on their little heads if my arm isn't in the exact right position beneath their spine, holding them up until their arms can do it for them.

Andrew's little sister shows off her almost-walkover.

"Miss Bellie I've almost got it." She puffs up her chest. She tells everyone else, "Miss Bellie has a boyfriend and he's cute …"

All the little girls look at me with big eyes except for Lauren, who is trying to do a back roll off a bleacher. I snag her and carry her in my arms like I'm a fireman rescuing her from a burning building.

"Do you kiss?" Andrew's little sister asks as I set Lauren down.

Lauren wiggles her eyebrows. "Do you make babies? My mommy is trying to make a baby. She's noisy. Making babies is noisy."

Oh yeah, I love gymnastics…

I actually do love it because I don't have to think about anything else while I'm there. I have to think about Andrew's little sister who is trying to do a perfect walkover. I have to think about getting some tissues for Callie Krauss whose nose is running. I have to think about bringing Nick Fowler, our only boy in the beginner class, to the bathroom because he's afraid to go alone.

I do not bring him in.

I get Mike, the swim coach, to do it.

I do not have to think about Em or my mother or Mimi. I do not have to think about seizures or about Tom hopefully coming over tomorrow night, and I don't have to think about the feel of his body against mine, the way his lips would look if they formed the words "I love you." I don't have to think about it at all, because every single part of my body feels it, a warm tingle, an expectation.

"THERE ARE THREE BASIC CHORDS in the key of C," I tell myself while I brush my hair in front of my bedroom mirror. "C. F. G7. There are three basic chords in the key of A minor. A minor. D minor. E7."

This little ritual is supposed to calm me down before the talent show.

It doesn't work.

I keep pulling the brush through my hair. "The ¾ arpeggio strum is a regular arpeggio with the last two notes repeated."

Gabriel sits in the corner, leaning against the wall. If guitars could sigh, I'm sure she'd be doing it quite theatrically right now.

In the mirror my mouth forms the guitar lesson mantras that I use to calm myself down. My hand pulls the brush down through my hair, up through the air, like the strumming of a guitar. My eyes, wide and blue, are my father's eyes. That's what everyone says.

I cross my eyes to blur my image and try to imagine my dad sitting there, on the other side of the mirror, staring back at me. What would he say?

You'll do fine, Bellie Bear, probably, something endearing. I cock my head like a dog, trying to listen.

Then I close my eyes and imagine a man's voice, sort of like mine, vocal chords shaped from genetics and war and aching across a grave. I imagine this voice, this father voice, and it doesn't say anything endearing at all. Instead it orders me, *Go out there and kick some ass.*

My eyes fly open, but it's just me in the mirror, no father ghosts linger there. I giggle and salute myself. "Sir. Yes, sir."

Then I straighten my legs, turn like an army man and haul butt over to Gabriel. I point at her. "You are commanded to kick some guitar ass."

The good thing about a guitar is that it can't tell everyone how crazy you are. It just makes the noise you tell it to. How great is that?

Tom was supposed to drive me over, but my mom pouted and fussed and guilted me into letting her drive. She drops me off and hugs me and tells me she loves me before she zooms back to the house so Jim can pick her up for her "LAST Big Date Before the Trip."

That's what she calls it. Her quote-unquote LAST Big Date. Is it any wonder where I get the dorkiness genes?

"I feel like a bad mother," she says, again.

I fake smile and say again, "It's fine. You aren't a bad mother."

But the truth is, I'm feeling a little abandoned. I'm feeling like this isn't the mother who has always acted like my mother. If I told her about my possible seizures she'd rush into supermom mode again, cancel her date and everything, but that's not what I want. If I told her about Em, she'd do the same thing. But I want her to be free and I want to be free, too. I want us all to be free.

So, I don't say anything, just rush inside the school and to the stage where I have nothing to do but wait.

Pacing back and forth on an empty stage while your classmates file into the audience just behind the fat, heavy blue velvet curtain, which looks like something out of an Elvis movie, is not a good way of dealing with stage fright but I do it anyway because that is the kind of idiot that I am.

From the other side of the curtain some other kind of idiot yells, "Who's gonna suck the most tonight? Any takers?"

"Dylan."

"Naw, that tuba-playing girl."

"Crap. Who cares. As long as we can see through her skirt again."

Last year, Amanda Duffy wore a see-through white dress with lime green Kermit the Frog underwear. Kermit's frog face was right in the front, smiling. Bad choice. People have been calling her Kermie ever since.

I punch the curtain. Dust billows out. A cloud of sloughed-off human skin.

It does not help things. I keep pacing and try to tune out the idiots who will soon be "my audience." One foot marches in front of the other across the wood stage floor, pivot, and back. One foot marches. The other foot marches. Pivot. Again.

Different folk singers have different ways of dealing with stage fright.

Some try to imagine everyone in their underwear. This is not a good idea unless your audience is fantastic looking. If they are not fantastic looking you run the risk of vomiting or laughing hysterically throughout your set.

Some try to imagine they're singing in the shower. That just worries me because then Gabriel would get wet and ruined. It just makes me more neurotic.

Some pretend everyone's paid twelve thousand dollars for their seat because they love them so much. That's a lot of responsibility. Twelve thousand dollars a seat.

I've tried them all and none of it works for me. So, I just clench and unclench my fists backstage. I pace back and forth. I run through the words of my song. I close my eyes. I open my eyes. I count backwards from ten thousand. Basically, it's ridiculous that I'm even nervous. This is nothing compared to what Em is going through, nothing compared to what Eddie goes through.

Dylan scoots up to me and hugs me. "Hey, sweetie."

I smile up at him and kiss his cheek. We do the kiss on the cheek thing that Dylan does with all his female friends. It's kind of funny actually. Now that he's come out, girls are always kissing him.

"You nervous?" Dylan asks me, smiling and showing off all his perfect white teeth.

"Yup."

"Palms tingling?" he asks, grabbing them in his hands and rubbing them.

"Yup." He knows me way too well. "How about you?"

He laughs and puts one of my hands over his heart. "My heart's beating like five hundred times a minute."

"You'll be great," I say, breaking our contact and rocking backwards. I jump up and down on my feet to try to get rid of all this extra energy. "You are a *fantastic* singer."

"So are you."

I shrug.

"You are."

I fake hit him in the shoulder. "Aw, shucks sir, you tell a girl the nicest things."

Anna scoots towards us because she's stage managing and she's all hectic, frazzled and crazy. "You two cannot flirt. You are no longer compatible. Now help me with the lights. Somebody forgot to lift up the lights. Crap-crap. Crap-crap."

She races off and we follow her. Dylan shouts at her butt, "Gay men can still flirt with hot folk singers."

I punch him again. "You think I'm hot?"

He touches me with a finger and makes a sizzling noise. "In that outfit? Obviously."

Anna whirls around. "Oh my God. I'm dying here. Just help me haul up the lights."

We heave on the cord to pull the lights to their proper

position above the stage and then tie them off. Anna leans against the wall, sweating and looking like she's going to puke. Dylan rolls his eyes and heads off to the greenroom to wait his turn.

My hand goes to her shoulder. "Anna, it's going to be alright."

"I get so nervous," she says, wiping her head with the back of her hand. "So many things can go wrong."

"They won't," I say. But I'm not thinking about Anna. I'm thinking about Em telling Shawn, wondering if she's told him, wondering if they are here.

Anna stands up straight, grabs her Palm Pilot where she's got a little checklist going. "How do you know? How do you know they won't go wrong?"

"Because they can't."

She stares. She puts the stylus in her mouth. It dangles like a cigarette.

"You are such an optimist." She puts her arm around my shoulders and pulls me along with her. "Come on and help me make sure everyone's here. We only have twenty minutes 'til show time. Did you know Mimi Cote has an act?"

I freeze in place.

Anna pushes me on. "It's okay. Really. It's a dance number."

"Oh my God. She's never been in the talent show before."

Anna shrugs. "She says she's only doing it to kick your butt. She likes Tom again, you know."

"I know." I clench my fists and realize that I have become a cliché, clenching my fists…in competition with another girl. Who will win? The sweet folk singer or the hideous slut girl who's really just troubled? Folk singers are not supposed to be clichés, easy to read. We are supposed to be originals, pushing beyond societal norms. Okay, we occasionally include a cliché or two in our songs, but still…Oh. Blah. Blah. Blah.

But here I am, a cliché. It's Mimi's fault, of course. She was the cliché first, right? I wear canvas Snoopy shoes. Nobody wears canvas Snoopy shoes, therefore I am not a cliché. Unless I'm the cliché of the girl trying not to be a cliché and assuming she isn't merely because of her offbeat shoe choice…

My head hurts.

I know we were all heart-to-heart this afternoon, but still…

Cliché.

Why is it that the self-realization of your cliché status does not make you stop caring or stop being a cliché? What's the next step? Is there some sort of twelve-step program for this?

"I hate Mimi," I tell Anna. I suppress the urge to stomp on the floor with my Snoopy shoes.

"I'm sure she'll suck."

We enter the greenroom and there she is…Mimi Cote, preening herself in one of the big mirrors. She hikes up her Daisy Duke shorts a little higher. She looks like a hooker or a contestant on some surreal reality show about girls competing to get a job dancing on bars. She catches my eye in the mirror and scowls at me. She checks out my ripped-knee jeans and black off-the-shoulder shirt ensemble and hisses at me. "Sometimes I can't believe you aren't the one that's gay. Where are your hiking boots?"

I glare at her and try to think of something brilliant to say but all I can do is sputter out, "There's nothing wrong with being gay."

This is true, but not a good comeback.

She rolls her eyes. "Tommy could do so much better than you. Like maybe actually date a girl who's not so self-involved."

My mouth drops open. What happened to this afternoon? To our sort of peace? I can't understand anyone. I pivot away, step closer to Dylan.

"Like you aren't." Anna grabs my arm. "Shut up, Mimi. I'm trying to see if everyone's here."

Mimi smirks and moves away, but only an inch.

Dylan gives me a thumbs-up sign from the couch. He's perched on the edge. Bob has his hand on Dylan's thigh. Bob's other hand is on his saxophone. Self-involved. The whole room seems to spin. I back up and zip out the door, intending to race down the hall and get some fresh air.

But instead, I slam into Tom.

"Hey, Hot Stuff, where you going?" he says. He has an armload of irises, my favorite flower.

"Are these for me?"

He smiles big and passes me the flowers, wrapped up in crinkly green paper. "Yep."

I breathe them in. They're beautiful and my heart gets all pitter-patter good. I look up at Tom. "Did Emmie tell you to get them for me? Is she here? Is Shawn here?"

"Of course they're here. They wouldn't miss this. Shawn's already perfecting his whistle." He shakes his head. "Belle. I've watched you do this talent show for three years and every year I've wanted to give you flowers."

My lips tremble. "Really?"

"Really." He leans in and touches my lips with his. He's been chewing cinnamon gum. My knees wobble. He laughs and catches me so I don't lose my balance.

"You are a good boyfriend," I tell him.

"What? There was doubt?"

"I don't deserve you." I rub at my eyes before I remember I'm wearing mascara.

He looks skyward. "Commie…"

"I don't. Do you think I'm self-involved?"

"What?"

"Do you think I'm self-involved?"

If Em and Shawn are here and acting like everything is normal then she hasn't told him yet, right? Ack.

Tom shifts his weight. He's wearing his jeans with the hole in the knee. I love those jeans. "I think it's human nature to be self-involved, Belle."

"So I am?"

He doesn't answer. Instead, he pulls out another flower, a gray duct tape replica of an iris. It's attached to a long, thin, duct tape stem. Tom is really into duct tape.

"This one won't die," he says.

My heart flutters. "I'll keep it forever."

"Promise?"

"Promise."

I point at his jeans. There's a piece of duct tape slashed across his thigh. It says, *"Tell me whom you love and I will tell you who you are"—Houssaye.*

I have no idea who Houssaye is, but I like the quote. I try to flash Tom a sexalicious look. "Nice."

"You knock 'em dead, okay?" He raises his eyebrow. "That's what I say, right?"

"Yeah. Knock 'em dead."

"Knock 'em dead, Commie."

I laugh and start to spin away. "Tom?"

"What?"

"Mimi likes you again."

His cheek muscle twitches. "Commie…"

My heart stops. One beat missed. Two.

His hands move up to my shoulders. "I like you."

"Promise?"

"Promise."

"Would you like me if I started having seizures all the time again?"

His hands drop. "What? Did you have another one?"

I shrug. "No."

"Commie? Did you have another one?" His face pales and whitens.

"No, I was just wondering."

He pulls me back to him, crushing flowers and me against his warm chest. "It wouldn't matter. I swear it wouldn't matter."

In an attempt to calm myself down I pull out my cell and start to text out a list of things to worry about before you go onstage. This is probably not an extremely mentally healthy thing to do.

1. Worry that you will be booed off the stage. Think about Lauryn Hill who this almost happened to at the Apollo. She survived and won Grammys. So will you. Okay. Maybe not a Grammy.

2. Worry you will forget your words.

3. Worry that you will say the wrong words like your mother does when she sings songs. Pray that you will not substitute the f-word for the love word. Start laughing because you imagine your principal, Mr. Raines', reaction to this. Mr. Raines is so uptight, he yells if you hold hands in the halls. "No personal touching, people! Unhand yourselves!"

4. Worry that you will laugh hysterically throughout the entire song because you will imagine Mr. Raines saying, "Unhand yourselves!"

5. Worry that you will look like an idiot. Worry that Mimi Cote will throw used tampons at you, because this is the worst possible thing you can imagine.

Except, maybe, used condoms. Used tampons inside used condoms?

6. Worry that you have a rip in the crotch of your jeans that you do not know about, but everyone will see. Worry that you are somehow magically wearing Kermit the Frog underwear like Amanda Duffy, tuba player.

7. Worry that your gauzy shirt is see-through. Realize that even if it is, the chance of seeing a nipple will make more boys pay attention and vote for you.

8. Worry that you should have definitely worn something see-through because Mimi probably has.

9. Worry that you'll have a seizure.

10. Delete this list.

I can't help it. I'm weak. I sneak out of the greenroom to watch Mimi's act.

She's bumping and grinding to a hip hop number that if I were cooler, I would know what it was, but I am not cool. It has to do with humping or something, but all the hump words are bleeped out. So basically the vocals are, "Let's *bleep*. You want to touch my *bleeps* and *bleeping bleep* my *bleeps* …" etc.

Mimi's mouth gapes open and she rocks her pelvis back and forth, while slinking her hands up her body right by her private parts. I suddenly feel like my mother, talking about private parts instead of just using the proper name. Her pelvic region? Her vagina? Her humps?

I glare at her. In thirty seconds of humping dancing, not only has she turned me into a prude like my mother, she's really just like stripping without taking off her clothes. A lot of the boys in the audience are hooting and whistling.

Tom. Is Tom hooting? Whistling?

The little red light on the sound monitor blinks out a warning.

She's actually good. I mean, I can see her doing this for a living. I can see the balding insurance CEOs sticking their meaty fingers into her G-string along with hundred dollar bills.

The monitor light turns a steady red.

I lean around the curtain and search for Em, Tom and Shawn in the audience. Shawn's fingers are in his mouth, whistling and Em's hitting him in the arm. Gulping, I look for Tom, afraid to look but knowing I have to see. I mean, what if he likes it? What if he's waving?

A giant gulp seems to fill my entire body and jealousy slings through my blood, because I know, I know that no matter how ridiculous Mimi's act is, I could never do that, never just be so openly sexual. I mean, this is me, the girl who dated a gay guy for almost three years, the girl who still hasn't had sex with her current guy, even though she really wants to. And you've kind of got to be proud of Mimi in a way because she isn't afraid of being sexalicious, it's just...it's like it's all she is, or all she pretends to be, really.

My eyes focus on Tom. He doesn't drool. He doesn't look all excited. Instead, he laughs, puts his head in his hands, and doubles over.

I smile and say, "Good boyfriend."

But I don't get to enjoy the feeling long because Mr. Raines bashes past me, a man on a mission. He bangs into my side without even seeing me. He pushes me against the soundboard. My hip shrieks out pain as it accidentally flips some switches.

"Off! Off! Off the stage now!" Mr. Raines screams and grabs Mimi's bare arm. He yanks her towards the side. The music shrieks out something from The Phantom of the Opera instead of the humping song.

I jump away from the soundboard. I must have hit something. There are four red lights showing now. Frantic, I search for the right switch. Grab it and turn it off. The world is silent. The lights are now green.

I press my hand against my hip. It is going to bruise.

Anna comes trundling into the area as soon as Mr. Raines shoves Mimi to stage left. She puts her hands on her forehead, frantic. "Oh my God. I am so dead."

She whirls on Mimi. "That was not the song you rehearsed."

Mimi smiles. "I wanted more of a reaction."

"Well, you got one," I say, putting my arm around Anna, who is shaking she's so mad.

Mr. Raines' footsteps echo across the stage. Nobody in the audience says anything.

He takes center stage. "I am appalled at the lack of judgment that has just been displayed here and I apologize to any parents that might be in the audience. This talent show is canceled."

My heart thuds into something painful. Canceled?

No one says anything. I swear no one is even breathing. It's so silent as Mr. Raines stomps off the stage. Dust falls off the velvet stage curtain. It spreads into a cloud and mixes with air.

Mr. Raines points a long, thick finger at Anna and then at Mimi. "You two. In my office now."

I cling to Anna's shoulder. "It wasn't Anna's fault!"

He whips his finger at me. "Do you want to join them, Miss Philbrick?"

"It wasn't her fault. That's not what Mimi practiced," I

say in a softer voice as Anna moves away from me so I don't get in trouble too.

Mr. Raines stares at all of us, one at a time. His hawk eyes glint in the darkness of the offstage area. The green lights on the soundboard blink.

And in the audience I can hear Shawn's voice. "Bell-ie. Bell-ie."

Em's voice chants with him and then Tom's. "Bell-ie. Bell-ie."

The chant becomes a roar that is my name, but is bigger than my name, really. My cheeks flame red, but my heart, it starts a happy little dance number in my chest...not a Mimi-style slut number, but more like a gigantic puppy doing the hokey pokey.

"Bell-ie. Bell-ie."

Mimi squints her eyes at me and her pointy, painted red nails squeeze her naked arms so tightly that they make marks. I toss an embarrassed smile at Mr. Raines. He wants none of it and storms out onto the stage.

"There will be no bellies on this stage tonight. There will be no derrières, no shoulders, no arm pits, groins or any other body parts either! Now go home or you will all have detentions!"

He roars off the stage, grabs Anna and Mimi by the arms and flies off to his office. I can't help it, I double over laughing. It's like "unhand yourself" or even better. It's amazing that someone who has no clue can be in charge of a school.

I stand there for a second, watching them. The must of the stage curtains heavies the air. Behind it come the sounds of people in the audience figuring out the rest of their nights. Tom and Em and Shawn are out there, waiting for me and we'll all do something. Maybe go get pizza. Maybe we'll drive out to Mount Desert Island and hang out at the beach, look up at the stars.

There's this part of me that wishes I were more like Mimi. Em would say that I wish I were a little more slutty, but that's the wrong way of putting it, that's an anti-woman way of putting it, like having sexual needs equals being a slut.

Of course, saying "I have sexual needs" sounds like some sort of self-help mumbo-jumbo that menopausal woman in an Explore Yourself! (And You'll Find Love) Group would say.

My Snoopy shoes are old and comfortable and goofy. My shirt is slightly sexy. What am I, though? That's the big question. And the truth of it is, I'm sure that Mimi would have had sex with Tom by now. She would have worn her Daisy Dukes and smiled and that would be it.

Me?

I'm stuck taking cold showers after every time we kiss, but tomorrow night things will change, I think, if I still want them to.

I grab Gabriel, tell everyone in the greenroom what happened. They all start shrieking and swearing and condemning Mr. Raines for being a dictator. I leave them raging and meet Tom, Em and Shawn in the hallway.

Tom hugs me while Shawn announces to the universe, "Mimi sucks."

"And she thinks she's sexy. She is so stupid." Em is all anger and indignation. Her head wiggles while she talks. "She ruined the entire talent show. And you!"

She jabs her finger at Shawn. "You thought she was sexy!"

He steps back, laughing and shaking his head. "No. I didn't."

"You whistled." She narrows her eyes at him.

"It was funny."

"You're telling me it was a mock whistle?"

"Yeah."

She crosses her arms and stares at him.

Tom kisses me on the top of my head and lets me go. "I'm sorry you didn't get to sing your new song."

I shrug just as Shawn grabs me by the shoulders. He spins me around to face him. He's a real physical guy, Shawn. He handles people like they're baseball bats and soccer balls and he's got this energy that just overwhelms you. It's hard to imagine anyone more alive or happier. Em starts smiling again at him, so she's probably forgiven him for whistling at Mimi. I know I have.

He beams at me. "You want to sing your song?"

I bite my lip and nod. "Yeah."

"Then you will," he says. "This whole thing is just shit. I can't believe Raines. I've got an idea."

----o----

Shawn calls his mom, who is pretty poor, but kind of a hippie and really, really nice. She's the mom who will always say okay to anyone's plans. She's a cashier at Green Whole Planet Foods, the health food co-op. After the call, Shawn, Tom and Em race around the parking lot rounding up people and telling them his idea.

We all drive to his house.

I grab Em before we go in. "You haven't told him?"

She yanks a sweatshirt out of the car. "It would've ruined the talent show."

"Em…" My voice is almost scolding.

"I didn't want to ruin your night." She yanks her arms

through the sleeves. The zipper gets stuck. I pull it out of the fabric for her.

"You want me to tell him?"

She shakes her head.

Shawn yells back from the front door, "You guys coming?"

"He's so happy," Em sighs out. Then she sturdies herself up. She takes my hand. "Come on. Stop worrying. It will be fine."

Shawn's mom has already started popping popcorn on the stove and in the microwave. She smiles her movie-star smile and moves some of the dirty blonde hair out of her mouth. "You girls help me with the popcorn while the boys move the furniture."

Shawn and Tom head into the basement and start moving couches and chairs out of the way so that there's a big space. Em and I set out bowls of popcorn. When we run out, we put the popcorn in canvas grocery bags and in glasses.

Shawn's mom hugs me and smiles. "This is so fun!"

"We're taking over your house," I say and then I imagine a white highchair pushed in the corner, felty baby toys tossed all over the floor.

She shrugs, fingers the rose quartz crystal that hangs from a chain on her neck. "Just the basement. Plus, I get my own private concert. Some day, I'll get to say the famous Belle Philbrick gave a concert in my basement."

"I doubt I'll ever be famous," I say.

Em groans, peers into the microwave and announces, "Needy, fake self-deprecation alert!"

Shawn's mom just shakes her head, leans against the kitchen counter. "I know you will. You know you will. Shawn talks about how good you are all the time."

"Really?"

She nods and this time we both smile.

Em crosses her arms and sputts out a breath. Then she gives up and shoves a handful of popcorn in her mouth. Shawn's mom notices and rushes over to her and wraps her arms around Em's rigid shoulders. "He loves you, little pumpkin. Don't you worry about that a bit. You should hear him talk about your pictures. He is so proud of you."

"Yeah?" Em asks, chewing.

Shawn's mom pushes Em's model hair away from her face so that she can look into Emily's eyes. "I swear. There's a lot of talent in this room. Eastbrook's a lucky town and Shawn's a lucky boy to have you as a girlfriend and Belle as a friend."

"I'm the lucky one." Em's eyes actually water. She rubs at them with the back of her hand. I've never seen her cry over a boy our entire lives. I pour some popcorn into a bag and try not to look.

Shawn's mom just nods. "We all are."

It seems like the entire senior class (minus Mimi) and half of all the juniors show up and smoosh into Shawn's basement, which is unbelievable.

"Did you lie and say you had a keg?" I ask Shawn.

"No. They're here for you, Belle." Shawn shakes his head at me.

"No, they aren't."

"Yeah. They are." He eyeballs me and says, "When are you going to stop pretending you aren't popular?"

"I'm not popular," I insist. I check out the crowd a little more. "I'm really not. It's not like I'm a blonde cheerleader or something, or one of those fashionista girls with all the clothes."

"Nobody in Eastbrook is like that, Belle." Shawn takes me by the shoulders and turns me in a circle. "That's media crap. That's what they pretend real people are like, but that's not what we are. So suck it up and admit it. You're popular."

I shiver, because to me being popular is being shallow, but what if that's just what I've been programmed to think from books and radio and movies? What if that's not really how it is at all?

"I'm not 'popular,'" I say again, making finger quotes, but even I can hear the weakness in my voice.

"Then why are all these people here?"

"Maybe because you're popular. Maybe because they want to just hang out."

Em comes over and hugs herself into Shawn's side.

"What's up?" she asks.

"Belle's pretending like she's not popular again."

Em glares at me. "You are so stupid sometimes, Bellie. I love you, but sometimes you're stupid."

I swallow hard, angry.

Tom duct tapes a couple of planks on top of the pool table so it is like a stage and I look to him for help, but he has no idea anything's going on.

"Hey Belle," Andrew says, smiling at me.

Anna and Kara give me big hugs and tell me how psyched they are. Crash bounces down the stage and yells, "BEL-LIE!!!"

"See?" Shawn says.

"She craves attention but her craving embarrasses her," Em says.

"Will you shut up?" I yell at her and turn away towards the stage. I slip through the crowd and get to Tom's side. He grins when he sees me and puts his hands on either side of my waist.

I whisper into his ear, "Do you think I'm popular?"

I sound like a fifth grader.

He laughs. "Yes."

I shake my head.

"You like your stage?" he asks me, waiting for approval, I guess.

"It's beautiful. You are so good with duct tape."

He smiles broader and lifts me up. His eyes twinkle. Then he hands me Gabriel. I pull her strap over my shoulder.

Standing on the stage, Gabriel in my hands, I survey the crowd. Dylan gives me a thumbs-up sign. Tom just leans against a wall and smiles. Then it's her. Mimi. She tromps down the stairs with Brittney. She snarls, I mean, smiles, at me. It's fake.

I clear my throat, try not to be nervous. "It was really nice of you guys all to come here. I mean, there's no free beer or anything."

People laugh. Anna yells, "Aw, darn, I'm leaving."

Nobody moves except Crash. He's short and super energetic. He's jumping up and down trying to see. He gives me the finger, smiling, and starts laughing.

"Um, I hope I...um...don't disappoint you or anything." I shiver. I can't believe they all came, just to hear me. Realizing you might be popular carries a certain amount of responsibility, maybe that's why I never thought I was, maybe I was just trying not to live up to it, not to deal with another responsibility.

Mimi is still standing on the stairs with her legs wide apart like a country singer on stage. She's changed into a mini, which you can totally see up. How do I know this? I know this because of the two guys beneath her who have this look dogs get when they see a rump steak. She is getting the attention she craves, yep.

"Um..."

Maybe Em's right, I crave attention too but I don't want the crud that goes with it. I shiver again and tuck some hair behind my ear. God, I am so not focused.

"Just sing, Bellie," Shawn yells.

Tom winks at me and my hands warm up. Mimi trots down the rest of the stairs and starts pushing her way towards Tom.

I catch Shawn's mom's eye. "Okay. I'm going to do a new song. And I'd like to dedicate it to Shawn's mom, because, well, she really rocks you know…I mean she's let us take over her house."

"To MOM!!!!" Shawn yells and he grabs her into a bear hug and lifts her tall, thin body up into the air and swirls her around. She giggles and pumps her fist. Everyone yells, especially Crash. He's convinced Kara Raymond to let him balance on her shoulders. She cringes even though he's light.

So when Shawn puts his mom down, I start my song. I do not like Mimi standing right behind Tom practically pressing her boobs into his back. I don't look at Tom. I decide to look at Em and Shawn and Shawn's ridiculously in-love, happy face because I want his face to stay that way forever.

Okay, there's something about song lyrics that always make them look trite and corny when they're written down. Music inflates them to another level, I think. But I sing,

> *There's a girl sitting in a cemetery, clutching*
> *her stomach, all alone.*
> *There's a boy who's gone. He's never coming*
> *home.*
> *There's a mother with her head buried in her*
> *hands.*
> *There's a coffin shipped in from foreign lands.*

I brave up and catch Tom's eye. He nods at me, tilts his head, and smiles. His fingers are quiet, not a piece of duct tape anywhere in sight, while mine fly through the chords.

> *We journey through lost in silence and alone.*
> *We journey through when we feel it's gone on*
> *too long.*

Em gives me a thumbs-up sign and smiles. Shawn's arms wrap around her, like he's holding her into forever. They sway to the music. And I know it's corny. I know it's all corny, but it's also good you know, right in this second, if I could just stay in this second.

It's funny because the walls of the basement are reflecting the sound, which means that my notes hit them multiple times; first when I sing them, but then when they bounce off the ceiling and the walls. It's like there's true sound and reflected sound and it's all mixing up, adding layers and vibrations, but still sounding good.

I keep singing.

> *We journey through when we can't anymore*
> *We journey through*
> *Past the truth of broken hearts and fallen*
> *dreams.*

Shawn's mom flicks on a lighter and sways on the basement stairs. It's so funny and cheesy that I almost start to laugh, which would be horrible, because it's the emotional crescendo part.

> *We journey through.*

After I sing a couple of Cliff Eberhardt covers and put Gabriel down, Tom lifts me off our little makeshift stage and twirls me around, just like Shawn did to his mom. The world dizzies in a good, good way. I will not be jealous. I will not be jealous of Mimi. I will not be insecure. I will not be jealous. It's like I'm chant-chanting this in my head.

"Do you know how proud I am of you?" Tom says. And I slide down his body, pressed up next to him and he kisses me full and long on my lips.

People whoop and Emily yells, "Well that's a little bit hotter than a Mimi Cote dance."

Tom laughs and touches my cheek. "You're blushing."

"I'm embarrassed."

People press in around us, telling me how cool it was.

"But happy?" Tom asks.

"Yeah, happy," I say, looking for Mimi. He keeps me close as everyone starts milling around, shoving popcorn into their mouths, wondering what to do. I catch Dylan's eye. He's standing by the couch. Bob's right at his elbow, as usual, but I'm not worried about Bob. I'm worried about Dylan and the longing look in his eyes. That longing isn't for me. That longing is for an audience.

"We need a slow song," I yell. "Dylan, why don't you sing us a couple slow songs?"

He smiles and all the people who were calling him fag and queer a few months ago cheer him on. Dylan's their golden boy again. Thank God. Even small towns that pretend to be cities can learn, I think. Or at least most of the people in small towns can learn.

"We need someone who can actually sing is what we need," Mimi says.

I ignore Mimi.

"Kara," I grab her elbow. "Want to play Gabriel? And help him out?"

Her eyes light up. "Really? You'd let me play her?"

"Yeah," I nod.

Shawn helps Kara up onto the pool table where she and Dylan confer. She smiles when she plays Gabriel, tentative and competent. Dylan's voice mellows out into the basement and wraps itself around all of us. Tom holds me against him and we dance. It isn't like we're in a basement with a concrete floor and exposed pipes in the ceiling. It's like we're somewhere else entirely, somewhere with stars and dreams and magic.

Tom touches my face so that I look at him, and whispers, "You're thinking goofy girl things aren't you?"

"Yeah."

His lips move into a smile and then he brings them next to my ear. "I like those goofy girl things about you."

I lean in. Shiver. I inhale his smell and lean my face against his chest. "You do?"

"Yeah, I do."

- - - - o - - - -

I think I've just squashed a mosquito.

- - - - o - - - -

When Tom brings me home it's all I can do to let him drive off in his black truck with all the duct tape everywhere. I know this is all about lust, which research shows is a chemical reaction that eventually wears off…blah, blah, blah. Yeah, I'm up on my Internet science. Still, it's like this physical ripping when he goes away.

"I don't want you to go," I whisper and it's suddenly so urgent, like if he leaves I'll never see him again, like he's going off to war, or college, or something, like he'll die. Every single atom in my body just leans towards him and wants to mingle with his atoms, or something. "I wish you didn't always have to go."

"Me too, Commie," his voice is husky, almost a whisper, but not quite. It makes me swallow.

We stand on my front steps. I hold my flowers in my hand. Gabriel leans up against the railing. All the lights in all the houses on my street are off. Everybody's in bed and happy with their dozing dreams. Then there's us under the front light, leaning into each other like trees that have been blown by too much sea wind, weighed down by too much ice, leaning into each other because that's the only way we'll keep standing up.

Wow. I'm thinking in song lyrics when I really shouldn't be thinking at all.

Tom's mouth finds my mouth. Tom's mouth finds my ear. Tom's mouth finds my neck. Tom's mouth would be very good at hide-and-seek.

"My mom's going away tomorrow," I say even though he already knows this.

He pulls his mouth away, just a whisper-inch. "Yeah?"

He says that like he doesn't know.

His breath hits my neck. I tremble. I tuck my head down against his chest so I don't have to see his reaction.

"Maybe you could stay over tomorrow? We don't have to do anything. We could just platonically sleep together, hang out, you know…You wouldn't have to leave?"

My words trail into the air, move past the circle of light, float into the darkness of the street. I cannot believe I said that. For a second I almost wish I could text Mimi Cote and ask her what to say.

Tom cups my chin in his hand, raises my head so that our eyes meet. He studies me. "Yeah?"

I shrug like it's no big deal. "Yeah."

He takes a step away but keeps his hands on my hips. He shakes his head. His voice deep like the sky at night. "Belle, if I stay here all night with you…I don't know if I could not do anything."

He moves one of his hands, lifts up his knee and rips a small piece of duct tape off his shoe. He folds it onto itself with one hand. I grab his hand in my own. "Tom?"

He looks at me again. The sky has no stars.

"That's okay," I say. "I mean, I don't think I'd want to not do anything. I mean…"

Words suck don't they? Because words just can't explain anything. I keep trying. "Because I mean, I think I want to, you know…"

His cheek twitches but his fingers are still beneath mine. "Yeah?"

"Yeah."

And I do. I do. I do. I do, but also what I really want, what I really, really want is to not connect this want with Em and Shawn and what's happening with them. And what I really, really, really want is to know that Tom loves me. I mean, I think he does, but how do you ever know? I thought Dylan did and I was wrong, wrong, wrong. How do you know when you're right?

How can I even want this when Emmie is pregnant? I don't know. I don't know, but I do.

One of the worst things about a bed is when it's empty and you want someone in it. It's like all the space around your body, all that space that was so normal before, it becomes a

vast plain, a prairie land. It becomes longing and the empti-
ness of the cold sheets presses against you.

I flop down on it, pull my covers to my chin, and stare
into the darkness of my ceiling.

"Honey? You have a good time?" my mom's sleep voice
calls from her bedroom.

"Yep. How about you?"

"It was nice."

"He didn't try anything did he?"

She giggles. My mother actually giggles. I sit up in my
bed. What has happened to my world?

"No. He was a perfect gentleman."

"Oh," I say staring into the blackness. "That's too bad."

My mom starts laughing really hard and yells good night.
I flop back down. Muffin jumps onto my bed and lands on
my stomach with an oof. She rotates so that her tail brushes
against my nose.

"I'm glad you're home safe," my mom calls, breaking the
nothingness again.

I groan and throw the pillow over my head, breathing in
the fabric softener smell. I am safe, safe, too safe and I want to
be wild, to tell Tom I love him, to sleep with him in my bed
and be free, free, free like words that float into the night.

She starts singing a lullaby in her sleep voice, screwing
up the words: "Rock don't lie lady, on the tip top. When the
wine flows, the candles will rock."

God. I want to be like Muffin and arch my back and
purr and do whatever is necessary to get my tuna and to have
people scratch me under my chin.

But instead I'm "safe."

What Is Safe?

1. Safe is not having sex.
2. Safe is not doing everything to get what I want.
3. Safe is a label.
4. Safe is very cool for fundamentalists. I am not a fundamentalist.
5. Safe is something I never used to be, not before, not with Dylan.
6. Safe is something Em and Shawn obviously weren't.
7. Safe is a word, just a word.
8. Safe is not having sex. I said that already.
9. Wait. It's more than that. It's more than just the sex thing. I just want to wake up in the morning with Tom beside me. I want to see pillow creases in the side of his face. I want to watch him stretch and open his eyes. I want the comfort that married people have, that sort of security. Yeah, it's false security. Married people cheat. Married people die. But I want it anyway. I want that dream.

SHE'S PREGNANT.

How can she be pregnant?

AT THE FRONT DOOR, MY mother kisses me on the top of the head for the 178th time. "You're sure you'll be okay?"

Her shaking hand picks up her suitcase. I take it from her and load it into the back of her car. "I'll be fine, Mom."

"You'll call me if you need anything?"

"Yes."

"You know my cell phone number?"

"Mom, I've known your cell phone number since I was like seven."

A yellow school bus bumps down the road in front of our house. Some little girls wave at us. Bethany, Toni, Samantha. I teach them gymnastics. I wave back as the bus swings away. Then I slam the trunk and pull my mom into a hug. She leans in and hugs back, tension easing out of her muscles for just a moment.

"You don't feel like I'm abandoning you," she says into my hair.

"No. I don't feel like my mommy's abandoning me. I'm a berry brave widdle girl," I say, because the only way my mom's going to make it through this is if I make her laugh. "I am a berry, berry responsible widdle girl."

It works.

She tweaks my nose. "You're fresh."

"Better than stale."

My mother doesn't care about whether I sometimes lapse into geek talk or not, she just hugs me again, makes me recite her phone number and then waves as Eddie Caron's dad backs Eddie's truck out of the driveway. He looks so sober and calm, even kind, but he hit Eddie the other night, just hit him.

"Where's your car?" my mom yells to Mr. Caron.

"Getting new tires!" he yells back. His hand smooths his bald head. "You have a good trip. We'll keep an eye out for your Belle for you."

My mom smiles, all lit up. "Thanks."

He drives off. My mom shakes her head. "He's such a nice man, it must kill him to have Eddie turn out the way he did."

Such a nice man?

"Eddie's not that bad," I say, opening her car door for her. "You're going to be late."

"He hurt you, Belle," she says, forcing me to look in her eyes. "You didn't deserve that."

"It's over now."

She shakes her head. "Thank goodness."

When she's finally in the car and driving off to the airport I realize it. This, this little conversation that just happened between the two of us, this is what Em will be doing some day. She'll be hugging the secret in her belly goodbye. She'll be worrying that her little girl or her little boy will get into trouble when he or she is out of sight. She'll be acting like a mom, not like a goofy girl dancing in the hallway, teasing the teachers. That Emily, my Emily, will be gone, forever gone.

I gulp and swallow. I go back inside my mom-gone house and get ready for school.

Since Tom drives me to school today, I don't see Em until I get to her locker. She's standing there, just staring into the mess of it. Her Hello Kitty mirror is crooked. Books pile on top of crumpled papers.

"Em?"

I'm almost afraid to speak her name.

"Em?"

Dylan saunters closer. He cocks his head at me and stops.

"What's up?" he asks. His green eyes narrow a little bit, like he's trying to figure things out. "You and Em fighting?"

I shake my head, try again, this time reaching out to touch her shoulder, "Em? You okay?"

She jumps, whirls around. Sorrow coats her features. "What?"

I drop my law notebook. Dylan scoops it up and in that second Em recovers. She manipulates her mouth into a smile. "I must've been zoning out."

Dylan hands me my notebook. I hug it to my chest. "Thanks."

"No problem." He eyes Em, shifts his backpack's weight on his big shoulder. "You need more sleep, Emily. You're looking pale."

"Thanks. Nice thing to say," she says. She starts walking away from her locker, doesn't even shut it.

"Em," I grab her arm. "Your notebook."

"Oh, right." She pivots, grabs it, shuts the locker and starts walking away again.

Dylan doesn't even bother to pretend not to notice. "Is she okay?"

"No," I say.

"What's up?"

"I can't talk about it." I cringe. I can actually feel myself cringe. "I'm sorry. It's not because I don't trust you or anything. It's just...Everything will be fine."

And I give this pathetic finger wave and race to catch up with Emmie.

"You have to tell him," I say. "This is killing you."

She glares at me and we scramble into Law just as the

late bell rings. We slam our butts into our desk chairs before our teacher can give us detention.

Stupid idiot Mimi Cote says, "I think Em and Belle are late, Mr. Richter. Shouldn't you give them detention?"

He tugs at his chinos, making them a little higher. Mr. Richter has pants-falling-off-the-buttocks disease, which most often manifests itself in plumbers and grandpas who wear tightie-whities.

Unfortunately, the disease has spread to teachers. Mr. Richter also wears "briefs." Em and I believe there is a definite link.

"They're fine, Mimi," he says. "But thank you for your vigilance."

Mr. Richter's eyes try to keep away from Mimi's cleavage, which is quite ripe today, almost as if she's planning on breast-feeding, right here, right now. She probably is, only not a baby. She doesn't have a baby. Just guys she wants to make babies with. Tom, of course, is at the top of that list.

She pouts and slams back in her chair. Her cleavage responds appropriately. Mr. Richter's eyes bug out and then he looks away, tugging up his pants again. "Today, class, we'll discuss the writ of habeas corpus."

Shawn winks at Em across the room and mouths the words, "I love you."

She mouths back, "I love you, too."

Like the evil, psychic bitch she is, Mimi leans forward and whispers loud to Brittney, "Tom still hasn't said the l-word to Belle."

"Really?" Brittney's voice goes snarky. "He's smart as well as cute."

She puts all the stress on smart, like she's brilliant for knowing a word that's over four letters and doesn't end in "ly."

"He's got standards," Mimi laughs.

They both turn and stare at me. They wave. I swallow and smile like I don't care, but this big cough starts rumbling up from the center of my chest and it threatens to swallow me whole.

How Not to Kill Someone in Law Class

1. Smile at them, because that's almost as good as murdering them with a pencil sharpener blow to the temple, because they can't figure out why you'd be smiling.

2. Do not think about what they said. Instead, focus really, really hard on the phrase, writ of habeus corpus.

3. Try not to think about how corpus sounds like corpse-us.

4. Realize that making someone a corpse means you will probably go to jail.

5. Realize that women prisoners always seem to have split ends and really dried-out broom witch hair.

6. You do not want that kind of hair.

7. Tom will never love you if you have that kind of hair.

8. That's not true. He's not shallow.

9. It's not like he loves you anyway, is it?

10. Wonder why you start referring to yourself as you in these lists instead of I. Is it for some emotional distance? Some way to make it easier to deal?

11. Give up thinking altogether. Doodle pictures of Mimi in her hideously bad clothes. Do not feel guilty. It's not as bad as murder is it? There's no jail time for doodling.

12. Wonder if you would have seizures in jail because life in jail has got to be stressful. You'd hit your head on the concrete, because jail cells are concrete, aren't they? That would most likely result in brain damage or something. Wonder why you had a seizure the other day at all.

Despite the tiny segment on habeas corpus, we spend the class jawing about abortion again. Em takes off before I can talk to her. Shawn rushes after her. I bump my hip into my desk. Andrew comes over.

"You okay?" he says. He's wearing his baseball shirt. They've got a game this afternoon. I wonder if Em will use that as her new excuse not to tell, not that she needs an excuse but...

"Belle?" Andrew touches my shoulder. "I was talking to you."

My stomach cramps up. "I'm sorry. I'm so zoned out."

"Your hip okay?" he asks. "You smashed it."

Bob comes into the room. It's already filling up with people.

I nod. "I'm good. Just an idiot."

"You and me both," he says as we take off into the hall, which is swarming with people. Soon they'll all be talking about Em and Shawn. Soon nobody will be asking me if I'm okay because they'll know that I'm worried about Em.

"We're going to be late for English," I say.

Andrew shrugs.

I shrug too, because really I just don't care.

Tom finds me right before lunch. He flashes this killer smile that almost makes me forget how worried I am about things. I touch the sleeve of his baseball uniform. It's such a funny material, stiff and starchy.

"You want to take off?" he asks.

I lean against the locker next to mine. "We're not supposed to leave the building."

Tom whips up two pieces of paper from behind his back. "I've got passes."

Snatching them out of his hand I say, "How'd you do that?"

"I've got my ways."

"You were flirting with Mrs. Romer again?"

Mrs. Romer is the high school secretary. She responds very well to flirting baseball boys, especially ones named Tom who have a proclivity towards duct tape.

"I can't reveal my sources. It ruins the mystery." He slings a backpack that was on the floor up onto his shoulder and reaches out his hand to me.

"What about Em and Shawn?"

"They're having their own romantic dinner in the cafeteria."

"So they know we're ditching them?"

"Yep. C'mon," he says and wiggles his fingers, which are amazingly free of duct tape and just show dark, naked skin.

I take those fingers in my pale ones, my pale guitar-callused ones, and follow him out of the school. In that second I would follow him anywhere.

He takes me towards the baseball field.

"Oh, this is romantic," I say, joking. "Baseball."

He squeezes my hand tighter. "Give it a second, Commie."

We walk around behind the dugout. There's a blanket spread out already and a little duct tape vase with real roses inside of it.

"I'm sorry there's only three," he says, gesturing at the roses. They are pink and lovely, delicate and colorful against the gray of the duct tape and the washed-out boards of the dugout. My breath sucks into my lungs in a good, good way.

I shake my head. "They're beautiful. How do you keep the vase from falling over?"

I turn my face to smile up at him. He smiles down at me and leans in. His lips, soft and warm, brush against mine. My body gestures against his. He lets it, leans in and then steps away, sighing.

My body feels suddenly empty. Someone honks a horn up at the school parking lot. Then a car alarm goes off. Tom gives his half smile and says, "This was supposed to be romantic."

"It is," I say and pull him down to the blanket. A little ant parade marches through a far corner. I do *not* point it out, but it makes me think of Em having lunch inside with Shawn. I wonder if she'll tell him. I wonder what he'll say.

"Em and Shawn must be wondering where we are," I say, trailing a finger down the muscle line in one of Tom's calves. I will not feel guilty about this. I refuse.

"Commie, I told you I told them." He pulls out a bottle of ginger ale (aspartame free) and a couple of plastic wine glasses. He holds them up. "It's not the real thing, but...we don't want to get expelled."

"Mrs. Romer would never forgive me," I giggle. Yes, I have lost it. I have actually giggled. What would my woman friends in Students for Social Justice think?

Tom pulls out sandwiches. God, he is so sweet and nice and good. And sexy. Very, very sexy.

"Cucumber," he announces.

"Those are my favorite."

"I know," his eyes twinkle.

I forget about the ants. He pours the ginger ale.

"Can I help at all?"

"No." He gives me a glass. He raises his. I raise mine. My hands shake. The glasses catch the sunlight. Little bubbles float up to the surface, excited to be out into the big world of carbonation. They pop.

Tom clears his throat. I lean my head back against the rough wood of the dugout and watch him. He's so beautiful, dark and strong. He itches behind his ear and clears his throat again before he says, "Belle. I wanted to tell you this after...you know...after you told me or after we did it because I didn't want you to think that I was only telling you because I wanted to Andrew you, you know, because I just wanted to use you."

"I don't think you want to use me," I say, and I lose my toughness and I look down at the ants marching, their determined line. They know where they're going, even if someone drops a rock in their path, those ants will just find their way around it and keep on marching towards their destination. Why can't people be more like that? Why can't I? It would be nice to know where it is I'm going, and how to get there, to find that straight line.

Tom's voice makes me look up again. "I would never use you, Belle."

I swallow. It's as hard as swallowing an oyster. "Swear?"

"Swear. It's just, I mean, I love my mom, but I don't want you to end up like my mom. I mean, if something happens..."

Like it has to Em, I finish for him, but he doesn't know that. He only knows about his mom looking lonely, staring out the window. But it doesn't have to be that way, does it? She made choices. She keeps making choices. Then I think about something.

"Are you more worried about me becoming your mom or you becoming your dad?"

He rocks back on his heels. "Both, I guess. But my dad, he got his dreams sort of, you know?"

"I know."

"But I don't want you to think the reason we haven't done it has to do with me liking someone else, or you having seizures or anything like that."

"Or that I'm not sexy enough?"

He laughs. "You are definitely sexy enough."

Then his eyes soften into something sweet and good and my heart hiccups and my hands shake more because his mouth opens and he says it, he just says it. "I love you, Commie. I really really love you."

----o----

In books and movies the big music would swell up and loftily hit a crescendo. In books and movies I would immediately throw myself into his arms because he, Tom Tanner, love interest of the protagonist, has finally said he loves me. And it wasn't under duress.

Cue: protagonist looks in awe.

Cue: two white birds flying over head. Okay, yeah, they are seagulls, but whatever.

Cue: tears come to our heroine's eyes.

If it were a thriller then the bad guy terrorists with the German accents would start spreading sniper fire at the couple, causing them to dive behind the dugout before returning fire.

If it were a romance the heroine (me!) would fall into her man's arms, swooning and covering him with desperate kisses.

If it were a surrealist adventure a dead zombie pig decked out as a police officer/clown would walk across their picnic basket, snorting.

If it were a romantic comedy the female love interest would hit the male love interest and say, "What the hell took you so long?"

She would say this sweetly, yet with passion and good humor.

But it is none of these things.

I do none of these things.

And the zombie cop/clown pig does not show up.

Instead, I do something dumb and typical of me. I say, "Really?"

He nods. "Really."

----o----

I am unbelievably happy. Tom loves me. Tom loves me.

Whatever I said before, about that not mattering, about it just being words was total crap.

Tom loves me.

Em would say I already knew this, but I don't care. Hearing it, out loud, is the best thing in the world. Hearing it, out loud, makes it real.

It's not just words.

I am unbelievably worried. Em's pregnant. I am incredibly happy. Tom actually spoke the word *love* out loud and in connection to me, Belle Philbrick.

These two feelings bash against each other as I walk to biology class. My lips are red and puffy from Tom's kisses. My stomach flip-flops with cucumber sandwich and fear. What do I say to Em? What would a good best friend do right now? Probably not make out behind the baseball dug-out. That is definitely not good best friend behavior.

I pause outside the door and cover my face with my hands. Then I stop. This isn't about me. This is about her, Em. What can I do for her? I don't know. I don't know at all.

I'm afraid to look in my advanced bio class, but there she is, sitting at our lab table, smiling.

I sit down next to her and smile back.

She points at my mouth and wiggles her eyebrows. "Puffy lips. Looks like you guys had fun."

"Yeah." I plop my books on the black top of the lab table.

The bell rings. People still saunter in. Andrew gives us a little jaunty wave. I do not like Andrew anymore. I still wave back and even smile. What is wrong with me? I'm a wave slut. I will wave to everyone.

Em rips a piece of paper out of her notebook. "Did Tom finally say it?"

I nod, but I'm afraid to smile. I'm afraid of being too happy.

"Good," she says and she smiles a smile big enough for both of us. "Good."

----o----

We spend most of biology class with our secret building itself between us, but instead of linking us together it makes me feel further and further apart from Emmie.

I glance at her sideways while Mr. Zeki struts around. She is taking perfect notes in neat lines. Normally, Em is a messy note taker, big loopy letters all over the place. I am the neat one, with my lists and outline forms. She sighs and puffs air out her mouth so that the hair that fell on her face would get out of the way.

"Am I boring you, Emily?" Mr. Zeki approaches our desk. Everyone turns to stare.

Emily's face doesn't change, not even when the infamous Zeki chino crotch is right smack dab in front of her. Once again, like every day, the material stretches out as far as it can go. Once again, like every day, I have to look away and wonder, Does he really roll up a wool sock and shove it down there? Would any man be crazy enough to do that? Andrew. Andrew would. Maybe even Crash, but Crash would do it as a joke because Crash is cool that way.

"You're not boring me," Em says in a sweet, I'm-bored-shitless voice.

"Really?"

"Really."

Mr. Zeki arches an eyebrow. "Really?"

"Really," Em says again and holds up her notebook. "Want to see my notes?"

Mr. Zeki snatches her notebook, brings it to the front, perusing it. "These are actually good."

Em smiles and says in a tone that Mr. Zeki completely doesn't understand is absolutely bitchy and sarcastic, "Really?"

- - - - o - - - -

I give up and write her a note. Why? Because I am a wimp. That's why.

Em,

I think you should tell Shawn, or at least your mom, because I don't think this is something you should have to face alone. Not that you're alone, because I'm here

239

and I'll always be here for you, but I mean it's got to be killing you not telling anybody else and I don't want to see you taking perfect notes and forgetting to take pictures and blowing hair out of your face, because that's not who you are, Emily. This doesn't change who you are, Em. It'll change your life, obviously, but your essential Emily-ness, that's not going to change, and I just think you should tell somebody.

She writes back one word.

Really?

I write back.

Don't be a bitch. Although with all those hormones you probably are going to be bitchy now. So that's okay. Sorry. Forget I told you not to be a bitch. But you are going to have to tell someone. Please. I love you.

She writes back.

Okay.

I write back.

Really?

Really.

Em's Song, Take #2
She dances swirling on the staff notes
Beyond the treble clef
Where I'm left watching,
Emmie,
Emmie in a spinning skirt,
Emmie with the notes
All in front of her playing,
playing,
playing
Until the coda,
until it all ends,
until she falls
Off the sheet music,
waiting for someone to catch her.

WE RUSH OVER TO THE game after our Amnesty International meeting.

Dylan has spent the meeting riffing about these monks who live in Southern Vietnam mostly and who are being arrested and defrocked and murdered because they are Khmer Krom not the other kind of monks. Not one western nation has ever talked to the Vietnamese government about them, even though there's over one million Khmer Krom living there. It's like they don't exist.

"Dylan's really into the monk thing," Em says, flopping onto the grass in an entirely uncareful, unpregnant way.

"It's horrible," I say. "People do horrible things."

"I know," she says stretching her arms over her head. Her shirt rides up. Her belly is still so flat.

I wish I could shut off my brain instead of thinking about Emily's belly, Eddie's dad, or Tom at my house tonight. The sound of a bat whizzing through the air and not hitting anything makes me nervous, almost as nervous as the thought of Tom and me alone in my house, which is in just about two more hours.

Two more hours!

Everything is changing.

I sit on the grass next to Em. She gives me a half smile. She smells like ice cream.

"Strike!" the ump, Mr. Duffy, yells.

"That was high," someone yells back. It sounds like Mr. Haslam. His son is on our team.

"No, it wasn't," I mutter and then clamp my mouth closed because they are talking about the strike zone, not my vocal pitch.

I keep my eyes shut, but I rub my hands together to try

to get rid of the tingling feeling. Em punches me in the arm and I lose my balance, flop over sideways onto the grass.

"You're not watching the game," she says.

"I'm tired of watching games," I grump back and hoist myself back into a sitting position. "I'm worried about everything."

"I know. Me too."

She points behind the big chain fence thing that separates us and home base. Ha. How perfect. Home base, like a home run, like all the way. I groan.

"Your boyfriend's on deck." She chews a piece of her hair like she's five or something. She has supermodel hair, all wild and dark and wavy. She thinks it's a pain. She's so dumb sometimes and simultaneously smart that it kills me.

"On deck?" I ask and pull her hair out of her mouth for her. Pretty soon a baby will be spitting up in that hair, tugging on it.

"Yeah, he's going next." She places her camera on her chest-high knees, peers through the viewfinder. "Want me to take a picture?"

"I can't believe you know baseball terms," I say and grab the camera from her.

"You couldn't survive without me."

"You're the salsa to my guacamole, baby."

She sticks out her tongue.

"What? At least you aren't green and lumpy."

"You made me red and spicy."

"That's good," I say and focus the camera on Tom, zoom in close to his face as he takes practice swings in the batting circle thing. He has a piece of duct tape around the dark skin of his right hand for luck. God, I hope he doesn't have another Shakespeare death quote on there.

I zoom in on the letters: BELLE. He wrote my name. I smile and my insides get tingly just like my hands, only it's a good tingly. I zoom back out. His mouth is a taut, determined line. A muscle in his cheek twitches like it always does when he's mad or has something important to do. I snap the picture, check it out on the screen, and hand the camera back to Emily, pregnant Emily.

"When you're in love you try to learn everything about your significant other," she says, training the camera on Tom. "And you don't even know what 'on deck' means. I bet Tom knows what a G-string is."

"Funny," I say and laugh against my will, because it's funny that a G-string is both a naughty underwear style and a guitar string. I reach over to my gig bag and unzip it, taking Gabriel out. We are pretending everything is normal. Everything is not normal.

Just when I start to strum, Em presses my hand flat against the strings. "Now is not guitar time."

"It's always guitar time."

"No, it's not." A black fly lands on Em's cheek. She moves her hand to swat it off. "Now is Tom time."

I fake sigh and roll my eyes. "Yes, Mom."

I swallow hard. What did I just say?

She doesn't seem to notice, just pulls a *Cosmo* out of her bag and points at it. "Did you know now is a time of great romantic upheaval and confusion?"

"Really."

"Don't be sarcastic. The stars are aligned."

"My stars are always aligned for romantic confusion and upheaval."

"True." She starts sucking on her hair again. "But this is for everyone and for a week. A whole week. Starting yesterday."

"Great."

Andrew strikes out and heads back to the dugout, swearing under his breath.

"That's okay, Andrew," I yell, clapping, and watch Tom amble up to the plate. He looks good in his uniform. You can't have skinny legs in a baseball uniform. Tom doesn't.

"I hope he gets a hit," I say to Em in a much quieter voice.

"That's just so you can watch his butt when he runs," Em says.

"Is not."

"Is too. I'll take a picture of it for you," she laughs.

I perk up. "Really?"

Then I add, "He just gets so sad when he doesn't get a hit. He wants to be perfect."

"Who doesn't?"

Tom shifts his weight, waits out the pitch. It's high and outside.

"Good eye, Tommy boy. Good eye!" Mrs. Darrow, my next-door neighbor yells, clapping.

"Make it come to you!" shouts Coach Chase, smacking his hand against his ample thigh, turning around and spitting out sunflower seeds.

My heart pauses for a second. Baseball is a tense sport. Tom hits the plate with his bat twice and gets back into his baseball stance.

"He is really cute," I say.

"Stop looking at his ass."

"I can't help it. It's sticking out."

"That's how batters stand, Belle." Em sighs and takes another picture.

I tug on the grass and stare at Tom's bottom. Andrew's little sister starts doing cartwheels on the grass in front of us, one after another. She flops on her belly and giggles.

"Good job," I tell her. She smiles big, an ice cream smile. Em takes a picture.

Another pitch flies at Tom. His muscles move. I start sighing. He swings, connects and the ball flies out into left field. Deep into left field, I should say. I jump up and scream. He runs towards first and Em clicks a picture. He runs to second, slides into third.

"That's a triple!" I tell Em.

"Oh, good baseball term," she teases and snaps a picture of me.

"Your boy done good," says Dolly who works at Rite Aid. The sun glints on her blue hair. She takes a deep drag off her cigarette. Andrew's little sister starts with her cartwheels again.

"Thanks." I smile at her and sit back on Tom's jacket.

Em leans over and shows me the picture she shot of Tom at bat. "It's a good butt."

"One of the very best."

"That's for sure," Dolly adds, grabbing the camera. Then she flashes us a Polydent denture smile. She sees the expression on my face and cracks up. "I'm not that old, sugar."

Em bites her lip and Shawn trots up to the plate. He winks at her and then gets into position. It's like her whole body sighs when she sees him. She tucks some hair behind her ear and brings her camera back up to her face. "Did you ever think we'd be sitting here on a beautiful Tuesday afternoon watching baseball?"

"No," I answer honestly. "Did you know Tom is part Penobscot?"

She shrugs. "No."

"That's cool isn't it?"

"I guess, but why is it any cooler than being part anything, you know?"

I don't. I don't know.

"It feels weird that I didn't know that."

"Did you know that I'm one thirty-second Moravian and Jewish?"

"You are?"

"See. It's not like it makes me any different. You don't have to know everything about someone to love them, especially not their ethnic makeup."

"True."

Shawn rockets a ground ball but it's just foul of the first base line. I pick at Gabriel's G-string, plucking it lightly with my finger. One tiny note breezes out into the air.

"Never," I add. "I never thought I'd be watching baseball. I never thought a lot of stuff that's happening would ever happen."

Em doesn't hear me because she's too busy jumping up and down and screaming for Shawn. "Way to go, Baby!!! Way to go!"

Yep. Em gets excited over anything Shawn does, even foul balls, even now.

Andrew's little sister pulls on my sleeve and looks at me with giant blue eyes. "Will you help me with my walk-overs?"

"Okay, honey." I want to watch the game, but it's hard to resist such cuteness. I put away Gabriel, nice and safe in her little gig bag home, then I get on my knees near Andrew's little sister.

"Go into your bridge," I tell her. Shawn fouls off another pitch, this one crashing into the backstop. Em claps her hands and does this tense little bounce that makes her seem all goofy-mom.

"Crud!" Shawn yells.

"It's okay. Good eye! Good eye!" Em yells.

Shawn moves back to the plate.

I hate baseball. It's too tense. I turn back to Andrew's little sister. She bends her little body backwards so that her belly faces the sky and she balances on both hands and feet. I put my hand under the small of her back and try not to laugh at her T-shirt that says "Just Call Me Princess." It's got fudgicle stains all over it.

"Okay Princess, rock back and forth."

She rocks.

Wood hits ball. Shawn makes contact again, a real hit, not foul this time, which means Tom is coming home.

"Okay over," I tell her. I'm trying to hurry her up so I can look at Tom. She pushes up with her feet so that she comes back down to a standing position. It's her first walkover ever.

"I did it! I did it!" She bounces her cute self up and down and jumps into my arms. I hug her smiling and look just in time to see Tom cross the plate, Shawn cruising behind him. Tom pulls off his batting helmet and points at me in a totally on-purpose cheeseball way. I smile at him. He smiles back and the princess kisses my cheek. I tickle her side. She screams, all happy.

Em takes a picture of us. She takes a picture of Shawn and in that moment he looks so happy, but the picture is a lie, really. The picture just shows the surface of things, just one layer of what's happening, not all the truths, all the scariness underneath. It's like a bad movie that just shows two people falling in love, but not all the consequences underneath.

Instead of showing all their wants, all their problems, it just skims the surface, simplifying everything. It's really a lie.

I give up and just say it to Em, risk her being pissed at me. "Em. You don't have to do this. You don't have to be all brave and pretend like nothing is going on."

She glares at me. "Yes, I do."

And then she turns away.

The princess is still so excited she's jumping up and down on her bare feet and she says, "Let's do it one more time."

"Yeah," I say. "Why don't we?"

It's the top of the seventh and the other team is hitting and I have a hard time staying focused, as much as I want to. I am not a baseball person. I never played except in P.E. Why? Well, I stink. But it's also because I could never handle the tension of everyone watching you, waiting to see you drop the ball, miss the pitch, foul up. Baseball fans want so badly for you to win, but you can't win all the time and that's a lot of pressure. I am not into pressure.

I am not a lot of things.

This calls for a list, I think. So, I make one up in my head. I have a thing for lists; they give me a little order. I was one of those kids who had crumpled-up homework, smooshed into their books. I was always losing things, forgetting things. I was smart and everything, but disorganized.

Now, I try to organize everything. It's probably overcompensating, but I don't care.

Things I Am Not

1. I am not a baseball fan because it is too hard to be a baseball fan with all the tension and stuff. Plus, baseball games take forever, especially if they go into extra innings, which is what happens

when there is a tie. Although, to be fair, if a guy has a good gluteus maximus, those extra innings can fly by because baseball uniforms are good at defining the male figure.

2. I am not popular in the POPULAR way, which is that skanky, snarky evil way where people are popular only because they:

   - Drink a lot.
   - Are evil to everyone else, so you have to be nice to them and vote for them for MOST POPULAR or MOST SPIRITED or whatever, because if you don't they'll start talking trash about you and say things like:

     > "You take laxatives."
     > "You're mother spreads her legs for all the guys on her bowling team."
     > "You're a slut."

3. I am not a person who can drink caffeine or have aspartame without having seizures.

4. I am not anonymous, but I would like to be because being famous is too easy. And according to all the surveys, everyone wants to be famous, instantly famous. In a little town like this everybody's famous and everyone's paparazzi. It's anonymity that takes work.

5. I am not pregnant.

6. This list is so stupid.

Em nudges me and I clap because Tom has caught some ball and a guy from the other side is automatically out.

"That Tommy's a good player, Bellie," this crazy lady, who is always trying to convert everyone to her religion yells at me. She winks, and smooths her long, black dress underneath her as she sits down. "That's what happens when you have God in your heart."

I cough. "Yep."

Em stashes her *Cosmo* (TEN HOT TIPS TO MAKE YOUR MAN HOT AND HORNY RIGHT NOW) back in her bag before we get a lecture about Satan and sinners and all that good stuff, which is as American as a baseball game.

Even at a baseball game against the Sumner Tigers (a regional high school from three towns over) you know pretty much everybody. You know the crazy ladies. You know the sunglasses girls like Mimi who all stretch out in their almost-too-short shorts and spaghetti-strap shirts trying to get a tan and impress each other's boyfriends. They snap their gum and rate each other in their heads (fat ass, her left boob's too big, look her nips stick out way too much) and rate other people out loud.

"Look at her butt in those pants. Those are so Goodwill."

They take off their sandals so their feet are bare and they make sticky pink bubbles and blow them up big until they touch everybody around them.

Em and I do not sit close to them.

Mimi whistles and yells, "Way to go, Tommy."

Em stands up like she's going to smack Mimi.

I grab her by the arm and keep her close.

"She called him Tommy," she says.

"She's an idiot."

Tom looks up from the base and waves. At her. At Mimi.

"He waved at her!" I shout.

People look. Mimi looks. She smiles.

Em bites her lip and then says, "Maybe he thought she was you."

"What?"

"No. No. No. You don't look alike. You might sound alike though, and…"

"We sound alike!"

Em gets frantic. She reaches out with her hand and presses my jaw up. "Close your mouth. It's nothing. Okay? It's nothing. You do not sound alike."

My mouth pops open again. "I should have yelled his name."

"You weren't paying attention."

That's the problem.

"A good girlfriend would be paying attention," I moan.

"So, you're not perfect."

"Why aren't I paying attention?"

She lifts her shoulders up. "You're too busy obsessing about me."

The sunglasses girls start giggling and they all yell in unison, "We love you, Tommy."

"I'm going to be sick," I tell Em, rocking forward a little.

"Ignore them," she orders.

"Okay."

I snatch a glimpse. Mimi's tugging her cami down a little lower. Then Brittney points at her stomach. Other people gasp. Everyone on the bleachers stares at me.

"Ignore them," Em repeats.

"Okay…Okay. I am ignoring."

I look away. It's not just those girls who are here. There's the kid brothers watching the game, dreaming of being varsity some day, trying not to look at the bubble-gum girls. They race after the fly balls, diving into the woods. They hunker down and spit their own sunflower seeds. They go out by the church next door and play their own pick-up game. Can I focus on them? No. I focus on Mimi. Something horrible knots inside my stomach.

Even though Tom's not actually doing any baseball-related amazing thing right this second I yell, "Way to go, Fascist!"

There's no way he can't know that's me. He smiles and his dimples show. He nods at me. The muscle in his cheek twitches. I can tell. Even from here.

"You're biting your lip," Em says.

"Oh."

"You're drooling again."

How can I be drooling now with everything that's happening? Is it because I'm a pretender too? I punch her. "Shut up."

I try not to focus on Tom or on Mimi and her posse, which is spreading the Belle-is-pregnant rumor right now, I'm sure. I sniff in. There's the sugar soda smells of Mrs. Darrow, who doesn't have any kids but feeds us all anyway. Her cooler is like a fridge and before every game Tom and Shawn help her haul it over to her place almost exactly behind the plate. Somebody's dad always puts out her chair for her, takes her hand, and lowers her down and she always smiles, smiles, smiles at them like they are the angels, when she's really the special one.

She gives the princess that is Andrew's sister and the other tiny kids frozen fudge bars. She gives Em and me cookies and water. She clucks her teeth at Mimi and the tan girls and when one of them opens up a *Cosmo* she whispers, "Why can't they even pretend to watch the game?"

"Because they are idiots," Em says.

Idiots like me.

Mrs. Darrow laughs and then says to me, all whisper-serious, "Don't you worry about your Tommy, Belle."

She touches her chest and adds, "His heart is true."

Em and I give each other looks. Em's look says, *See.*

"Mrs. Darrow," I say, thinking about Eddie and his dad. "Did you hear anything funny Sunday night?"

"Sunday night?"

"Yeah."

She shakes her head. "No."

On the two-lane road we call a highway just beyond the field, logging trucks, SUVs motor on by pretty slow because even though the drivers have places to go, they'd rather be here with us, checking out the game. I'd trade places in a second. These people will be shocked by Em's secret and then they'll take care of her. They will. That's what we do here.

I hug my knees to my chest and then let go and grab Em and hug her instead. "I love it here."

She looks at me like I'm crazy.

I say it again. "I love Eastbrook."

"O-kay," she says and touches my forehead. "Are you on something?"

I shrug. "It's all going to be over soon."

"Because of me?" she picks a piece of grass out of the world, shreds it in two.

"Yeah and because we're seniors."

She nods and watches as Sumner's Blake Crowley gets called out at the plate. "Yeah."

The severed grass blade falls from her fingers.

"I thought you wanted out of here. I thought you were tired of being stuck." She takes a cookie from Mrs. Darrow, breaks it in two, rests part on her knee, offers me half. She smells like suntan lotion and long, sunny days that are

254

almost here, and that makes me smile. She breaks her half of the cookie again and inspects it before she eats it. She always does that, just stares at her food, looking for bugs or mold or something.

Finally I say, "I do, but I don't. How about you?"

"Not now, Belle. Now I don't have a choice, do I?"

Her fake-happy face cracks and she wants so hard to keep it strong.

So, I say, "Our white-boy baseball team looks like it's going to win another game."

Her lip quivers. "Yep."

I try again and whisper-ask, "Do you think having sex with a straight guy is different than having sex with a gay guy?"

Em loses some cookie. "Where did that come from?"

I pluck a cookie piece out of the grass. "I don't know."

Em thinks about it. "Maybe. I mean, the mechanics of it are going to be basically the same. The feeling underneath it might be different. But…um…is it different having sex with different guys anyway? I mean, it can be different with the same guy. But I don't know if the difference will be a straight guy versus a gay guy difference or just an 'it's a different guy' difference. Did that make sense?"

"No."

She snorts.

My guitar waits for me to strum her, make her sing out something that's trying to be true. Em turns the picked-up cookie piece over in her hands. Once, twice, another turn in her fingers and she eats it.

My half sits on top of Gabriel's gig case, untouched. I feel bad for it.

"You and me, baby," I tell it, and then I chomp it down.

Mimi starts her super giggling again. "Let's chant his name. Okay?"

The suntan girls start chanting, "Tom-my. Tom-my. Tom-my."

"Oh, he's going to hate that," Emmie says.

I grab her hand. "I promise you everything will be okay."

"Belle, you can't promise that."

----o----

When Tom drives me home, it feels like everybody in the whole universe knows that tonight is the night. Well, at least all those people who don't already think I'm pregnant, thanks to Mimi and Mr. Dow. Poor Mr. Dow.

Brent, this guy who works at the Y helping out with soccer and Little League sees us in the parking lot post-game and goes, "You gonna be okay without your mom home, there, Belle?

I nod and grab Tom's arm, which is warm from the game. Brent is one of those men who wear sweatshirts with the arms ripped off and although he's big, he doesn't exactly have muscle tone. This is a style that should be buried, but Brent is nice enough. He leans with his elbows over the back of his truck. It's all dinged on the sides.

"How'd you know my mom was gone, Brent?" I ask.

He shrugs. "Everybody around here knows everything. It's Eastbrook, remember?"

Tom smirks. "Oh, yeah, we remember."

Brent winks at Tom and says, "Well then, have fun tonight. Don't do anything I wouldn't do."

This is slimy because despite his unfortunate taste in shirts and overall lack of muscle tone, Brent is pretty well known for taking advantage of many a soccer mom who's been feeling underappreciated.

I shudder as we walk across the cooling air of the parking lot.

Tom bends down so his lips are near my ear and whispers, "In ten minutes we'll be at your house and it'll be just you and me. Nobody else. Okay Commie?"

More than okay. But worries of Shawn and Em and Eddie all swirl around my head. I'm not sure we're really going to be alone, not if my head has anything to do with it.

We've parked Tom's truck at the end of the cul-de-sac at the end of a dirt logging road so nobody talks about how it's at my house all night long. Elbow. Elbow. Wink. Wink.

"Food first or not?" Tom asks me. We're barely in the door, but we're already kissing. Tom kicks the door shut with his foot. Muffin prances down the stairs and then sniffs the air like we've brought a dog in the house and she promptly turns around, showing us her little kitty bum before she screeches back up the stairs and around the corner.

"I think she knows something is up," I murmur next to Tom's shirt.

"Something is definitely up."

"Ugh," I say. "Total slime ball thing to say."

He backs away. His lips look wet. He raises his hands, leans his shoulders against the wall and grabs me by the sides of my hips, so that our hips are still connected, very connected, but not connected enough. "Yeah, but it's true."

"Food after then," I say.

He presses his hips into me just a little bit more. Then, even with everything about Em, it just happens. It's hard to think you could ever physically long for a person more than I long for him right this second. In fact, even though long is an old-fashioned word, it doesn't work here. Yearn? Maybe yearn.

"I think I should make a list," I tell him.

"A new list?"

"Yeah, of words that describe how my body feels right now."

"Really?" He shifts his center of balance a little and the movement comes to his hips and then translates onto mine.

"There's the obvious ones…want, need, long for, and yearn, desire…" I say, "but they aren't good enough. I bet Germans have a word for it. Like BodyNeed or AllMoleculeCrave or something."

"Commie, you're crazy." He shakes his head, pulls his body straight again so our chests gesture against each other. His heart beats below ribs that touch my ribs, which cover my heart. Oh God.

"We could ask Herr Reitz," he says. "Want to give him a call?"

I pretend that I'm going to slug him. He grabs my hand and kisses it, one knuckle at a time. Then I catch his hand in my free one, clutch it and whisper my craving, "Please, Tom. Please."

----o----

Somehow we make it up the stairs and into my bedroom. I think Tom sort of carries me up, but I'm not sure. His lips are the only thing I really know. His hands against my back, in my hair, on my butt, are the only things I really feel. In my bedroom, I yank off my shirt and start in on his. He laughs because I'm so pushy and since we're still standing up, we're kind of off-balance.

"Belle…" his voice comes out deep and full of things, promises and emotion and the same craving I have.

I get his stupid sleeve stuck in his watch.

"I stink at this," I say. I wonder if Emmie and Shawn ever had stuff like this happen to them.

Tom fixes it, untangles himself and cups my chin in his hand. His hand is so steady.

"No. No, you don't."

My hands slide into the side of his jeans, land in between the hard denim and the soft cotton fabric of his boxers. I move my thumbs just a little and he moans.

His hands clutch at me hard for a second and then soften, like he's figuring out how to control himself. "God, Belle. Do you know how long I've wanted to do this?"

"Then why did we wait?"

"I want it to be right. I want you to be ready."

"You jerk!" I laugh at him and push him onto my bed. "I am SO ready."

"That's not the right word. I didn't want you to think I was using you, I guess. Or make a mistake, you know, like my parents. And I didn't want to scare you off. You're a little wimpy about things since Dylan."

This hits home.

"I guess there were a lot of reasons, not just one," he says. "I just didn't want to ruin us. I wanted to be ready."

"You are so nice to me. I don't deserve you." I flop down next to him. Muffin, who has been hiding under the bed, scoots out and makes a beeline for the door. "Poor kitty."

"I think we're traumatizing the cat," he says as I lie down next to him.

"Probably," I say as he starts to kiss my stomach, the skin

below my ribs. I can barely make myself speak. "It's worth it though."

Then I think of Emmie and her belly, and her face once we saw those pregnancy test lines. Poor Emmie...I hiccup. Tom laughs.

His lips linger at my bottom ribs. He lifts himself over me, his legs straddling mine. He brings his lips down low, and makes a trail, like a butterfly touch around the circle of my left rib and then my right. His hands grab my hands, holding them against the bed and he moves his lips to my collar bones, nibbling. He kisses my shoulders and then lowers his hips so they press against mine.

"Teenage boys are not supposed to be good at this," I manage to say.

"Oh? I'm good huh?"

I nod.

"Then stop thinking so much, Commie, and just let me love you, okay?"

"Okay," I say and he moves in again. The pressure of his hips change and my hips ride up to meet him. I moan. He breaks away to look at my face and smiles. He brushes hair out of my eyes.

"You're so beautiful, Belle."

I beg him with my eyes and since he is my Tom, my sweet, handsome Tom...not Shawn and I am not Emmie...he understands and lifts off of me so he can take off his jeans. It's painful. His leaving is painful, like having an ice cream taken out of my hand or something, like losing a friend. I kiss his stomach while he pulls off his jeans.

His leg gets stuck. He moans, not a happy moan. "Oh my God."

"It's okay," I whisper.

"I'm an idiot."

"You do not have to be Mr. Suave Man, Tom." I kiss his stomach. It's hard and dark and wide and has some hair on it, totally different than my stomach. "I am in love with your stomach."

"Really?"

"Swear."

He gets his leg out of his pants. His stomach ripples up and down. My hands move across it. My body slides up against the length of his body.

He grabs my face in his hands. "I just want to be good for you."

"You are."

"Perfect, you know?"

"You could start singing the Star Spangled Banner and it would still be perfect."

His fingers twitch. "What?"

"I don't know. I mean…Um, anything you do would be perfect because it would be you."

His eyes surrender. "Commie."

Then something rings.

What?

I'm not sure what it is at first, that dinging noise, is it like some sort of bells of love?

Tom's stomach tightens up. "Belle?"

It dings again. I pull myself up on my elbow. "Oh God, it's the doorbell. Shit."

Tom grabs his pants, makes a frantic effort to start putting them on and then thinks better of it, tossing me my shirt. I yank it over my shoulders and peer out the window just as the doorbell rings again. There's a little red car in the driveway.

"Oh God, it's Emmie," I say. "I have to go to the door."

"Why?"

He squints and his cheek twitches. It's like I can see his whole body sigh.

"Pretend we aren't here," he says.

And this is it. The moment. What will it be? My wants or Em's needs? What will it be? The boyfriend or the best friend?

There's no choice.

"I can't."

I race down the stairs, trying to tuck my hair back into the ponytail I always wear for gymnastics. I fling open the door. Em storms up the stairs. Her face is white and frozen. I follow her as she starts heading towards my bedroom, which is where we do all our big talks about important things.

She starts talking. "I couldn't do it. I just couldn't tell him. He'll hate me, Belle. I'll ruin his whole life. I think I should run…"

"Uh-Em, wait a min…" I say, but I'm too slow and she's caught sight of Tom in just his jeans, standing near my bed, having issues with getting his shirtsleeves right side out. Tom gives me frantic eyes.

Em stops and staggers against the wall. She backs up and then whips her head around. "His truck isn't here."

"We hid it," I explain.

"Oh…Oh…you guys. Oh, I'm sorry. I forgot your mom was gone…" She covers her mouth with one of her hands and then does a totally Emily thing. She pulls out her camera and takes a picture of me and then whirls around to get Tom, who is still struggling with his shirt. God, how hard can it be to get into a shirt?

"Emily. Jesus," he says.

His eyes are angry and I don't know if it's at Em or because of me, because I got the door.

Em's oblivious and she giggles. "I'm so sorry. I have to capture this moment, though. I mean, this is *the* moment isn't it?"

I stare at a picture of a sailboat in the hall. It's stuck, this sailboat. There's no wind. No wake. It's moored in a bay somewhere.

"I am so sorry I interrupted," she says.

She giggles again and stuffs her fist in her mouth trying to stop.

"It's okay." I grab her hand and lead her back down the hall towards the stairs. "Let's go talk in your car."

"I'll start dinner," Tom yells.

He gives me a thumbs-up sign. Everything inside of me unclenches. I flash him a smile, throw it over my shoulder. He smiles back. I am totally, hopelessly in love.

Damn.

"I CAN'T DO THIS," SHE says once she's stopped her hysterical giggling, which turned into hysterical sobbing and then finally ended in this sentence. I can't do this.

We sit in her car. The heat of the day presses against us. No wind to provide relief. Nothing moves outside. Not a leaf. Not an ant on my driveway. Nothing.

"Will you do it for me?" she asks.

The chords of the world silence themselves waiting for my answer. There isn't a sound. It's like everything is waiting for my notes to give some sort of direction, some way to go.

My hand wipes against my forehead checking for sweat.

"Okay," I say and the world starts again. Em looks up, tears in her eyes and I am the one who turns away first. One tiny chickadee flits across the driveway and settles into a branch, still again, but the rest of the world, it's moving forward.

"It's not fair of me to ask you, I know that," Em says. She swallows so hard I can see her neck move.

I shrug and open the door but don't get out. My legs stick to the seat. I take a deep breath, but it's just hot air.

"I'd do anything for you," I say. "You're my friend. God, I even buy your tampons."

She smiles but it doesn't reach her eyes. "You're the best friend ever."

My legs make a noise as they lift off the seat. "I know."

She follows me out of the car and I tell her that I'll do it tomorrow. After school. I'll blow off our Students for Social Justice Meeting, which is now on Wednesdays. I'll even blow off Anna's bike ride. I'll grab him before practice.

"I'm sorry I interrupted you and Tom," she says and hiccups.

She covers her mouth with her hand, looking surprised.

"You never hiccup," I announce.

She shifts against the tree and slow-walks to her car. "I know. It's probably hormones or something."

Guilt and fear wash over her face.

"You sure you're going to be okay?" I yell after her.

Her hand flits through the air.

"I love you!" I holler and swipe a mosquito off my leg.

"I know!" she yells back. "I love you, too."

And then she is gone. I wave to her. I wave and watch Eddie's truck back out of his driveway and follow her down the road. I wave to the truck too, even though I can't tell if it's Eddie driving or his dad. I feel like I'm waving goodbye to the whole world.

Then I climb the stairs back into my house. Inside, I snuggle up against Tom. There's a duct tape patch on his jeans, right near his hip. It says, *Do not forsake me.*

"All this stuff that's going on?" he asks me running his hand through my hair. "It's been about Em?"

I nod.

His hand moves to my shoulder, makes a circle there. "Is everything okay?"

"No," I say. "No."

"Can you tell me?"

I shake my head. "Don't get mad."

"I just want to help."

"I know."

Five minutes later we're kissing again, but it's not the same and we both know it and then my cell phone rings. It's Emily. Her voice rushes out. "I'm going over now. I'm going to tell him. I can't wait. I can't handle this anymore."

She hangs up before I have a chance to say anything. I can't even say good luck.

Tom and I make dinner. I'm too spazzed out to do anything

else right now and he's being all sweet boy, sexy hunk, understanding. We cook spaghetti in a pot.

"I think we've left it in too long," I say. "It's going to be all super limpy."

This is not supposed to be a sexual innuendo, but we both crack up anyway. Because everything we do seems to be charged. When I held the uncooked spaghetti in my hands. When the water bubbled to the top. The smell of tomatoes. Everything.

My cell phone rings. I check out the screen.

"Emily?" Tom asks.

"Uh-huh."

He takes out an ultra-limp spaghetti strand and bites it in half. It steams. I do not know how he doesn't burn his tongue. "You should get it. It's okay."

I answer.

There is nothing but the sound of sobbing.

"Are you home?" I demand. "Tell me where you are."

Tom's eyes go big. He can tell I'm panicked.

"Emily? Are you home? Are. You. At. Home?"

Her voice tiny, and sounding just like she sounded freshman year when her dad died comes back at me, "Uh-huh."

I cover the phone with my hand.

"It's Emily," I plead.

Tom nods. "I'll clean up here, and run to the store to get more spaghetti. You go."

"You sure?"

He kisses my head. "Just come back."

I'm already pulling on my shoes. "Turn off the stove, okay?"

"Hurry back," he says.

I barely hear him because I am almost gone.

I race my bike over. It takes two seconds. Almost. I don't

even put on my helmet. Em's mom's car isn't in the driveway, so I storm right in, up the stairs, through the hall, past the pictures, to Em's room.

She sees me.

"You told him?" I ask. I don't know why I ask her because I know.

"I lose everybody," she says. She hurls herself across the room, thuds the wall with her fists and then whirls around, screaming. "I lose everybody!"

For a second I stand there.

The picture of Kermit with a rainbow? It falls off the wall. She's had it forever. It bangs onto the floor and lands face down by Crocky Wocky. I make an oath: I will kill Shawn for doing this to her. I will kill him for not being supportive. My teeth grind together like I've bitten a bullet all the way through and I just want to keep biting. But this isn't the time for me to be mad. This isn't the time for me at all.

My feet take me across the floor to this bent-over girl who is my best friend, to this bent-over girl who is so much like me, who clutches her stomach because the hurt is too much. My hands reach out and pull her to me.

"You don't lose everybody," I whisper to her firm and real. "You don't."

She spits out the words. "What? Who do I have left? My mom? You?"

"Yeah. You have me."

She tries to break free, but I won't let her go and she doesn't really want me to. Instead, I hold her by the shoulders, wait until she has the will to look into my eyes. When she does, I grab her hand and bring it back to her stomach.

"You don't even know who you are, Belle. You're too afraid to face the fact that you love Tom. You're too afraid to deal with the fact that you don't always know who people are. You put us all in little compartments and then pretend like you're all open minded, but you aren't, Belle. You aren't, okay? And I'm not Good Emily, Best Friend. I am pregnant and in high school and I've lost everybody! Can you understand that? My mom is going to kill me. Shawn hates me. He's not mature enough to deal with this. My dad is gone. Everybody's going to be looking at me like I'm such a stupid slut. And you? What about you, Belle? How are you going to deal with having a best friend who's pregnant? How's that going to fit in your little perfect world? It won't. We both know that. Because you're too wimpy to accept the truth."

Her words crush me and for a moment I can't speak. Every single word she says feels like a guitar string breaking under too much tension, snapping in half, snapping against my face, a spasm of pain. Is that what she really thinks of me? That I'm a coward?

I am a coward.

But why the hell do I have to be perfect? Everyone's always telling me that I need to fix myself, but what about them? They aren't perfect. They aren't any better than I am. They're flawed too and I love them. I love Tom and his fear. I love my mom and her innocent sexiness. I love Emily even though she's being mean.

And I do.

Do not forsake me.

Okay, I do think she was stupid to get pregnant. I never thought she'd be that stupid. But that doesn't mean I don't know her. It just means that I don't know all of her. It just means I was wrong about one of her actions, but not her essence. And anyway, it's not the end of the world to be wrong. It isn't the end of the world to be uncertain.

I swallow and say, "You are my best friend and you are good."

She shrieks at me, "I. Am. Pregnant."

"That doesn't make you bad," I say. "A little bitchy maybe…"

"Will you just shut up, Belle? I am hormonal, not bitchy." She glares at me. Her hands scrunch into fists. "Ever since Dylan told you he was gay you've been an idiot. You're afraid of everything. You try to understand everyone because you're so scared you're going to be fooled again. Well, here it is. Dylan is gay. Tom is not gay. He is very, very straight. I am pregnant, very, very pregnant and you are selfish, very, very selfish."

"Selfish?"

"Always thinking about Belle. Always protecting Belle. Always trying to figure out who people are and what they're going to do because you're so afraid of being wrong about people again." She takes a big breath. "Listen to me, Belle. We are always wrong about people. We never really know people. I thought I knew Shawn. And look! Look at me!"

I want to reach out to touch her shoulder because even though she's hurt me to the core, she's hurting more. A lot more. A good friend would let her rant. A good friend wouldn't let her give up. I want so badly to be her good friend. I don't want to forsake her.

"Emmie?"

She hides her head in her hands and doesn't say anything.

"Emmie?" I touch her shoulder. "You haven't lost everybody Em. You haven't lost him. You haven't lost me."

Her lip trembles. "I thought he loved me."

"He does love you. He's just a frightened idiot asshole. He's a boy, remember?"

Her hand turns around and clutches mine and then my favorite super-strong friend crumbles, the most important person in my whole life other than Tom, sits back on her bed and cries some more.

"Can you go?" she says.

She stares at me hard and weak all at once. She says it again and each word hurts me more than anything Mimi has ever said or done. "Can you just go, Belle? Please."

I flinch. I need to be here for Emmie. I need it. "You want me to go? I can stay the night. It's okay. I'm sure you're mom will say it's okay."

She shakes her head. "Please, Belle. I love you, but I just need to be alone."

I nod, stand up, kiss the top of her head because I don't know what else to do. I bite my lip so hard it bleeds. The salt blood in my mouth makes me think of childbirth, or pain, of things that can't change, of hurting so much that blood is almost a relief.

I want to ask her if she really thinks I'm a delusional coward, but this isn't about me and I hate myself for even wanting to ask when here she is, my best friend, full of pain.

She was right. I am selfish.

"I'll have my phone on me," I say, voice cracking. "You call me if you need anything. Anything. Okay?"

She nods.

I don't want to leave her like this.

She was right. I am afraid.

"You sure you want me to leave?"

"I'm sure," she says and then she jumps up, running to the bathroom. She doesn't even shut the door, just throws up into the toilet, hands clutching her stomach, clutching at life, clutching, clutching.

I go in, kneel on the floor beside her, pull her hair out of her face and fix her ponytail. "Emmie, I don't want to go."

She wipes her face with the back of her hand. She grabs her car keys, which were abandoned on the floor. "I know."

Her tone tells me I have no choice.

I careen out of the room. My heart falls lower and lower with every step I take.

Her mom meets me in the hall. I don't know when she got home. I don't know how much she's heard. I can't even look at her in her mother eyes. She grabs me by the shoulders and says, "Emily's pregnant, isn't she?"

I swallow. "She's in pain."

Em's mom drops her hands. She nods and her eyes are empty pots waiting on the stove for something to fill them. But nothing does. "Go get some sleep. I'll take care of her."

I give her a quick hug. She's built just like Em. She's all hip and bone.

Then I struggle down the hall and let myself out the door. I do not wave because it is not goodbye.

---- o ----

I take off as fast as I can, just will my legs into supergirl mode because I want to get away, get away, now, fast.

Emmie was right. I am scared. I am selfish. But she wasn't all right. It wasn't just Dylan being gay that made me scared, that made me want to figure people out. It was Eddie too. When Eddie grabbed me in the hall that day, when his eyes went mean and hard, and when his hands became my enemy, that threw me. Neither Dylan nor Eddie were who they were supposed to be.

It's hard to trust people after that.

It's hard not to analyze people after that.

It's hard to live after all that.

But I have to try.

Tom isn't back yet. I can't believe I beat him back. Maybe Shawn called. Maybe he's over there helping Mr. I'm *So Not* a Supportive Boyfriend to deal.

I wheel my bike into the garage, glance across the street at Eddie's house. There aren't any lights on there, but it's still daylight. It's almost June. The days get longer and longer. The sun stretches out, shining its hot light on all our flaws, all the cracks in the road, in our selves.

I run across the street and right up to the window of Eddie's room. I cup my hands and try to stare inside.

When we were little we'd bounce a big, red ball across our driveways. We'd eat brownies together. He'd play at my house all the time, eat dinner, beat me at Go Fish. Then we kind of drifted away. I'm not sure why. I guess it doesn't matter. Em would say it doesn't matter.

I try to stare into Eddie's room beyond his dark green curtains. I can't see anything, but even if I could, I doubt it would make me understand.

The past is as much of a mystery as the present. It is as unavailable as the future. Nothing you do can get back people who are lost. Nothing you do can make change any more understandable. You have to accept it. I don't want to. But I do.

I will never have a father.

I will never not worry about having seizures.

I will never be comfortable with Eddie again, never be with him alone and not be just a little bit frightened, never not remember his hands on my throat.

I will never be friends with Mimi again.

I will never love Dylan the way I once loved Dylan.

I will never have a best friend Emily who didn't get pregnant her last year of high school.

This is the list I make inside my head. I do not like it. I do not like this list. It's all about me. I'm selfish. I'm human. I hate that.

Tears start flowing down my face. I can't stop them. They just run and run and run.

I don't know how I can help Emmie. I don't know.

The front door of Eddie's house opens and I jump, think about running across the street. But I don't. I'm frozen, stupid looking.

"Belle?" he asks.

"I was staring in your room," I say, wiping at my eyes. "I could probably get arrested for that. I think it's trespassing or peeping tomness or something. You'd think I would have learned that in law class, but I didn't, for some stupid reason he never actually taught us whether..."

I stop rambling.

He walks towards me. "You okay?"

I shake my head.

He starts to reach out his arms to hug me, but I step back. I can't help it. He puts his hands in his pockets and leans against his house.

"Do you think I'm a coward?" I ask him.

"You wouldn't be talking to me if you were."

"People are saying you do heroin. I think that's shit."

His eyes close up. Each word seems an effort. "People make up rumors, they try to explain things, to make sense."

He shrugs, scratches at the side of his nose. "Nobody could figure out why I did what I did to you, so they make shit up."

We both cringe. A chipmunk scampers across Eddie's driveway, stops in the middle of the road, looks both ways and then bounds to my lawn. The wind gusts, and blows my hair against my face. I pull it out of the way.

"I'm always trying to explain things," I say. "I make lists and stuff, try to organize everything. And it can't be, life can't be organized."

He watches me. I watch him. I bend down and pick up some grass, split the blade into three pieces and then try to braid it. It's not long enough though. I let it dangle from my fingers. The wind takes it away.

Finally I say, "Thanks for helping out when I had the seizure."

"I thought Tom was going to kill me."

"He probably wanted to," I say. "He's like that. Remember when we were little, and you always used to try to save me?"

He watches my grass braid blow into the culvert. It'll sink there, get muddy, ruined. "Yeah."

"I miss that."

"Me too."

"I wish you could save me now," I tell him. My voice breaks. "I wish you could save me."

He takes a step forward but stops, afraid, I guess. We are both afraid of who we are.

"Save you from what, Belle?"

"Everything."

He nods.

I risk it. "Do you think it's stupid if I sometimes miss my dad, even though I never knew him or anything?"

"No."

He grabs his forearms with his hands, rubs them like he's cold. "Sometimes I miss my dad, and he's still here, you know?"

"That's not stupid either."

We both shift our weight at exactly the same time. The wind gusts against us like it's pushing us forward, but neither of us, neither of us have any clue where it is we're supposed to go.

I LEAVE EDDIE. HE'S WAITING for his dad to come home. His dad is using Eddie's truck again and is supposed to bring back pizza. He's running late. Eddie's eyes wear worries about whether or not his dad will be sober. If we were placing bets, both of us would bet that he won't be. He is that late.

Kind of like Tom.

Gabriel and Muffin keep me company on the couch, waiting for Tom to show up.

He's turned off the stove like the good son of a police chief. He's left his book bag in the middle of the floor where everyone can trip over it. There's duct tape all over it. He's written out little sayings on the pieces, which is so cute. I don't know why he does this. I will not try to figure it out, or organize it, but I like it. I like that he does it. I touch the smooth-rough pieces of tape, the words he's written.

"April is the cruelest month" —*T. S. Eliot.*

Eliot was wrong about that one. It's May.

"When sorrows come, they come not single spies,
But in battalions!" —*Shakespeare.*

I hate Shakespeare.

I put Tom's book bag back down. Em's been acting like the Energizer bunny just hopping on and on, moving on batteries, moving on automatic, and she's finally stopped. She's no longer just going and going. She's stopped.

So, I do a Belle thing, a true Belle thing. I make a list.

What I Want to Do with Emily's Baby:

1. Hug it.
2. Not change its diaper.
3. Buy it really cute onesie pajamas, those baby clothes things made out of really soft cotton that have the little feet built in.
4. Buy a Fisher Price guitar.
5. Teach said baby to play said guitar.
6. Read it *Goodnight Moon*.
7. Not change its diaper ever.
8. Really. Have you ever seen green liquid baby poo? It's absolutely vile.
9. Love it. Love the baby and smell his/her baby powder smell (after Em's changed the diaper).

Then I do another true Belle thing, I pick up Gabriel. It really doesn't matter who people think I am:

Belle who dates Tom but hasn't had sex yet.

Belle who is popular.

Belle who has a gay ex-boyfriend that she had sex with all the time.

Belle who is best friends with Emily.

Belle whose dad died in the first Iraq war.

Em was right. I spend too much time worrying about who people are, afraid I'll be wrong about them.

I will always be wrong about them and they'll always be wrong about me.

That's okay.

That's just how this crappy world works, and it's kind of beautiful that way. There's nothing wrong with always discovering new things about people, is there? Even if it's yourself. Even if it's that you're a coward.

I am Belle who plays Gabriel. My fingers glide over Gabriel's strings. I close my eyes and play, just fooling around, making things up. The sound is too edgy though, too many tremble notes, too many tremble notes. The harmonic notes are stronger than the fundamental notes and it sounds raspy.

I am not in the mood for raspy music, so I stop, go back to the chords, basic progressions, deep and rich and full. That's the core of music. The base. The relationships between the notes are there, strong and ready.

I play them.

The phone rings. I grab it.

"Belle, I'm so sorry," Tom's voice comes through. He pauses. I know what he'll say, I can hear it in him already and everything inside of me curls into itself, closing, worried, hurting. "I went to Shawn's. Did you know? About Emily? Was that what was going on? Why you're so stressed?"

"I knew," I whisper.

A tree branch hits the window, like the wind is mad at me, trying to knock some sense into me. I am so jealous of the wind, of how it never stops moving, it goes and it goes.

I swallow and ask, "Are you mad?"

"Mad?"

"Because I didn't tell you?"

Because I still want to risk it, to have sex?

Another pause. I touch the hole where the sound echoes inside of Gabriel. My heart seems frozen in my chest, a big blob of motionless dough.

"No, I'm not mad."

The light bulb in the stairway flickers. Neither of us talk for a second, maybe because we know this will be all we talk about later, Tom and me. All of Eastbrook, talking and talking like we can get to the essence of it, figure it out. It's part of being human. We are all human. I have to remember that it's okay to be human. It's okay to be human. It's okay to be stuck sometimes. And it's even okay to have to rip up the duct tape sayings we've got stuck on our hands and to pull up the little hairs beneath it, to feel the pain.

He starts talking again. "And then I stopped off at home. My mom's freaking out because Shawn's mom talked to her…So, she's all, 'Are you having sex? Are you using protection? You don't want to make the same mistakes we did, young man.'"

"Oh God."

"I'll be there soon, okay?"

He is sweetness and stability. I don't care if I deserve him or not, I'm just glad I got him.

"Your mom's still letting you come?"

"I'm not telling her where I'm going."

"Oh. Okay."

When we hang up, I imagine Em holding the baby in her arms, silently moving back and forth on her long, naked feet, rocking the baby to sleep. Shawn puts his arms around both of them. I imagine them singing a lullaby.

"Things could be okay," I tell Muffin. "They could."

It is a lie a cat would never believe. She turns around and sticks her butt in the air.

"Okay, if Shawn is going to be an ass, then I'll take care of her," I say.

I imagine us taking turns feeding the baby at night, taking turns going to classes. One of us would have to transfer, because Em's not going to the same college, but that's okay. It would be worth it, tiring, but worth it. Right?

Oh God, it'll be so much work.

Muffin leans her head against my hip and snuggles in. Her paws knead the fabric of the couch. I start playing again.

The music is slow, soft. I don't know how it comes from my fingers. It just comes. It fills the house with its quiet noise. Sirens sound in the distance. I wait and wait for Tom to come. I play and play a lullaby song. Maybe I'll make it a present for Em and Shawn's baby. It will be my first lullaby.

I keep playing my guitar. This is what I do, and that's okay. No matter what happens, who people turn out to be, I have this. This and my lists.

I strum. I practice my chords, all in the right progression. It sounds good, just me and my guitar.

It's like a ritual, that no one else has to be a part of, something I can control, and feel good about. Me.

I play.

But, it's not enough. Playing is not enough. I grab some scissors from the kitchen cabinet and cut off a piece of duct tape, take a marker and write: *Do not forsake me.*

Still not enough.

So I cut off another piece and write in big block letters: I WILL NOT BE FORSAKEN.

I stick them on the fridge, like they're magnets. But they aren't. They're just words.

Then I make up one more list on some sheet music, writing in tiny letters between empty staff lines.

Things I Am Right Now

1. I am an Emily fan even though she's mad at me and I will continue to be an Emily fan and keep being her friend.

2. I am sort of popular and that's okay.

3. I am a person who sometimes has seizures and that's okay, too.
4. I am a person who does not think sex is evil.
5. I am a person who is really glad she isn't pregnant.
6. I am a girl who plays a mean guitar.
7. I am a fan of boys who wear duct tape.
8. I am a person who realizes that forgiveness is not the same as trust and that it's okay to forgive someone like Eddie and not trust him. It doesn't make you a victim. It doesn't make you anything.
9. I am Belle Philbrick.
10. I am me.

This is a fine list, I think.

About the Author

Carrie Jones likes Skinny Cow fudgicles and potatoes. She does not know how to spell fudgicles. This has not prevented her from writing books. She lives with her cute family in Maine. She has a large, skinny white dog and a fat cat. Both like fudgicles. Only the cat likes potatoes. This may be a reason for the kitty's weight problem (Shh . . . don't tell). Carrie has always liked cowboy hats but has never owned one. This is a very wrong thing. She graduated from Vermont College's MFA program for writing. She has edited newspapers and poetry journals and has won awards from the Maine Press Association and also been awarded the Martin Dibner Fellowship as well as a Maine Literary Award. She is still not sure why.

THIS IS A BOOK ABOUT love and friendship and I have been really lucky with love and friends.

So when writing a book about love and friendships, it's good to acknowledge the cool people who have supported you.

How to do this? Oh, thank them in list fashion, of course.

1. Thanks to Emily Ciciotte and Doug Jones. You two are angels, only without wings, or harps or anything like that, but you know what I mean.

2. Thanks to Jennifer Osborn for always letting me rant, for eating lunch with me, for being a cool reporter chick and the best grown-up friend ever. Understand, here, that I use the term "grown-up" loosely.

3. Thanks to Jackie Shriver. You were the best high school friend ever and such an inspiration for this book. May the Parallel Zone continue on! Thanks for finding me again. I missed you and Imaginary Land.

4. Thanks to Dottie Vachon and Alice Dow. Alice, you have saved my butt SOOOO many times. Dottie, you have kept me sane. I owe you both a lot of flowers. And to Mary McGuire for always making basketball games a lot more fun.

5. When it comes to butt-saving, Doris Bunker Rzasa has to be the ultimate. Doris, you are wise and funny. You've called out rescue teams for me (Really! She did! It involved a dog, a knee injury, cool hospital maintenance guys, and deep woods) and helped me in every way possible. I love you.

6. Thanks to Alison Jones, Kayla Gelinas, and Norah and Phoebe Clark for being the best relatives and readers possible. You four have already made the universe a kinder, brighter place.

7. Thanks to Maggie and Sarah Rausch for being the ultimate fan girls, for making me believe in writing, and for telling me the term Eye Orgasm. Thanks to Devyn Burton for being the ultimate cool fan boy/writer. You are always there. FTW!!!

8. Thanks to Melissa Love for making duct tape roses. Tom would be proud.

9. And when you talk about roses, you've got to thank Ellen for this amazing cover. I am drooling. You are incredibly gifted, Ellen. And so are you, Sandy Sullivan. Thanks for joining us on this journey and trying to keep it all straight. Thanks to Brian Farrey, super blogger and way cool publicist man. You are so graceful to put up with me. I owe you.

10. Thanks to Andrew Karre, Sweet Editor Man. Thanks for giving me faith, for caring about books, and for being so ridiculously competent and smart.

11. Thanks to Super Agent Guy Edward Necarsulmer IV and his amazing assistant/sidekick Cate Martin. She ain't no Robin, folks. You make being a writer a joyous thing. I never doubt that I'm in superhero hands. Plus, how many agents pick you up and spin you around in a hotel lobby? Only the best ones... Only the best...

12. Oh, yeah, thanks again to Emily Ciciotte and Belle Vachon for letting me use their names. There are betta fish named after you guys now. Really! How cool is that?

13. Thanks to Emily Wing Smith, Johanna Staley Arnone, Christopher Maselli, Ed Briant, Bruce Frost, Kellye Crocker, Cindy Faughman, G. Neri, Greg Fishbone and the Class of 2k7, Vermont College's Whirligigs, my lovely Livejournal friends,

the Cyber Girl Circuit and the cast of Tamra Wight's Schmooze and Robin McCready's PW's. You are all the best writing family a person could ever want. Thanks for writing good books for such good reasons.

14. Thanks to J. K. Richard, who knows everything about Postum and horses. You are a hero every day, even if you do think you're just a softie.

15. Thanks to Jo Knowles. Jo, you are the best advocate/writer/friend a person could have. Thanks for defending TIPS.

16. And finally, thanks to my family for being my family. I love you, Mom, Dad, Sis, Bro, Nana, aunts, uncles, cousins, nieces, nephews, the whole crazy she-bang.